A Madras Miasma

A Superintendent Le Fanu Mystery

Brian Stoddart

A Madras Miasma
Copyright © 2014 Brian Stoddart
This paperback edition first published in 2014 by

Crime Wave Press
Flat D, 11th Fl. Liberty Mansion
26E Jordan Road
Yau Ma Tei, Hong Kong
http://www.crimewavepress.com

Protected by copyright under the terms of the
International Copyright Union: All rights reserved.
No part of this publication may be reproduced or
transmitted in any form or by any means, electronic
or mechanical, including photocopy, recording,
or any information storage and retrieval system,
without written permission from the publisher.

ISBN 978 988 13510 1 2

This book is a work of fiction. All names, characters,
and other elements of the story are either the
product of the author's imagination
or else are used only fictitiously.
Any resemblance to real characters,
alive or dead, or to real incidents
is entirely coincidental.

Cover Design by Hans Kemp

To Eric Broom

For a very long
& treasured friendship

Very best wishes

Brian Stedder

One

He prayed she was already dead when pitched headfirst into the Buckingham Canal's putrid shallows.

With head and neck shoved deep into the rancid quagmire lining the Canal banks, her face was hidden. The body otherwise swayed rhythmically to the dank, oily water washing towards the edges. She lay on her back, grotesquely angled, neck evidently broken. Still standing a few yards away, he guessed her age at around thirty. The scuffed and sodden pale blue, mid-heeled shoes were recognisably expensive. So was the full length, layered, pale blue gown with intricate lace top. Matching pale blue stockings appeared briefly at the ankles before disappearing into the shoes. She was slim, but with curves, that much he could tell. A blue sapphire ring glinted on the third finger of the right hand that was floating on the surface. A plain, solid gold bangle encircled the left wrist. She was well out of place here, he thought, and a long way from home, wherever it was.

At thirty eight, Superintendent Christian Jolyon Brenton Le Fanu, MC, Indian Police Service, Madras Presidency, still looked more sportsman than policeman. He stood six feet tall, broad-shouldered, strong rather than elegant and with well-groomed swept back fair hair greying at the edges. Clean shaven, his lined face was more the result of more than four World War One service years than natural ageing. Prominent cheekbones highlighted an angular jaw. The grey eyes were lively, the nose suggested he was once a boxer, and he moved lightly but wearily.

The neat grey working suit, fresh cream shirt with regimental cufflinks, and innocuous blue tie looked odd above the knee-high rubber boots. He was ready for the Canal. As usual, he was alone onsite at the start of an investigation, apart from two uniformed Indian constables allegedly standing guard to one side, but smoking the acrid local bidis to pass the time just after dawn on this hazy, late-November day. The solitude helped him assess the surroundings and shape his ideas. At least it was not ferociously hot. It might reach 75 Fahrenheit by the afternoon, but not the relentless 100 plus of May or June in south India. He hated dealing with bodies then.

Now head of the Madras City Crime Unit created to apply the investigative techniques pioneered by Austrian criminologist Hans Gross, Le Fanu surveyed the "scene of offence" before approaching the body. He preferred "crime scene", but the "scene of offence" used in Gross' Criminal Investigation was favoured by the Inspector-General, Sir Maurice Wilson who had established the unit, so "scene of offence" it was. The I-G handpicked Le Fanu for the job, angering several officers already professionally and personally threatened by political reform. And Le Fanu had never travelled well with any of them.

The location of her body was ironic, he reflected. Here, south of the toxic Cooum River, the Buckingham Canal was all degraded water, debased soil and deteriorating locks. People dumped waste into the water fouled routinely by animals, rubbish jettisoned by the trading boats, with the accumulated nutrients producing the weeds now choking the waterway. That clag was aggravated by filth spewing from the shanty towns proliferating along the banks to shelter people come to Madras fleeing the rural famine now sweeping the Presidency. Some found no refuge, though, drowning/suffocating

A MADRAS MIASMA

themselves in the morass to escape despair. The uniforms had pulled six bodies from the Canal in the past two weeks alone.

Madras was a difficult place in which to live in 1920 and, for her, this wasteland a dreadful one in which to die, if she had died here.

The irony was that she lay behind one of the city's most beautiful buildings. Seized mid-nineteenth century from a Muslim prince by the British, the Chepauk Palace now housed the powerful Board of Revenue whose four Members ran the Madras Presidency government. The Palace's elegant lines and red and white stone texture symbolised the Indo-Saracenic fusion of Eastern and Western architecture that gave the city a rare claim to fame.

The social distance between the Canal and the Palace was far greater than the physical one. But that was Madras, Le Fanu lamented, a cruel place where "haves" and "have nots" were separated more than in most cities, even in India.

Over on the Cooum's north bank, the deserted Madras Gymkhana club golf links reminded him and others that, at the end of the world's worst war, a tiny European elite still controlled one of Asia's fastest growing cities, but could not manage its mushrooming misery, poverty and exploitation. Beyond the Gymkhana soared the Madras High Court buildings, repeating the style of the Chepauk Palace. British law had suppressed local legal and political traditions long ago, but this dominated land and people were retaliating with political unrest, reaching into labour discontent and rising costs, to challenge a government accustomed to automatic subservience.

Le Fanu envisaged the trading city turmoil sprawling beyond the High Court. Tight lanes and dilapidated buildings struggled to contain bewildering numbers of people, occupations, religious beliefs and social rankings. Among the pungent smells and confronting sights of the flower, meat, vegetable, livestock and fruit markets, Indians eked out a living, almost despite the British presence. Throughout the laneways specialising in clothing, fabric, metalware, household goods and all the rest, traders clamoured to attract haggling customers. Shops sat hard against temples. Butchers hacked at meat piled on wooden blocks standing out in the open and attracting squadrons of flies. Barbers cut the hair of customers squatting on the streets. Alongside them, fortune tellers and astrologers promised a better future to all takers.

He remembered his first encounter with a Madras seer, back in 1905. The man crouched at the base of a wall outside the police station, commanding a bird in a cage sitting on a plain cloth. Along the front of the cloth lay a row of cards, face down. Having been persuaded to part with a coin in order to learn his fate, Le Fanu watched the man open the cage. The bird hopped to the opening, then climbed down a short ladder. It strutted up and down the row of cards several times before seizing one in its beak. After delivering the card to the seer, the bird climbed the ladder and re-entered the cage. Naturally, the news was good. Le Fanu was guaranteed a long, successful career and a wonderful personal life. In retrospect, not a very good seer, he thought. This new Crime Unit should set him back on track, he hoped

Returning to the present, Le Fanu was forced to absorb the constant noise of the trading city. Bullock carts competed for alleyway space with hand barrows, cyclists, rickshaws and pony carts. In larger streets, crowded trams added further confusion. Broken-bodied beggars filled muddy, rubbish-strewn streets, jostling alongside naked children, bustling hordes, wandering cows and tattered dogs. Thatched lean-to hovels housed entire families outside better off homes whose fences and walls served as toilets for the poor. Once experienced, that smell stayed in the nostrils for life.

This "real" rather than British Madras carried defeat, despair, disillusion and dismay for over half a million people whose sounds and behaviours overwhelmed most European newcomers. He remembered that after his first two weeks on patrol he had just wanted to go "home", even though India promised an escape from what lay back there. The new political challenge now, though, came from this cacophony even if its leaders lived in leafier, more prosperous suburbs to the south and west of this wretched murder scene. Most of the new leaders, in fact, lived near Le Fanu's house. That alone roused suspicions about his loyalties among many members of the small, resentful Madras European community. Even other British communities elsewhere in India considered their Madras cousins to be overly conservative, the "Benighted Presidency" label deriding a hidebound mentality rather than a shortage of natural resources. Madras had changed for the worse in a short time, Le Fanu thought, and its new paranoia made him increasingly uncomfortable.

The victim should be enjoying Gymkhana life, not lying dead in this squalor. Board of Revenue bureaucrats would never have found her, with neither the need nor desire to investigate the detritus immediately over their back wall. A passing boatman had spotted her an hour earlier. He despatched a cyclist to the Triplicane suburban police station where the desk sergeant telephoned Le Fanu's office.

One of the force's new black American police cars rattled up to interrupt his thinking, its thin and solid rubber tyres struggling to grip the Canal-side muddy track. A stocky man with broad shoulders and what seemed like no neck, clambered out, clutching a small Gladstone bag. Spying Le Fanu, the newcomer advanced with a rolling gait. His dark blue suit, shirt, tie and wellington boots matched his complexion, the jacket barely containing his barrel chest. The thick hair was jet black. So was the luxuriant beard, masking much of the face.

"Good morning, sir, I am assuming you are Superintendent Le Fanu." The voice was firm, the tone rich, the words well-articulated. His engaging smile displayed broad, white teeth.

"And you must be Sergeant Habibullah."

Le Fanu had read the personnel file the previous evening, and come away impressed. A Muslim from the Telugu-speaking country north of Madras city, Mohammad Habibullah's home town of Nellore hosted frequent Hindu-Muslim squabbles. His father, a mid-level Forest Service employee, realised his son needed an edge to advance. Money was found and Habi sent to England, where he attended a Hampshire boarding school for two years. Le Fanu knew just how difficult that English life would have been for the young Muslim, having endured such a school himself.

Habi survived, though, returning to Madras and Police College three years before the war, fluent now in English as well as Urdu, Tamil and Telugu. He never returned to Nellore, holidays aside. Following successful postings in various districts, he arrived in Madras in 1916 to serve on several teams that solved some important cases. He was marked out as bright and a local with a future. That was why the I-G posted him to the Crime Unit as its first Indian member, further provocation to disgruntled European officers already fearing for their futures. Indianisation was a dirty word, Habi's appointment an unwanted symbol of change. Like Le Fanu, Habi was watched closely by conservatives inside and outside the force. Now teamed together, they would be natural targets for the diehards.

"I'm delighted to have you here, Habibullah, you've an excellent record." Le Fanu shook the newcomer's hand enthusiastically.

"Thank you sir, I'm honoured to work with a senior officer of your high reputation. And you might call me Habi, people find that easier."

Closer up, Le Fanu saw a resolute, intelligent man with intense dark eyes framed by the beard.

"Right, Habi it is. Call me 'sir' when Europeans are around, but otherwise call me LF."

"Sir, thank you, but I'll call you 'sir' at all times. I find it easier that way."

Le Fanu let it go. Never warm at the best of times, relations between British and Indian members of the Madras police were now at their worst. That annoyed him. During the war, he worked closely with his Indian troopers, many of whom died fighting for British ideals and standards they had never nor ever would enjoy back home under current conditions. Britain would happily use men like Habi when it suited, but withhold career progression from them whenever possible.

"Fair enough. Let's get started. I've had a preliminary look at the scene of offence, so we should now search more extensively. What have you got in your bag?"

"Sir, a copy of Hans Gross which I've re-read over the past two days, some small bags to isolate any items found, some tweezers to pick up those items, a magnifying glass, some string, a tape measure, marker flags, a brush, a compass, some glass test tubes in case we need water samples, and a torch. And my notebook and pencils, of course."

Habibullah was more impressive by the minute.

"Good man. If you can find a way over to the far bank and see if there's anything significant there, we can then either follow up or cross it off our list of things to do."

"Yes, sir, right away."

Habi rolled away back along the bank.

Le Fanu breathed deeply, removed his jacket, hooked it on a nearby branch, removed his cufflinks and tie, rolled up his shirt sleeves, stepped into the Canal shallows, and waded towards the body.

Two

As he neared the victim, Le Fanu was swamped by his feared mix of despair, humility, disgust, guilt and anger at a pointless waste of life.

It began during 1914. As a British Indian Army Sixth Division lieutenant, he led a unit against Ottoman Empire divisions in Mesopotamia. The campaign never matched the savagery of the Western Front, but the slaughter still numbed him. His increasing anathema turned permanent at the 1915 battle for Shaiba, as the Turks set out to retrieve Basra. The 6,000 British and Indian troops withstood 18,000 Ottoman soldiers, but among the 4,000 casualties lay a Le Fanu friend, Major George Wheeler, VC (posthumous), and too many of the men under Wheeler's command.

From that moment, Le Fanu vowed to avoid losing his own men or killing too many enemy ones, a military minimalism that angered his commanding officers, won support from his troops, and allowed him to live with himself. Even so, whenever he encountered a body now, his mind retrieved images of too many soldiers killed for too small a purpose.

Standing calf-deep in the Canal, he confirmed his earlier observations. Stepping carefully around the body, he saw nothing that might have belonged to her. The stink of the water intensified as he crouched lower, putting his hands under the surface to feel along the Canal bed for evidence. He dared not think about what he was touching, or the innoculations he might need later. There was no purse or evening bag to be found anywhere, but he assumed its colour would be pale blue.

Her clothing looked intact. The stockings were snagged, a slight tear marred the dress hem, and one shoe heel was broken. He lifted her right hand, the one with the ring. Two jagged scratches scarred the back, three fingernails were broken, but he found nothing under the others. Had she known her killer and been unprepared for the attack?

Reaching deeper into the water, all but retching from the stench, he felt around her shoulders and neck. Her head was wedged in sludge, but the bed was soft, so she should be removed easily enough. That meant the killer had jammed her in there just as easily. In turn, that suggested she was killed elsewhere then dumped here, the killing planned rather than spontaneous.

Who was she? The missing bag was the most obvious source of an answer. If she was well off, as the clothes suggested, then somewhere in Madras her absence would soon be noted. There were few young, unattached (he saw no engagement or wedding ring) European women roaming the city. Whoever she was, her death would bring uproar from the growing "law and order" brigade.

Finding nothing around the body, he widened his search until the water became too deep mid-Canal. He scoured along the bank in both directions for two hundred yards, pushing fifteen yards back from the bank and right up to the Board of Revenue wall. The Chepauk Palace chiefs would arrive at work soon, and no doubt complain about police investigations disrupting their tranquil daily habits. Le Fanu had little time for the Board and its officers. He repeated the search, still finding nothing.

Habibullah appeared from further along the Canal, apprehensively poling a flimsy raft towards the opposite bank.

"Best you could do, Habi?" asked Le Fanu.

"Unfortunately, yes, and while in England I never learned to row."

"Well, try not to fall in, the water's rancid. Never know what you might catch. Can you see anything over there?"

"Nothing floating, sir, and if there's anything underneath we wouldn't see it anyway, the water's too murky."

Le Fanu wished his Tamil was as good as Habi's English.

"Quite right. We may need some constables to search with nets later if we find nothing else to identify her. Can you get on shore over there and see if anyone noticed anything?"

Le Fanu doubted Habi would find anyone willing to talk, but it was worth a try. The police were unpopular enough, but these Canal dwellers lived in constant fear of being forced back to the countryside. They would say nothing and remain invisible if at all possible. It was like dealing with a city within a city within a city.

Habi steered his wobbling craft towards shore. It spiked into the muddy bank and tipped precariously, its commander struggling to stay upright as he leaped for semi-firm ground. Barely making it, he lurched straight into a row of shanties where Le Fanu heard him rousing the residents.

A few minutes later, as Le Fanu retraced his search steps, Habi re-emerged.

"I'm going further along," the sergeant said. "These people say they saw nothing and heard nothing, but I've recorded their names and we can return later if necessary. However, one fellow reports a rumour that someone along the bank heard something last night. I'll go and see what I can discover."

It was better than Le Fanu had expected.

"Well done, Habi," replied Le Fanu, "take your time and I'll keep searching here."

The temperature was climbing but remained bearable. Movement along the Canal increased as Madras awoke. Men and women squatted to relieve themselves, some lifting their clothes while crouching in the shallows. Le Fanu was glad he had completed the search, though he knew the Canal was already well polluted before he waded in. He remembered, too, that some days in India it was easier to stay indoors with a book than venture out to face reality. The sight of people shitting in public disturbed him.

Two flimsy, barge-like country boats ambled along the Canal, connecting Madras markets with provincial rice, cotton and tobacco suppliers. The boat crews looked curiously at the police from under semi-circular thatched covers serving as cabins. The Canal had enriched traders and growers for seventy years, yet now they funded the rising political unrest. No wonder Le Fanu's civil service masters were aggrieved: London was ramming through unwelcome change, and former local allies were transferring their loyalties to new Indian leaders like Gandhi and Nehru nationally, and the troublesome C. Rajagopalachariar locally. That perplexed older Madras European hands, mystified as to why all their glad-handing had come to nought.

The boatmen remained poor, though, living either on their cramped boats or in low, fragile board, mud and tin hovels like those lining the opposite bank and whose inhabitants were sitting Canal-side to better observe both police and body.

That body would complicate the Inspector-General's life far more than the ones found normally in Madras. Any murder was bad enough, but one involving a European, a woman to boot, in the midst of political turmoil, falling profits and rising labour problems was a genuine crisis. If the already nervous European community sniffed a rising crime wave that threatened whites, then the Governor would be pressured and that pressure relayed down the police chain of command. Le Fanu was glad all he had to do was solve the case, even though that might prove difficult.

He looked skywards. The Madras carrion vultures were

assembling overhead, drifting easily on the rising heat currents, awaiting opportunity. She must be moved soon. There was nothing more to be learned here. The autopsy might be revealing, but he was not optimistic.

◻

Three

"Le Fanu, what the bloody hell are you doing here on your own? Where's your team and why's nothing being done? You must get on top of this, now."

The strident voice interrupted Le Fanu's swirling thoughts, many not about the body – among other things, the woman currently sharing his bed was a complication, but at least she was alive.

He peered back through the haze and groaned. It was his immediate boss.

Arthur Jepson's appointment as Commissioner of Police for Madras City astonished the force, given his reputation for little skill and less patience. At forty-nine, he was short, round, red-faced, narrow-eyed, and devious. He was fussily trying to avoid marking his new uniform with its Commissioner's insignia and the dazzlingly polished black dress shoes so sensationally misplaced at a scene of offence, especially this one.

To Le Fanu, the shoes belied a desk man and political manipulator. At least Jepson was wearing trousers, he conceded, not the God-awful bloomers and long socks still favoured by some senior officers. Jepson's police hat covered a close shaven skull, Le Fanu knew. He had met Jepson twice since his appointment and been underwhelmed both times, confirming sour memories of earlier clashes.

The Commissioner's appearance here was as rare as meeting a civil Board of Revenue servant, Le Fanu thought. The violent death of a white woman was a political disaster, so Jepson was covering his arse. An underling would carry the blame for whatever bad news emerged later. Of course, if any credit was available for the taking, Jepson would be first in line.

Le Fanu was stymied. While appointed to the Crime Unit by the I-G, a mentor, for obscure technical reasons he had to report first to Jepson, an oddity emerging only after confirmation of his appointment. Le Fanu would not have worried had the previous Commissioner still been in office, but Jepson was a different matter entirely. Given the man's manner, reputation and behaviour, along with their previous history, Le Fanu proceeded to ignore the official report line and go direct to the I-G. It was dangerous, but showed how much he distrusted and despised Jepson.

Le Fanu tried to anticipate the criticisms.

"I arrived here a short while ago, sir," Le Fanu explained, hoping he sounded calmer than he felt, "and my sergeant's along the bank chasing up a possible witness. Things are following their normal course, as required by the I-G."

He regretted that last comment immediately, watching Jepson react to an imagined taunt and turn even more red-faced.

"Listen to me, and listen carefully, you shit," hissed the Commissioner, "I despise this Gross nonsense, so whatever the I-G wants is his affair. But you report to me, and do what I order you to do. Is that clear? What I want from you is decent police work, not that I think you can do any. What the hell have you achieved so far?"

Le Fanu saw this getting worse. Jepson would pull rank to get authority, the needs of the case a distant second to his need to appear to be in charge.

"Sir," Le Fanu began, "the victim was found an hour ago. We haven't yet discovered anything that will help us identify the killer, or her for that matter. Sergeant Habibullah is along the bank, as I explained, but neither of us has had a chance to make any immediate progress on her name and movements."

Jepson soured further. "I always thought you incompetent, Le Fanu, an incompetent propped up by the I-G for God knows what reason. I'll have you busted back to the ranks quick smart if you continue like this."

As Le Fanu struggled to hold his temper he saw Habi returning from the far bank, appearing through a hole in the fence several yards behind Jepson. Anxious that his sergeant avoid the imminent explosion, Le Fanu tried surreptitiously to signal him away. Habi kept coming. Le Fanu wasn't sure, but it looked like Habi was deliberately ignoring the signals. The sergeant was soon a few steps behind the Commissioner, grinning.

Le Fanu had no choice but to introduce him. Drawing Habi's presence to Jepson's attention, he began, "Sir, this is..."

"Not now for God's sake, Le Fanu, this is too bloody important."

Habi's grin widened, quickly replaced with a serious stone face the moment Jepson, not able to help himself, whipped around.

"And who the bloody hell are you?" roared the Commissioner.

"Sir, allow me to introduce myself, I am Sergeant Mohammad Habibullah." Habi had turned on his very best public school voice, sounding far more polished than Jepson.

Jepson looked at Habi malevolently, sneered, and returned to the attack on Le Fanu.

"You don't even know who she is yet?" Jepson's face was crimson by this point. "What kind of a slack bloody answer is that? You're a fucking disgrace." Fists jammed on hips, he was a barrel about to burst.

"Sir," Le Fanu resumed, attempting calmness, "Sergeant Habibullah's an excellent addition to the unit and will report on his searches. "

"Never mind that," shouted Jepson, "have you found anything, or are you just as bloody incompetent as your so-called superior officer?" He glared at Habi who looked evenly at the fuming Commissioner.

"As I said earlier, I arrived just ahead of you, sir," Le Fanu intervened," the sergeant came later and we've had only a brief chance to search the scene of offence."

With Jepson losing both control and patience, Le Fanu sensed the investigation was already at risk.

"Sergeant," he said, "could you brief us on what you've found along the bank?"

Le Fanu hoped Habi had something because, if not, there was no predicting what Jepson might do or say. Among his other faults, Jepson persistently made racist comments about Indian personnel, some of whom complained officially in earlier days. The all-white inquiry panels cleared Jepson, but Indian members of the force remained wary.

Habi picked up on Le Fanu's anxiety, and began reporting .

"Sir, I've found nothing physical to help us yet. There's still no sign of a bag or a purse. She is still wearing all her jewellery, we think. None of her clothes were removed, it seems, and there was certainly none found anywhere along the bank."

Jepson looked to intervene. Habi hurried on.

"However, sir, there's one piece of possibly good news. We believe a man from near here may have heard something last night. He is not here presently because he went off to work on a country boat about two hours ago, just before we reached here. But we have his name, know where he lives, and I'll interview him immediately upon his return. He might be helpful."

Le Fanu admired Habi's insight and quick response, but they were a weak defence against Jepson's onslaught.

"Not bloody good enough." Jepson was incandescent, and Le Fanu wondered if the government provided life insurance for senior officers. The Commissioner looked ready to have a heart attack.

"Sir," said Le Fanu, "this is a serious and different crime…"

"What makes you think it's a crime? You don't know anything yet, you fucking idiot," Jepson snarled.

Le Fanu was stunned. Desperate to make this case disappear and avoid political complications, Jepson was ready to argue that a woman found speared into the Canal and suffering a broken neck had died from natural causes.

"We're considering all possibilities, sir," he replied, guardedly, "but it's unlikely to be suicide or accident. A European lady would not come here willingly, and this one scarcely threw herself headfirst into the Canal."

He could not resist the barb, and heard a feigned cough behind as Habi covered a laugh.

Jepson looked around rapidly at Habi, who returned an innocent stare, then lashed a polished shoe with the riding crop he was carrying. The affectation amused subordinates who immediately lit upon "Jockey" as a nickname. Privately, Le Fanu preferred "Olli," as in oleaginous. The Commissioner was certainly oily enough to earn that nickname, and he scowled anew at Le Fanu.

"We'll do the basic things immediately, of course," Le Fanu continued quickly. "However, there's still no sign of her evening bag. Given the dress, it's likely pale blue and our best immediate chance to identify her, so locating it is a priority."

"You should have found something by now. This is just bloody pathetic. Swanning about here on your own when you should have had a whole squad in." Jepson was working himself into another tirade.

That was the approach the I-G had hoped to avoid by setting up the Gross approach, thought Le Fanu. A squad bumbling about this murder site would be hugely unhelpful. But getting Jepson to see that was impossible. So, too, was getting change into the Madras police force.

Commissioner Jepson was now stomping around the

scene of offence. Le Fanu feared any remaining evidence would be trampled by this dinosaur.

"Sir, we're going by the book, and that means methodical analysis rather than undue haste and irrational guesswork."

Jepson reddened further at another suspected attack on his professionalism.

Habi suffered another coughing fit.

"Don't bloody provoke me, Le Fanu, I know what you're up to, and it won't work. I want results, and you'll produce them or you're fucking out."

"I understand, sir, we'll make progress as fast as possible," Le Fanu replied.

The riding crop thrashed the other shoe.

"I'm telling you, Le Fanu, I-G's pet or not, your career's finished if you fuck this up. I've never liked you or your methods. This Crime Unit is a farce. It'll be disbanded when this case collapses. Now just get on with some half decent work. The dumbest constable can do that, so it should not be beyond you."

Still within earshot, the two uniformed constables bristled behind their smoke clouds.

"Report back to me by the end of the day and, by God, you'd better have some results."

Jepson stared at Le Fanu for several seconds, ignored Habi, spun on polished heels and swaggered off, slapping his shoe with the swagger stick as he went while stepping around the bank's muddier patches.

Le Fanu watched Jepson's retreating figure until it disappeared into a waiting car that slithered off down the track.

He had feared this, but not thought it would happen so quickly. Given more time, he might have produced a name for and a story about the victim. Jepson knew that, so the quick belligerence was a deliberate tactic to wrong foot the investigating team. The Commissioner was not after information, he was establishing a scapegoat for whatever poor publicity might emerge.

As Le Fanu watched the car disappear around a bend, he knew he had a management problem again.

Four

Habi was already in the water by the body as Le Fanu edged back into the Canal, still rattled by the Jepson onslaught.

Hundreds of shanty town onlookers thronged the far bank, women wearing plain saris and men just loincloths or the long, sarong-like cotton lunghis and no shirts. They all jostled for position to better see what happened next, the hubbub rising along with the speculation. A dead white woman would be news for weeks to come.

If Jepson's dinosaur feet had left any clue undisturbed, it would soon be lost under those of the crowd, thought Le Fanu, but Habi had searched thoroughly, he knew. They had all the information they would get here, precious little. Jepson's threats and deadline added even more urgency to confirming this woman's identity, and her movements over recent days. Her body was found less than three hours ago, but they were losing time already.

"Odd she ended up here," Le Fanu murmured as he moved closer, more to himself than to Habi who responded anyway.

"She was most likely brought here later. By the look of her, I'd say she was killed elsewhere, so that raises questions about time, place and intent."

Le Fanu looked up, pleased. Habi really was sharp. He had just read Gross but already absorbed the methods and analytical thinking. The two of them stood a good chance of finding her killer, despite Jepson's derision.

"Time to move her, you think, Habi?" he asked. "There's nothing left here, we know, and nothing to help us identify her."

Habi nodded.

Le Fanu moved towards the victim's head and worked his arms under her shoulders, preparing to lift her out, an unpleasant prospect. He stopped, stood upright again.

"I'm sorry, Habi, I should've asked earlier: can you do this, touch a dead European woman?"

Before the war, Le Fanu thought, he would not have considered let alone asked the question. Back then, he had the same amount of empathy for Indian officers as most other Europeans – little or none. But amidst the war's trauma and grief, he learned much from and about his troops. He was now more sensitive, he hoped, and embarrassed by memories of his younger approach, but there were still times when he wondered just how ignorant he and other British officials could be.

"Thank you for asking, sir, but it's alright. I'm a Muslim, yes, but in the way you're an Anglican, I suspect. The messages and lessons are there and I remember them, but I also lead a secular life, and wouldn't be a policeman if there was any part of the job I couldn't do because I'm a Muslim."

Le Fanu suspected he was far less a thinking Anglican than Habi was a thinking Muslim, but said nothing. Instead, he bent over again and took a firmer grip on the body.

"Good," he said, "can you support her back and legs while I lift her shoulders?"

As they settled into position, the onlookers crowded closer with those at the front struggling to avoid being pushed into the water. The noise levels ratcheted higher as the pushing and shoving intensified. The two constables were still nearby, still smoking, still watching on, still doing nothing. They could provide little control, Le Fanu knew. The best strategy was to get the body out and away as rapidly as possible.

Neither man mentioned how he was feeling, but Le Fanu was queasy.

He crouched lower still, slipping his hands further into the murk either side of her neck to strengthen his hold, trying not to breathe in through his nose. The stench was intensifying and the temperature climbing so he was starting to sweat. Sensible or not, a suit was not the best clothing for this job, but protocol demanded it be worn. Would he ever buck any of that protocol, Le Fanu wondered.

"Alright," he said, "gently."

Habi angled the body up while Le Fanu extricated her head from the ooze. It came out easily enough, face and hair caked in the foul-smelling sludge infused with the myriad wastes jettisoned by local residents and passers-by.

"There should be an ambulance here by now," Habi remarked softly. He is as moved by this as I am, thought Le Fanu.

"Probably can't get close enough, we should have a stretcher brought in."

He shouted to the two constables who scurried off in search of the ambulance.

Le Fanu and Habi almost lost hold of her and their footing as they struggled up the slippery grass, the crowd roaring at every near miss. After a few minutes manoeuvring, they laid the body on the cleanest part of the bank before wiping their hands on the grass.

Le Fanu broke the silence.

"Thanks Habi, that was difficult, you did a great job."

"Thank you, sir, but I'll be delighted if we do not have to do that every day."

"The medical examination will clarify things." Le Fanu changed the subject, not wanting to voice his own thoughts. "Can you spot anything immediately?"

"No obvious marks on wrists or ankles, so she wasn't tied."

Habi looked sombre.

"Nothing other than the pearls around her neck, either. Any other jewellery we couldn't see before?"

"No," replied Habi. "The fact that the jewellery is still present suggests murderous intent rather than death by botched robbery."

They looked at each other, and nodded. Jepson's attempt to brand this a non-crime was ludicrous, but he would hold that line as long as possible for his own purposes. That complicated the investigation, another reason they needed information sooner rather than later. The medical examination was assuming even greater importance than usual.

A dead white woman, political trouble, a belligerent Commissioner, an anxious and aggrieved British community, and a truculent police force made the worst possible combination. And Le Fanu and Habi had to steer the investigation, both of them already under pressure from superiors and peers.

Le Fanu sighed. Just two hours into the case and there were more obstacles than evidence.

Habi suddenly grinned at his boss.

"I say, sir, you did put the Commissioner in his place."

Le Fanu acknowledged Habi's insight.

"I didn't mean to, it just came out that way."

"How on earth did a fool like Jepson get appointed anyway?"

"I'm not sure I should let your disrespect go unremarked, Habi, but I can tell you he was a compromise. Two leading candidates cancelled each other out, the brass disagreed on everyone else. Some fool who didn't know him or his reputation mentioned Jepson. Next thing we know he's here."

Habi looked thoughtful, assembling his next words carefully.

"There's no good enemy, sir, but the Commissioner could be a really bad one, especially given the history between you."

"How'd you know about that?"

"I heard stories, sir, and did some background checks on both of you. The service records are easy enough to find. You both served in Chingleput straight after the war. You personally resolved a couple of difficult cases but then got transferred immediately. Rumours in the ranks suggest you two clashed seriously over an Indian sergeant whom you defended and Jepson wanted sacked."

"I'll have to watch you, Sergeant, I think, you know way too much already, but good work. Yes, there's history between me and Jepson. However, I've no time to worry about an incompetent Commissioner disrupting my life."

Even Le Fanu thought he sounded unconvincing.

"Who polishes the Commissioner's shoes, I wonder?" Habi changed tack. "He doesn't trust his servants, apparently, at least according to the gossip I've heard. Perhaps Mrs. Jockey has that task?"

"Again, not my concern, but she's widely described by many Club members as long suffering."

"One of the many things I like about the English language, sir, is the way we can use words to say one thing when we mean quite another."

The two Indian constables arrived back with a stretcher, looking sideways at the body.

"Never dealt with a dead European before?" Le Fanu asked them in Tamil. "And never a European woman I'm guessing? Don't worry, put the stretcher down, Sergeant Habibullah and I'll deal with the body. You carry her back, then we'll place her in the ambulance."

The bearers were relieved, and soon stretchered the body back along the rough track after Habi and Le Fanu had lifted her gently on to the stretcher.

Habi lit a cigarette without offering Le Fanu one, his homework also telling him that refusal was certain. Was the Superintendent the sole non-smoking returned serviceman?

"Watch Jepson, though, sir," Habi resumed. "He's petty

minded, vicious and ambitious. My friend ended up in a one-man, no-dog punishment station because of him. Jepson made a serious mistake in a case, and shifted the blame to my friend. He's not the only victim I know about, either."

"Thanks Habi, I'll watch out. A quick solution here would help."

"If we don't discover who she is tout suite, you'll be mid-Canal sans my raft let alone a paddle, sir."

Le Fanu patted the sergeant's shoulder as they laughed.

The two constables waited behind the ambulance. Le Fanu took a thin sheet from inside the vehicle and placed it over the body. He and Habi slid the stretcher into a rack on one side of the van.

"What a terrible end for such a young woman," Habi spluttered through his last mouthful of smoke.

"Agreed. Let's get her to the hospital and see what our expert there can divine."

Five

Inspector-General Sir Maurice Wilson gazed out through the open French doors of his Police Headquarters first floor office, grateful for the view towards Marina Beach where Indian Ocean waves crested in, white caps sending off spray. It was often calm, sometimes stormy, and always mesmerising. A lot like his job, he mused. He had read somewhere that during the later nineteenth century, before Madras had a real harbour, ship crews simply dumped horses overboard hoping they would swim ashore. That seemed like his current job, too.

The office was large, the French doors opening to a wide, covered verandah. The building dated from the early nineteenth century and looked stately, all white and simple lines, but no longer met the needs of a modern police force. A new wing had been built to the rear but even that was crammed already. Le Fanu's unit was over there. Wilson had not wanted it taken hostage by the Commissioner's office over in Egmore, so crammed Le Fanu and now Habi into the Criminal Intelligence Department area.

The I-G's desk faced the French doors so he could keep the view while he worked. It was soothing, and God knows he needed that. It was sad, he thought, that his peers and rivals sat facing their internal doors, fearing anybody or anything they could not see coming. That anxiety symbolised the present state of the force, he thought.

On one side of the room a long, elegant table was surrounded by a dozen equally elegant chairs where he held "prayers," as he termed his morning briefings and consultations with senior officers. In one corner, two club chairs sat either side of a small circular table. At day's end he frequently took a whisky or three with someone from among his few trusted subordinates. That was often Le Fanu.

The room was dominated by bookcases, glass fronted and replete with legal reports, crime statistics, crime technique volumes, including his prized signed copy of Gross, large runs of the Government's district manuals and gazetteers, biographical sources, a complete set of the whimsically named Asylum Press Madras Almanack going back over sixty years, and a motley collection of other publications. The Almanack was indispensable: it listed every city inhabitant, at least those who counted - not all the criminals appeared in there but most troublemakers might be found, along with all those whose sensibilities must be considered. That was especially important with this wretched dead European woman.

One modest bookcase tucked away in a darkened corner was rarely noticed by visitors, but contained Wilson's treasured collection on the 1799 Seringapatam campaign when Arthur Wellesley, later the Duke of Wellington, defeated Tipu Sultan and set the course of British power in India. Wilson's grandfather served Wellesley as a raw staff office subaltern and the core of the collection descended from his possessions, including a sword said to have been used by Tipu. Wilson sometimes wondered if he might not have enjoyed those times more than these, command seeming more straightforward back then.

His secretary knocked, then entered. "The Commissioner is here, sir."

Jepson stormed in.

"Good morning Arthur. I take it you want to discuss this European woman?"

"Yes, I-G, I want Le Fanu off the case, he's useless."

"What makes you think that?" Wilson's voice cooled.

"He's given us no results yet."

"Let me see: the medicos are only now examining the body, Le Fanu has just done the preliminary scene analysis and identified some possible witnesses. The case is about four hours old."

"But still no results." Jepson sounded vengeful rather than professional.

"I expect we'll get the victim's name today," Wilson responded.

"Perhaps so, I-G, but that gets us no closer to finalising the matter, and we need a result. Some senior people at the Club are very unhappy already."

"Jepson," said Wilson in aggravated tone, "Club talk mixes gossip, fact, fantasy, wishful thinking and sour thoughts. Those "senior people" can comment all they like, but we'll run the case as we always do, on police lines. And if you've spoken to those Club idiots just four hours into the case, then it occurs to me you might have better things to do with your time." "

Jepson turned crimson. "I still think we should replace Le Fanu."

"What's your real agenda here?" shot back Wilson. "Le Fanu has an excellent record, yet you want him sidelined."

"He's not a team player, sir, never thinks like the rest of us."

Wilson stood up from the desk, shaking his head. "By now, Jepson, you should've realised that's precisely why I gave him the unit. He gets results because he doesn't think like the rest of you."

"Perhaps so, sir, but he's not popular." Jepson was struggling now

"Le Fanu won't be bothered by that, and neither am I. It's not a popularity contest."

"That's my point, sir, he's not a team player."

Wilson slammed a hand on the desk. "Jepson, get back to your office, and find a way to work with Le Fanu. It's bad enough a case without us having an internal brawl over who runs it."

That signalled the conversation's end, but Jepson missed the signal.

"I-G, I want him replaced."

Wilson turned towards the Commissioner, looking calm but the words suggesting otherwise.

"Jepson, I've given you an instruction. Your best course would be to scuttle away and obey."

Jepson reddened further, the anger palpable.

"Sir."

He left, Wilson knowing the problem would only get bigger. The sound of riding crop on boot resounded down the corridor outside. Jepson's intransigence would rub up badly against Le Fanu's commitment to principle and disdain for anything unprofessional.

It had always been that way, Wilson thought. He had watched Jepson then Le Fanu enter the force. Le Fanu was all hard work and shrewd insight, while Jepson cultivated his immediate superiors and avoided responsibility wherever possible. Le Fanu returned from the war an improved man, in Wilson's view, but Jepson used those years to ingratiate himself to all and sundry. That was why he became Commissioner, not because of his crime-solving skills. Of all his officers, Wilson reflected, Le Fanu was best placed to deal with the new political order because he now had a deeper understanding of Indians than anyone else. The war made him bitter, but also better. If it was simply down to merit, Le Fanu would be Commissioner now, even at his relatively young age. The politics of fear and change worked against him, though, and the state of his marriage had not helped. Now Jepson, a throwback if ever there was one, had to be dealt with.

He returned to the sea view, seeking solace. Tough days lay ahead.

Six

Le Fanu returned home briefly to take breakfast but, really, to think hard about this new case.

His choice of home was another source of irritation within official and commercial Madras. At the end of the war he had several months leave owing, but instead of going to the UK he returned to Madras, looking for a house in which to live a quiet life.

To widespread condemnation, he bought an old villa in the heart of Mylapore, paid for out of his accumulated savings and service pay. It was a lovely, tree-lined suburb close to Police headquarters. The houses were large and stylish with extensive gardens. It hosted two of the great Hindu temples and was home to the traditional Carnatic music movement. Throughout its streets and byways, tiny shops housed instrument makers and musicians. But Mylapore was also the city's heartland for the push towards political independence. It was lawyer and, to many senior British administrators, agitator land. Some of those lawyers once served the Madras government, but most now supported the Indian National Congress and argued for constitutional change if not complete political independence.

If Le Fanu chose to live there, thought the more conservative Europeans, he must be an Indian sympathiser. His wife had obviously thought so because she left him, returned to

England and never came back. No decent senior police officer would live in Mylapore.

Like most Mylapore homes, Le Fanu's was large, on a big plot of land behind a wall. He loved the garden, the first thing that attracted him upon seeing the place. It was mostly lawn which he used as a chipping and putting green to keep up his golf game, not that he played much anymore given a lack of time and a dearth of pleasant playing companions .

The garden perimeter was lined with dense shrubbery and the tall, established trees so typical of Mylapore. Streets here were over-arched with dense green trees that provided shade and ambience, especially during the really hot weather - those who disparaged Madras described the four seasons there as "hot, hot, hot and hotter." Le Fanu had also installed bird feeders to attract species other than the ubiquitous crows.

Like all Madras "great" houses, his was very open. Wooden slatted doors on the lower floor opened onto broad verandahs overlooking the lawns, but also giving protection from the sun and maximising the breeze. The extensive servant quarters and kitchen areas were at the back of the ground floor behind the big dining room, two general reception areas, and a library where Le Fanu spent a lot of time.

There were four bedrooms upstairs, each with a bathroom and dressing room. They stood two by two on either side of a wide, high-ceilinged hall, now served by electric fans but which not too long ago were operated by servants, the legendary punkah wallahs who would sit outside each room, pulling on a string to operate a fan inside.

Le Fanu returned home to experience the same sensation every day, relief at leaving the office mixed with the joy of being in a place where he could relax. He loved the house from the moment he moved in, and even his wife's departure had not reduced his pleasure. If he was honest, her departure made the house even more pleasant. They were happy enough in the two years before he left for the war, but by the time they shifted into the house they were very different people trying to find a reason to co-exist. He never found out, but suspected her war in Madras was much more pleasant and pleasurable than his at the front.

He took breakfast on the verandah, south Indian coffee washing down the steamed rice idlis, fried chickpea vadas and tamarind-based vegetable sambar that long ago replaced his English breakfast. Work papers lay on the table, along with the mail he was opening and mostly discarding. One letter, though, raised a frown before being set aside.

"Ro, could you bring some more coffee, please?"

A woman arrived bearing a smile along with a copper coffee pot, and refilled his cup. She was about thirty, tall, well-built, dark hair cut short. Her face was angular, the mouth full-lipped, and the eyes dark but bright. She was much better dressed than the normal house servant, a stylish dress falling to her ankles.

She was neither local dark nor European white but more latter than former. Roisin McPhedren was Anglo-Indian, the daughter of a mixed marriage. Her father came from Ireland to work as a railway manager, then met and married a local woman working as an office clerk. Like all such marriages it was despised by European society, so her parents were posted to every possible remote Presidency railway office, and she went with them. When Ro was twenty, she met and married another Anglo-Indian who died in a railway accident towards the end of the war. When Le Fanu arrived back in Madras, a friend suggested she would be a good household assistant. She needed a job because times were difficult, so arrived as general chatelaine.

"Thanks Ro. Do you need money for supplies today?"

She shook her head, smiled again, looked at him for a moment, then left.

A uniformed constable arrived at the gate on a bicycle, dismounted, and walked towards the house.

"Good morning, Mudaliar, this is unexpected."

C. Muthiah Mudaliar worked in the Inspector-General's office support unit, but few other Europeans could have named him. To them, such lowly people remained nameless.

"Sir, the Inspector-General is asking me to be giving you a message."

"I guessed that – what is it?"

"Sir, the Chief Secretary himself has been calling to the Inspector-General and maybe having some information on the dead woman."

Le Fanu stopped eating. If the Chief Martinet was involved, this case just officially got that much harder. "Thank you Mudaliar. I am guessing the message is that I should go to see the Chief Secretary?"

"Yes, sir."

"Thanks Mudaliar, you'd better get back."

Le Fanu left the table, placing in his pocket the letter set aside earlier.

A few minutes later he wheeled out his motorcycle, a 1000cc Indian Powerplus bought from an American met in the Middle East, then shipped back to Madras. With a top speed of sixty miles per hour and an extended cruising range, it was perfect. His favourite adventure was to ride up to Ootacamund from Madras on the occasions his presence was requested there, when senior Government officials sought hill station relief from the hottest seasons on the plains. It was the only bike of its kind in south India, another sign of eccentricity, according to his critics.

He kicked the bike to life, idled down the gravelled driveway and into the quiet dirt-based, tree-lined lane that led down to Bishop Weller's Road then onto his normal route to the Marina and HQ. That was not the most direct route, because he went across to Luz Church Road and down to the beach where he turned left towards Police headquarters instead of going directly there down Elliot's Road. The reason was simple: he liked time on the bike, because it helped him think.

Le Fanu observed the street life as he went. Men were returning from their morning temple visits, most dressed in the lunghi and bare-chested apart from the sacred thread looped across a shoulder that marked them as Brahmins, and bearing the distinctive forehead markings identifying them as followers of either Shiva or Vishnu. Then there were the roadside breakfast sellers who specialised in the idlis and sambar he now favoured. Fruit and flower sellers were everywhere. Kids emerged from small houses, immaculately dressed and on their way to school. Mylapore took education seriously. It was just so different from where he grew up.

There was also the poverty most people associated with India, even in this well-off suburb. Tiny lean-to squats and hovels stood up against house fences, entire families crammed into a couple of square yards of covered space. Toilet facilities were those same fences, a little way off from the huts. On some corners small kids begged from people riding bicycles or riding in the few pony-and-carts still to be seen. Beggars got small return from the now more numerous cars because sitting behind glass made it easier to ignore the supplicants. Would political change do anything for these people, Le Fanu wondered.

He turned onto the Marina, buoyed by the sight of the sea and the smell of salt. The bike created its own breeze and he opened the throttle to create more. He was wearing goggles but no helmet, so the sense of freedom increased momentarily, subsiding as he slowed near the office.

Most cases allowed him to be self-contained but this one meant too many other people, like Olli, had a vested interest in his actions. He could not be his own person, the quality he appreciated most when Wilson offered him the post.

He stopped outside the columned main entrance to the building, and a groundsman came over to wheel the bike around to a small space commandeered for the bike in the stables. The need for horses was declining and the emerging government economy drive saw several of them sold off, creating space for newer transport options like his bike.

Once inside, he climbed the wide, winding stairs towards the I-G's office where he was immediately shown in.

"I-G, the message was to go directly to the Chief Secretary," said Le Fanu," but I guessed I should check with you personally first."

"Well spotted, LF. There's little I can add, however, because the Chief Secretary has not enlightened me on any new information. I fear this will get even more complicated, because he obviously knows something but is reluctant to make it widely known."

Le Fanu nodded. "That had occurred to me, sir, and it's worrying."

"He doesn't like either of us," the I-G continued, "so for heaven's sake try not to upset him too much. You know what he's like."

"Unfortunately, sir, I do, and I'm not looking forward to this. But I'll report back to you as soon as possible."

Once back in his own office, Le Fanu had Habibullah set up the usual crime analysis blackboards, listing all lines of inquiry and the state of their progress. That list would lengthen in the coming hours and days, Le Fanu thought as he returned to the front entrance where a police vehicle awaited to take him to the Secretariat.

Seven

By now it was eleven am, five hours since the CID duty office gave him the news now spreading though the European community with senior officials being pestered for information and pressured on the need for action. As the car travelled north towards Fort St. George and the Secretariat, Le Fanu contemplated his next appointment.

Sir Charles Whitney, the Chief Secretary, was a notorious conservative who brooked no dissent. A year from retirement, he loathed reform and was incensed at the prospect of more Indians entering "his service". He was a dedicated "law and order" man which meant he disliked liberal policemen. Whitney had orchestrated local European opposition to the proposed reforms, and masterminded the Indian Civil Service Association's bitter rejection of proposed changes to service conditions. A couple of months earlier he had called out the army to confront political demonstrators, threatening to have live ammunition fired at any protesters refusing to disperse. He might have been the mould for the "Steel Frame" the ICS was said to give administration in India.

The car cruised past the stately buildings of Queen Mary College, Presidency College then the University of Madras whose domes and turrets looked more Arabian than Indian, Le Fanu all the while thinking about Whitney's possible involvement. The imposing Public Works Department sat in front of the Chepauk Palace behind which they had pulled their victim from the Canal mud. The four Members of the Board clashed frequently with the denizens of the Secretariat, particularly the one Le Fanu was on his way to meet. Away on the beach side, the fishing boats were drawn up on the shore, some of the morning's catch already on sale by the roadside. The two sides of Madras life could not have been more obvious.

Le Fanu always experienced culture shock when entering Fort St. George through the tiny arched gate designed for horses but now used by cars. Still surrounded by its moat, the Fort was really a small town complete with its own church. Yet it was so unlike what lay immediately to the north in commercial Georgetown. Europeans had been in Madras for three hundred years now, the Fort the constant symbol of British power in the south. Somehow, though, it remained remote and aloof from the political and social change going on outside and that made life more difficult for people like Le Fanu, especially when Fort officials like Whitney began interfering.

Standing at the bottom of the Secretariat steps, he wondered again why people enthused about this building. Yes, it had those four black pillars at each side and a storied past, but inside it was a rabbit warren of offices with files everywhere and an army of people employed to shift those files from one pile to another. He walked up to the hallowed top floor and the office of the Chief Secretary where one of the army, a trusted younger ICS man marked out for greater things and posted close to power in order to be groomed, made him wait "until the Chief Secretary was ready."

That turned out to be another twenty minutes. So much for the urgency, thought the policeman.

When he was finally shown into the spacious office lined with paintings and relics from earlier great days, Sir Charles was standing in front of his desk, smoking a cigar and drinking coffee. A compact little man, he wore a conservative dark, pin striped suit matched with a white wing collared shirt and dull tie.

"Coffee, Le Fanu?"

"Yes, sir, thank you very much."

The rising star looked miffed when asked by his boss to serve morning tea, but withdrew gracefully enough.

"Thanks for coming over so soon, Le Fanu, I appreciate it and I do apologise about the wait. These damned strikes have the business community up in arms and I have to calm them down. Damned box wallahs, would not have them here if I had my way, but I suppose commerce has to flourish."

The Chief Secretary moved to a small table in the corner, sat, and invited Le Fanu to do the same.

"Sir, I understand you might have some information or ideas about our dead woman."

"Quite so. The thing is, from the description I have, it seems she might have been a fishing fleeter."

The fishing fleet, young women come from England in search of husbands, was the butt of many jokes but also the source of several marriages, some successful. Before the war, Le Fanu became the target for several fisherwomen, but once married he lost contact with the fleet's activities, except when encountering its passengers at dinners and dances. Once his wife left, however, more desperate trawlers still considered him a possible catch.

"Is there anything specific that leads you to that view, Sir Charles?

The bespectacled Chief Secretary delayed his answer.

"Well, as you will understand, it is a little delicate."

Le Fanu became more gloomy. Delicate meant that a prominent or connected name was involved, so the investigation would have more than the normal egg shells to be avoided.

"Delicate, sir?"

Le Fanu hated the charade demanded on these occasions,

but hoped enlightenment was imminent.

"Yes," replied Whitney, "don't want to start a search unnecessarily, but one fleet member seems unaccounted for."

The Chief Secretary was visibly worried. Given his reputation for being imperturbable, that was even more concerning.

"Perhaps if you…."

"Yes, of course. You're an experienced man, and we have to trust someone."

That seemed a backhanded compliment, but Le Fanu let it slide by.

"The fact is, one of the fleet has been staying with Sir Roland Wark but did not appear as expected this morning."

Le Fanu's gloom deepened - Wark was the city's most senior businessman, a Madras resident for over forty years and a confidant of every senior administrator.

"As I say," the Chief Secretary continued, "we don't want to panic unduly. The young lady wouldn't be the first fleeter to drink too much at a dinner, then wake up in some chap's bed with a massive hangover and no further chance of finding a husband."

Among other conservatisms, Whitney reportedly had little time for the younger generation.

"Quite so, sir, but if someone is missing, perhaps we should investigate discreetly to satisfy ourselves one way or another. Do you have a name?

"Jane Carstairs. She's twenty nine and has been at Wark's for about a month. I have not seen you at too many of the season's functions, so you wouldn't be aware of her, or any of them really."

Le Fanu had no idea how to take that remark.

"She has been at all the functions and taken up all the usual invitations, mainly in the company of her friend, Virginia Campbell, who is also out fishing. It was Miss Campbell who received the invitation to Wark's. She has some sort of connection through Edinburgh. On the strength of that, Miss

Carstairs also arrived at Wark's."

"Do we know anything about her background?"

Sir Charles picked up the cigar previously deposited on an ashtray, took a deep pull and became even more disdainful.

"Well, both of them were educated beyond any necessary level. Jolly hockey sticks at Rodean, then both went up to Girton at Cambridge. No wonder they're out here searching for husbands."

The Chief Secretary had evidently never recovered from Mrs. Pankhurst and the vote for women.

Le Fanu restrained a smile. "Miss Carstairs did not appear for breakfast, then?"

"No, which is why Wark called me, given the spreading news about the body. Looking out for fear of his own reputation, too, I would think."

"Were the two women at any particular function last night?"

"There were evening drinks at Wark's, then Misses Carstairs and Campbell went off by car to a garden party given by the Secretary to the Board of Revenue."

Could this get any worse? The tension between Secretariat and Board was legendary, aggravated by their physical separation between the Chepauk Palace and the Fort. The Secretary to the Board, Arthur Jamieson, was below Whitney's rank but that did not prevent the Chief Martinet from looking lemon lipped.

"Who was there, and what time did the women leave Mr Jamieson's, sir?"

"I don't have the detail, of course, so you best pursue that with the man himself. No doubt he'll be of assistance."

For a small community a long way from home, Le Fanu reflected, Madras hosted enmities, divisions, and personal struggles in great number and considerable intensity.

"Yes, sir, thank you. I will conduct discreet inquiries with Sir Roland and Mr. Jamieson. The Inspector-General will get my reports but I know he'll forward them to you. Thank you for the information."

As Le Fanu left the building and entered the waiting car, he wondered how much more complicated this could become, and just how hard it might be to unravel this woman's story.

Eight

The answer came quickly, because he returned to his office only to leave again: the morgue's medical examiner already had a preliminary report. Le Fanu had anticipated this, but hoped it would not happen quite so quickly. Part of his aversion to the loss of life had transmuted into a pathological distaste for morgues and discussions about autopsies. Given his profession, that was like a golfer being allergic to grass.

His visit to Habi's office was more procrastination than anything else, as a result. Habi had lined up several blackboards, all recording the few case details yet available. There was a wall board on which they could pin papers, and a large map of Madras pinned on another wall with the location of the victim's body already marked. There was little else Le Fanu could do, other than ask Habi to check diary commitments for the coming days and eliminate anything non-urgent. Their time would be precious.

Le Fanu now had no other excuse to avoid the morgue.

He willed the driver to go ever more slowly as they tracked back along the Marina, past the Fort, over the bridge, and into Georgetown proper before reaching the General Hospital. The city was crowded as always. Bullock carts blocked motor vehicles, rickshaws and handcarts challenged pedestrians. Traffic policemen struggled to impose order on chaos. Traffic snarls were everywhere. These people were going about their lives while he was going to find out how another life ended. That was depressing.

The morgue was difficult to find in the labyrinthine hospital buildings, hidden away as if death was embarrassing both for the victim and those left behind. It was an old facility, scarcely updated since the late nineteenth century, further suggestion that authorities were loathe to admit its presence, let alone its necessity.

Dr Ramachandran worked on police cases sometimes, and Le Fanu knew him to be an excellent analyst. Among the first Indians from Madras to train overseas, he spent several years in London developing a taste for classical music as well as his medical skills. Ramachandran was among the first in Madras to buy a record player. Technically he was not attached to the morgue, being an Assistant Surgeon, but he was interested in medical jurisprudence more broadly so found the morgue compelling. Erudite, charming and professional, even he could not lift Le Fanu's dismay at having to be there.

"I see, Superintendent, that you are your usual happy self upon entering my domain?"

"Rama, you know me too well."

"Shall I do the autopsy now for you?" Ramachandran asked, the whisp of a smile at the corners of his soft mouth.

"What an offer. I would take it up, but I know you've already done your work to spare me discomfort."

"Come through, I'll tell you what I've found."

Ramachandran led off back through cramped spaces, the hospital smells Le Fanu found so nauseating strengthening by the yard. Specimen shelves lined the corridors for lack of space elsewhere, their contents further upsetting the policeman's mental and physical condition. Through small, dusty windows he could see Ramachandran's assistants cleaning up after one examination - perhaps the woman - and preparing for the next, a body already on the table. Le Fanu looked away hurriedly, following the doctor into an office the size of a broom cupboard.

"Rama, you're a professional and highly qualified man, excellent at your work. Why do you put up with these conditions?"

The Indian looked up, bemused. "It's my duty. I owe it to people to help find out why their loved ones died."

"But we give you so little support."

"Even more reason I should be dedicated."

"You did all that training, and could earn so much more based in a practice in one of the good suburbs."

"I have all I need for myself, the rest I give in service to my country which surely needs it, even you would agree. Now, where's that report?"

He picked up several papers. Le Fanu had assumed there would be little to report, so wondered what was coming.

"Do you have a name for her yet?" Dr. Ramachandran inquired.

Le Fanu knew him well enough to know that he was not after gossip material.

"No, but we have a possible candidate, a missing woman visiting from England, name of Jane Carstairs."

"A fishing fleeter?"

"Probably, but after we finish here I have to go and follow up on the possibility. If she was a fleeter, would it have an impact on your findings?"

"It would not change my findings, but it might help explain some of them. However, let us start at the beginning, all good things to those who wait."

In spite of his surroundings and feelings, Le Fanu could only smile, Ramachandran was a rare human being.

Ramachandran thought the woman had died four to six hours before she was found. That placed time of death somewhere between midnight and two in the morning. If it was midnight, then most garden parties were finished at least three hours earlier. The obvious question, then, was what had she done and what had happened to her during those missing three hours? Part of that query concerned her location. She was found in the Canal behind the Chepauk Palace, about midway between the Madras Cricket Club ground and the Island where the Gymkhana was located. That was quite a distance across the city from the garden party at Jamieson's home, an elegant spread in Nungambakkam. So, how did she get from there to where she was found, and how had those three hours been filled?

"That gives me some questions, Rama."

"I fear I'll give you even more."

It was no surprise she had alcohol in her bloodstream, these parties were awash with the stuff and especially where fishing fleeters were involved, hence the Chief Secretary's lurid suggestion about a possible scenario. The victim, though, had not consumed much, perhaps two to three glasses of wine.

There were two surprises, however, about what else she had taken or not taken.

The first was that she had not eaten since breakfast the morning before her death. So, what had she been doing all day, and why had she not taken food when there would have been a good offering at Jamieson's?

The second surprise was much more significant.

"Superintendent, according to my tests she had some sort of drug in her system, and it looks like morphine."

"Are you sure, Rama? That's astonishing news if true."

"The science doesn't lie, and the science says this woman took morphine in the hours before her death."

"That news will delight the powers that be, I can tell you."

Le Fanu was thinking of Sirs Roland Wark and Charles Whitney, in particular, but there would be others.

"And in case you're wondering," Ramachandran continued, "she also had sex in the hours before she died, and if you are still wondering, it was not her first time."

"Forced?"

"Doesn't look that way. There are no signs of bruising or bleeding, and her underwear was intact. Looks like she had sex somewhere, got dressed again, then ran into trouble."

By now Le Fanu was convinced there was nothing else that could further complicate this case. A friend of a family friend arrives in Madras as part of the fishing fleet, stays with the city's most illustrious businessman, moves around for three weeks, goes to a garden party hosted by a senior ICS official, at some point that evening takes morphine and has sex, then turns up dead in a wasteland.

"Given all that," Le Fanu asked, "what exactly killed her?"

"Very good question - because it was not the broken neck. That probably happened later when whoever disposed of her body was trying to plant her head in the canal. Too much pressure was applied so her neck snapped."

"That means she was killed somewhere other than where she was found."

"Yes, certainly."

The precise time of death was now crucial, because somewhere in those three hours she died and was transported to the canal. In seeking a killer and a site for her death, he and Habi had to know her detailed movements last night.

"Alright," Le Fanu continued, "if the broken neck came later, what killed her?"

"I have two tests left to do," Ramachandran replied, "but if I'm right, there might have been an adverse reaction between the drug and the alcohol and that compromised her breathing."

"So she might have died unexpectedly, and whoever was with her panicked?"

"Possibly, or that the someone gave her something further to aid the process."

"But that would require a knowledge of chemistry or medicine or both, surely?"

"Yes," replied Ramachandran, "but that's just a theory at present."

Le Fanu wondered how the I-G would take all this.

"Would you like to see her?" the doctor inquired, mischievously.

"I don't want to, but I have to," replied a disconsolate Le Fanu.

They returned to the examination room where the woman lay on a table, covered by a sheet. Ramachandran turned the sheet back from her face. The staff had cleaned the mud from her face and hair. She was brunette, hard to tell if that was natural or not, with high cheekbones. The lips were full, complexion fair and smooth, delicate features. She had been very attractive.

Le Fanu took a deep breath, then motioned Ramachandran who removed the sheet from the body. He tried to control his breathing, feeling his pulse start to race and the sweat begin to appear on his face. The autopsy marks were disguised as much as possible but still looked ugly on what had been a beautiful body. She was not a natural brunette, it transpired, more a fine dark coppery red. She had slim, shapely legs, carried no excess weight and had prominent breasts.

She would have attracted many men in the past three weeks so who were they, were any of them in attendance last night, and to whom were they connected in this large Asian town that was still, in many ways, a small English village?

"Anything significant about her clothing, Rama?"

"No, but we have it in bags so you can examine it more closely: the dress you saw her wearing, stockings, shoes, standard underwear with suspender belt."

"Thank you, Ramachandran. As always, you've given me a lot to think about."

"As soon as I have the other results, I'll let you know."

Five minutes later, having run the gauntlet of the jars, Le Fanu arrived outside to gasp in what passed for fresh air.

Nine

It was now two in the afternoon and Le Fanu had forsaken lunch. He could not face that after the morgue, so set off for the Board of Directors office at J. Taylor and Co. (import, export and shipping specialists) where Sir Roland Wark was Chairman and Managing Director.

The offices were on Broadway, Georgetown's magnetic centre for trading companies close to the port that was now far more substantial and efficient than when those nineteenth century horses arrived. Le Fanu entered the building to be greeted by a doorman who phoned Wark's office to say the police had arrived. There was a lift, but Le Fanu walked up the four flights of stairs, a concession to exercise. An Indian male secretary received him in the outer office, then ushered him into the all-important one where Wark slumped behind a desk remarkably free of paper for the boss of such a prominent company.

If bulk meant anything, Wark had enjoyed India. The local chatter was that he grew up in a struggling English family that scrimped to get him into a half decent school. Not wanting to go to university, and with no chance at Oxford or Cambridge anyway, he set on a business career but even openings there proved difficult in England. At twenty he sailed for Madras and did not look back, physically or professionally. He joined the firm which he now led, that position owed at least in part to his marrying the boss' daughter.

He had dominated business circles for years. Somehow avoiding the Arbuthnott banking crash of 1905, he supplanted several Taylor partners on his way to the top, and Le Fanu had heard that many people in Madras still distrusted Wark as a result. Along the way, though, the man became a director on several other firms' boards and ranked among the wealthiest Europeans in Madras. Turning up at all the right charity affairs and supporting all the right social activities, like the races, he was the quintessential business figure before whom most bureaucrats quailed.

Wark's tailored, checked grey suit stretched tightly over the ample belly onto which a trickle of cigar ash fell periodically. Good living made him look far older than his sixty years, the florid complexion suggesting health problems. The jowls were large, his face chubby, eyes set in such puffy slits it was difficult to determine their colour. His gray hair was receding but still slicked back and oiled into place with a severe part to the right. The suit was matched with a white shirt and floral tie with matching handkerchief tucked into the jacket's breast pocket. It was just three in the afternoon, but Wark had a whiskey at hand, apparently the latest of a few.

Le Fanu declined the offer of a drink.

"Sir Roland, I believe you're worried about someone who appears to be missing from your home?"

Wark was grateful for the opening.

"Yes, Superintendent, and thank you for coming personally, the Inspector-General tells me you are his best man."

"He is too kind, sir. Is it a Miss Jane Carstairs who is missing?"

"Yes, it is. We invited Virginia Campbell to stay, she's the daughter of some old friends, and Miss Carstairs came as part of the package, as it were. She was travelling with Virginia, who asked if she might stay as well, and we agreed as any decent people would."

"When was the last time you saw her?"

"Last evening about six or so. We served pre-dinner drinks for some other guests. Virginia and Jane joined us before going off to whatever it was they were doing. You know what it's like this time of the year, very sociable, and with all these young women receiving innumerable invitations. That's what they are here for, after all."

The last sentence carried a distinct edge, Le Fanu thought.

"You disapprove?"

"Not really, but it makes one's house rather like a railway station."

"You knew where they were going?"

"We knew where they were going first, at least. Jamieson was hosting a garden party at his place in Nungambakkam. Virginia and Jane were taken there by our driver at about six forty-five."

"Was he to bring them back?"

"No, they agreed to find their way back independently, as they have done for the past three weeks. No shortage of gallant chaps ready to provide transport."

"Miss Campbell arrived back?"

"Yes, but I've no idea when. A servant took her tea in this morning but I came to the office before she appeared. It was later that my wife telephoned to say Virginia reported Miss Carstairs absent."

"I will need to speak to Miss Campbell, obviously."

"If you go directly from here, I'll make sure she is available - the house is in Adyar, but I'm sure you know that."

Le Fanu did, and lamented the fact because it would be a trek at this time of day. Many of the city's elite had built grand houses near the banks of the Adyar River, and Wark's was among the grandest along with those owned by a couple of minor local princes. It was only six or seven miles, but poor road conditions and increasing traffic made the journey seem endless .

"Le Fanu, do you have any news at all about this?"

Le Fanu ignored the question. "Perhaps, Sir Gordon, you might describe her to me?"

"Never been any good at that sort of thing."

"As best you can."

"Well, she was twenty-nine, according to Virginia. Brunette, not very tall. Slim thing but not flat, if you know what I mean. Bit of a looker, actually. Attractive mouth, nice features."

"What was she wearing when last you saw her?"

"Good God, man, I have no idea."

Wark refilled his glass and took a long sip.

"Perhaps you can recall a colour?" Le Fanu persisted.

"Oh, some sort of blue, I think."

Le Fanu lamented that he was close to naming the victim. While it was confirmation rather than a surprise it still depressed him when these moments arrived, but it would be far more depressing for those who knew her. Finding the evening bag was now less urgent, but its recovery would still be helpful.

"Sir Gordon, this is irregular, but time is shortening and I must speak with Miss Campbell as soon as possible, as I am sure you will understand".

Wark looked uncomfortable, not knowing what was coming but fearing it could only be bad.

"If I arrange for you to be met at the morgue by my assistant," Le Fanu continued, "could you find your way there to make a possible identification? I know you will be discreet."

"Is that really necessary?" the businessman squeaked.

"From your description, I fear that Miss Carstairs is the victim we found in the Canal a few hours ago. We need to have her identified, and you seem like the best person."

"It was that news about the body that prompted my telephone call to Wilson, obviously." Wark looked like he wished now never to have heard the news.

"Unfortunately, the only reliable people for identification purposes are you and Miss Campbell, and no doubt you would wish to spare her that?"

Trapped now, Wark poured and downed another whiskey. At this rate, Le Fanu thought Miss Campbell might have to do the identification after all. He had heard Club whispers that Wark's drinking was attracting attention, but the man still had clout. Other whispers suggested he was tough to deal with, but Wark did not look tough at present.

"Well, of course." Wark ground out his assent, but clearly wished to be going elsewhere.

Le Fanu telephoned Habi who agreed to meet Wark at the morgue. Le Fanu wondered how Wark would react to having an Indian, and a Muslim at that, accompany him to identify a dead white woman. Wark himself called Virginia Campbell to confirm Le Fanu's visit. Le Fanu went downstairs, found his car and driver, and began the trek to Adyar.

Ten

Le Fanu normally enjoyed the journey up Mount Road, but not this time. A young woman had suffered a violent death, yet the self-interests of highly placed Madras citizens were already threatening to restrict his investigation.

The Hindu offices passed by on the right, the Madras Club on the left. It was wonderful, he thought, that these symbols of the competing forces in modern India sat cheek by jowl. The Hindu was no radical rag, but for conservative Europeans it was positively communist compared to their preferred read, The Madras Mail that opposed any political reform whatsoever. Yet across from The Hindu, the Madras Club reminded everyone just where Presidency power still lay. The Club was the social bastion of European authority and, he reflected, of male dominance. It was as if the two buildings represented all the warring parties struggling to determine India's future form and function.

Further along, the Thousand Lights mosque was a reminder that Hindus and Muslims had long co-existed peacefully in Madras. They were joined by communities from all over India, drawn to commercial, professional and educational opportunity. Next to the light green coloured mosque sat a prestigious Catholic girls school. All over the city Hindus, Muslims, Jains, Gujaratis, Sikhs, Telugus and all the rest co-existed, for the most part peacefully. Every Christian missionary group in the world was here, it seemed, trying to convert non-believers. Another irony, he thought – there were Europeans here who feared Muslim proselytism, yet supported the same zeal among Christian missionaries. Then there were the Europeans themselves, along with Americans and Antipodeans among others, many blinded by the Eastern light and come to Madras to set the world to rights. Could he set things right for Jane Carstairs?

They passed St. George's Cathedral, Anglican heartland of the European community and where he married with all the usual enthusiasm and expectation that life would be straightforward. His police, then military life thwarted those hopes, and here he was alone again, almost.

Passing the Cosmopolitan Club golf links, he remembered how long it was since he had played. Many Madras Club members had misunderstood when he took a Cosmopolitan subscription as well. He simply wanted to play the Cosmopolitan course as well as the Gymkhana, but diehards thought joining the so-called "mixed race" club (but which, really, was predominantly Indian) signalled he had finally "gone native."

By the time the driver reached Chamier's Road, then found Boat Club Avenue, Le Fanu was depressed. The case weighed on him, but so did the reality of British Madras.

Though well out of the city, Boat Club Road was the place to make a statement about being someone in the European community, and Wark had made his. The mansion sat on four acres of land with "In" and "Out" gates sweeping in a semi-circle across the front of the house. The gates alone, massive wrought iron things about nine feet high, probably cost half the total price of Le Fanu's house. Those gates cut into a hedge that otherwise hid the house from public view.

The "In" gate opened, revealing a small guard box to the right. A uniformed servant checked Le Fanu's business, seemingly unsurprised that it involved the police, and waved him vaguely towards the main entrance of the three-level house.

It was standard Madras style, flat roofed with wide verandahs and full door-windows opening to the rooms within. The gardens were immaculate, Le Fanu counting at least a dozen people working to keep them that way.

Another uniformed servant appeared on the steps and led him in the front door where Le Fanu found himself in front of a regal staircase, the walls of which were lined with what looked like expensive paintings.

"Lady Wark will be here directly," said the servant, directing Le Fanu into a reception room to the left of the stairs. Le Fanu realised he should have expected to see Wark's wife, but her presence might alter his approach.

Lady Wark appeared a couple of minutes later, far better preserved than her husband. In her late fifties, she stood straight-backed to reveal a spare frame. The grey hair was pulled back neatly and severely, highlighting the fine-featured face, dominated by the round, heavy-framed glasses that added to her authoritative air.

"Superintendent, thank you for coming all this way. But before we start, a Sergeant Habibullah has asked that you telephone him immediately upon your arrival. There is a telephone over in that corner, and I will leave you in private. Just let the servant know when you have concluded, and I will return with Miss Campbell."

When she had left, he called the office.

"What's the news, Habi?"

"As anticipated, I'm afraid. Sir Roland identified our victim as Miss Carstairs."

"How did he take that?"

"Not well. He needed another drink, so headed to the Club. That's why I wanted to talk to you, because as soon as he gets there the news will be all over Madras."

"Understood, Habi, good thinking. Anything more from Ramachandran yet?"

"Afraid not."

Le Fanu rang off.

Lady Wark returned, accompanied by a tall, elegant, beautiful woman of about thirty, dark hair cut short, green eyes set in a perfectly oval face. Virginia Campbell was dressed in a close fitting, floral patterned and apricot coloured, short-sleeved dress that reached calf length, with a belt of the same material slung across the hips. The shoes were flat, black leather. There was little jewellery he could see, apart from a thin gold bracelet that showed up against her olive skin. She looked tired and worried, but he detected a shrewdness in her eyes.

"Miss Campbell? I'm Superintendent Le Fanu, thank you for seeing me."

She nodded, and Le Fanu steeled himself.

"Miss Campbell, Lady Wark, I'm afraid I have some very bad news for you."

The two women gripped each other's hands and sat down next to each other.

"I am extremely sorry. Sergeant Habibullah has informed me that Sir Roland has just identified Miss Carstairs as the young woman found dead in the Buckingham Canal this morning."

He expected histrionics but they did not appear.

Virginia Campbell looked out a window, closed her eyes briefly then looked back towards Lady Wark. They looked sad, but seemed unsurprised by the news, bad though it was. Le Fanu was confused.

"It might take some time for the shock to set in," he said. "During the war I experienced…"

"Thank you, Superintendent." Virginia Campbell's voice was light but strong, almost musical, with a refined Edinburgh accent.

"It is a shock, of course," she continued, "but after what we had been hearing through the day, it is not a surprise, sadly."

So the Madras intelligence system was already at work.

"Even so," she continued, green eyes glistening, "it is hard to imagine this has happened to Jane. Can you tell me what happened?"

"We are still investigating the actual cause, so I cannot say much just now. Not because the details might be upsetting for you, but because we need to keep our investigations confidential for the moment until we determine exactly what did happen."

She smiled. "Thank you for that, I would not want to be thought of as constitutionally weak."

He was unsure, but was she flirting with him, even at this sad moment? Surely not? She was certainly attractive, and accustomed to manipulating men, he thought. He felt uncertain, less in control, and with a sense of being drawn into a spider's web. A beautiful spider, yes, but possibly a dangerous one.

"Perhaps you can recall some details from last night for me?" he said, hoping to move things on and restore his authority. "What time did you leave here, and where did you go?"

Lady Wark answered. "The girls had pre-dinner drinks with us before leaving for the Jamieson garden party."

This woman was used to running things. Did she run the business as well? After all, it was part of her family's life. Her husband merely married in and might not be fully focused, given his drinking. Perhaps there was a reason for that increased drinking?

"Thank you, Lady Wark, that helpfully confirms Sir Roland's recollections. It will be important now, though, that we get Miss Campbell's version of events. I'm sure you understand the need for that."

Lady Wark looked to respond, hesitated, then nodded, settling in her chair.

"Miss Campbell?" Le Fanu continued.

"Well, yes, we left here about six-thirty, perhaps six-forty-five. Lady Wark kindly allowed her driver to take us in the car, and he left us at the Jamieson's."

"That's in Nungambakkam. How long did it take to reach there?"

She looked surprised. "I'm not sure, really. Jane and I were talking, so I took no real notice."

Le Fanu estimated a twenty-minute journey at least, so they would have arrived no earlier than seven-fifteen, but he would check that at the Jamieson's.

"I understand. What were you talking about?"

Her expression changed. She looked briefly troubled, then reverted to the calm role. What was that about?

"Oh, you know, the sort of things women talk about when going to parties."

That was one thing Le Fanu did not know and never had. It was always a complete mystery to him, and that gap in understanding had always made his relationships difficult.

"Perhaps you might give me some details?" he said, hesitantly.

She smiled widely. "I'm sure you know the sort of thing," teasing him with a lowered, throaty voice, another strange moment of lightness amidst the gloom of a friend's death. Even he knew that was a flirt.

Lady Wark intervened. "Superintendent, Miss Campbell has had a trying day. This can wait, surely?"

Virginia Campbell took pity on him. "We were actually discussing the previous night's party, a dinner at the home of a junior ICS member."

Lady Wark decided she had pressing business elsewhere in the large house, and left them alone.

Misses Campbell and Carstairs had done well, he thought, given that ICS officers of any rank topped the social pecking order, at least in their own minds and those of the fishing fleet.

"Did that officer have a name?" he inquired.

"You really are quite the policeman, are you not?" The husky voice again.

He felt himself blush, and cursed inwardly.

"We were at Jamie Wigram's," she continued, "He has a nice little house in Egmore, reasonably close to the railway station. There were about a dozen of us at dinner."

Le Fanu hoped he would not have to check them all, but feared there might be even more candidates as the story deepened. Fleet members were on a mission to pack in as many social engagements and meetings as possible. That increased their chances of netting a catch, good or otherwise. This pair would have met a lot of people.

"Did you discuss anything in particular about that evening?"

She considered an answer. "Well, yes and no: Jane inferred something had upset her but we arrived at Jamieson's before she could tell me."

Something else to be followed up.

"After you arrived at Jamieson's, how did the evening develop?" Le Fanu prompted. "Were you together the whole time?"

"Good heavens, no! The whole idea was for us to split up and spread out, as I'm sure you know." She produced the powerful smile again and he felt like the spider was advancing on him. He was intrigued, though.

"But you saw Miss Carstairs during the evening?"

"Yes, she was off talking with several people and we encountered one another perhaps four or five times while circulating."

"Did you recognise any of the people with whom she was talking?"

"I recognised some faces, but could only put names to three or four of them."

It had already been a long day, and Le Fanu could think only of the many investigative lines already opening.

"We'll need a list of those names tomorrow, if you could. I'll send someone to fetch them from you in the afternoon. But one last thing for now - what time did you leave Jamieson's, and do you know if Miss Carstairs was still there at that time?"

"Billy Walsall from the Madras Artillery took me off at about nine, and we went for a few drinks at the Connemara. He then drove me back here at about midnight. Well, it was midnight when we arrived."

"And Miss Carstairs?"

"I honestly don't know. It was possibly about eight-thirty when I last saw her, but whether or not she was still there when I left, I have no idea."

"Miss Campbell, that's enough for the present, thank you, but I'll need to speak with you again, I'm sure you understand."

"It will be a pleasure to speak with you any time, Superintendent." The voice was warm, welcoming. For someone who had lost a friend, Virginia Campbell was holding up well to the point of still playing the fishing fleeter with a net. What did that mean? But he admitted to himself he did find her attractive and that worried him. He had enough problems already on that front.

Lady Wark was lurking outside when he left, ensuring he left the premises before she grilled Virginia Campbell. He would be back here, certainly, because he needed to learn more about Jane Carstairs besides her status as a fishing fleet member, and he was sure that Virginia Campbell could tell him much more.

Eleven

There was one more stop to make before finishing the day. Early in his police career, his superiors reckoned that if a day had been sensational, then a trip to the Club was mandatory before going home. That way, the facts and fantasy of what "society" knew or thought it knew could be assessed, and the opportunity taken to sow seeds of wisdom, doubt or facts.

Today was sensational.

The car carried him up the gravelled way towards the white colonnaded entrance, immaculate lawns and shrubs on either side, the ladies pavilion to the right. Women were not allowed in the Club proper, another sign of how British Madras clung tightly to the older social habits. There since 1832 and immediately off busy Mount Road, the Club was an oasis in one respect, a trial in another. Members took a slight quickly, relinquished a grudge reluctantly, and hunted in professional packs, so many a junior had run afoul of someone or other throughout the Club's history, often ruining a career. Attending was a necessary evil at any time, even worse this day.

He was scarcely across the threshold of what was still considered "the longest bar in the East" when the questions began:

"Le Fanu, I need you to answer a couple of questions."

"Le Fanu, could you clear something up for us?"

"Le Fanu, is it true that…?"

"What is the next step, Le Fanu?"

He knew the questioners and their motives but made the excuse he had to consult the I-G first, knowing Wilson was there to update him on current Club opinion and fantasy. He spied his boss at a far corner table, near an open door leading out to the terrace and into the gardens. The I-G was with a Member of the Board of Revenue, a senior judge, and another senior official from the Madras Chamber of Commerce. The subject of conversation was obvious.

Wilson signalled him over and had a white-coated waiter place another chair at the table. "What will you have, LF?"

"Whiskey, thank you, sir, it has been a long day."

The drink arrived quickly and they all toasted each other.

The I-G began immediately. "What more can you tell us, LF?"

Le Fanu looked around the table.

"It's alright, LF, feel free to speak. A fair amount has gone around here already, as you would imagine."

Wark, of course – he was already here and voluble, no doubt, having had time for a few more drinks.

"The victim is formally identified as Miss Jane Carstairs, sir. We have an incomplete, but developing picture of her movements last night. There are time gaps to be accounted for, and by tomorrow we'll have a preliminary list of people to question. That list will grow, I think. Some names we have already, but will keep those confidential for obvious reasons. I have spoken with Miss Carstairs' friend, Miss Virginia Campbell, and that was after discussing matters with Sir Roland Wark who was most helpful."

Wilson was nodding but the others wanted more, which Le Fanu was reluctant to deliver.

The businessman reported Club speculation about Jane Carstairs' cause of death.

"Sir, we have a preliminary autopsy report, but the full report has yet to arrive so, again, we can't speculate."

The Board of Revenue man speculated on those who were or might have been at the garden party hosted by Jamieson, his colleague (but not necessarily friend, thought Le Fanu).

"There is no full list yet, sir, but we'll be talking with Mr. Jamieson in the morning."

It felt like every person in the Club was watching them, edging closer in the hope of learning something new. His whiskey had no taste, and he no taste for it, given the atmosphere. He would leave as soon as possible. But not just yet, because Wark was rolling towards them, his bulk accentuated by the alcohol-influenced lack of physical control.

"Wilson," he slurred, "glad to see you and your chap here. Need to clear up a few things. One of the worst days of my life, having to identify that girl. Would've been easier had your chap here been with me."

Le Fanu began a response but Wilson waved him off.

"Quite understandable, Sir Roland, and we really appreciate your effort. We know it was an ordeal for you. Never an easy thing to do. As you know, though, time was of the essence and we needed Le Fanu to speak with your other guest as soon as possible. I ordered him to do that."

"Well, yes, of course," spluttered the lurching Wark, "but..."

Wilson cut him off. "Le Fanu tells me your guest and your wife are very upset by all this, naturally. Might be a good idea if you went off to see how they are bearing up, don't you think? They'll need you."

Wark took that as a compliment to his strength and decision-making, so bade his farewells and rolled away.

"Getting worse, I'm afraid," the Chamber of Commerce man observed dryly. No one else commented, and Wilson and Le Fanu were soon left alone.

"Come out to the garden, LF, I need a cigar and another whiskey."

Wilson signalled the waiter as they went outside. For Madras it was cool, unlike the mid-year dog days of heat when it was impossible to stay outside even in the evening. Rather than sit, they set off through the gardens, the waiter catching them after a few steps to hand over two more whiskeys rather than one, to Le Fanu's regret.

"What do you really think, LF?"

"It will be complicated, I-G."

"More than normal?

"Much more."

"Why?

"Ramachandran's autopsy shows Miss Carstairs took morphine in the hours before her death."

Wilson stopped walking and looked shocked. "Is he sure?"

"I asked the same question, I-G, and he was adamant. And Ramachandran is good, as you know."

"That's what worries me. He's never wrong, so this could open some nasty options."

Le Fanu got the feeling there was something he did not know.

Wilson looked at him, and smiled. "I have another small group like yours working on some drug issues. Mostly small time things going on among the local population, but we received a couple of signals there might be a connection into the European community."

"If that's true," Le Fanu suggested, "then these cases might be connected."

"I agree, said his boss, "because there is a small suggestion that a European rather than a local is behind the whole thing."

"So it's possible Jane Carstairs somehow or other stumbled into something to do with this?"

"Yes. It's a long time since there were a lot of drugs about in Madras, of course, but we've noticed an increasing trickle in the past few months, which is why I set up this other unit. Nobody knows about that, by the way, not even the Chief

Secretary or the Governor, and I want to keep it that way."

"Of course."

"This lot here would have a field day if they knew." Wilson gestured back inside.

Le Fanu imagined the Club discussions if that news got out, and realised Wilson was under more pressure than he had thought. "Ramachandran also suggests she had sex shortly before her death, was killed somewhere else then put in the Canal, and that her neck was broken after she died."

"Sex and drugs! Wonderful." Wilson threw his hands in the air. "Now we definitely have to keep this quiet and that won't be easy. Better restrict circulation of the report to those who need immediate use, and that's almost no-one apart from us. I'll brief the Chief Secretary, who can brief the Governor."

They meandered towards the bar. Wilson extinguished the cigar, dropped the butt in a sand bin, and they re-entered, watched by every person there. Wilson went to speak with other senior officials, and somehow Le Fanu left without having to give up any more information.

The driver took him home in the car, the bike safe in the stables. That exhilarating morning ride to work seemed a long time ago now. He walked into the house, and remembered the letter placed in his pocket all those hours ago. That would have to wait. Roisin appeared, asked if he was ready for dinner, and he was soon eating roast duck and vegetables washed down with a glass of red wine.

By nine he was ready for bed, so took a shower. He had become used to showers while in the army, so modified the bathrooms in the house as soon as he moved in. Each one now had a shower. Somehow it was more refreshing than a bath and less time wasting.

He turned off the light and fell into bed.

Half an hour later his door opened then closed, quietly. He heard the susurrus of fabric dropping away from skin, and felt the sheet shift imperceptibly.

"Sorry I was late back, Ro, it was a long day."

There was no reply, just the feel of her breasts as she lowered herself towards him, and of her fingers sliding down his belly.

Twelve

He awoke alone, as usual.

Breakfast appeared as soon as he arrived downstairs, Ro bearing it in with a smile, but no other acknowledgement. It had been this way for months, a further confusion in his life. He was not the only man in this town with a mistress, if that was what she was, but most avoided Anglo-Indian women for fear of being ostracised by their colleagues once word got out. The Madras Cricket Club, another Europeans-only bastion, recently hosted an Anglo-Indian team at the Chepauk ground. The visitors were not allowed inside the clubhouse, but consigned to a verandah corner containing a few tatty chairs. The visiting players ate sandwiches out there while the MCC team and members enjoyed a full lunch in the dining room. Caste separation was not confined to the Indian community, and the Anglo-Indians suffered more than most. He had no idea where this relationship with Ro was going, but he knew the possible social implications were serious.

Having fed him, Ro retreated to her room in the servants quarters. While small, it was comfortable and had doors that opened onto the garden where she could see the birds at their feeders morning and night. Le Fanu had found her a bookcase that fitted the space, so she could line up all her literary classics. That made her feel more at home than having her clothes lined up in the wardrobe. Her mother made her read, believing that an educated Anglo-Indian woman had a better chance of surviving than the others. Ro doubted that was true, but thanked her mother daily for the pleasure of the reading.

Like Le Fanu, she had no idea where this relationship was headed, but knew that it could cause both of them trouble. She had not even thought about a relationship with him, but as soon as she arrived in the house she was drawn to this troubled but kind man with such a different outlook on British India from his ruling colleagues. The question now was what they might do. A Dickens helped divert her mind from that line of thinking.

The car arrived, and took Le Fanu to the Board of Revenue offices in the Chepauk Palace. He disliked the inhabitants but loved the building. Ornate but elegant, it epitomised the original Indo-Saracenic style that later become more flowery. As always, he thought about the current Prince of Arcot, descended from the one who built then lost the Palace. The descendant lived in the splendid isolation of the Amir Mahal palace, guarded by its ceremonial cannons not far away in Triplicane, surviving on the pension endowed by the British, a pitiful recompense for the lost building.

Le Fanu reached the second floor, seeing more order and less bustle than in the Secretariat. The Board's work involved the all-important revenue collecting that kept the Raj afloat financially. Out in the country, much of his old police work concerned revenue collection: pursuing recalcitrants, collecting taxes or impounding goods in lieu of taxes not paid. It was dull apart from the odd disturbance, theft or sudden death. Now there was more to do in suppressing political movements, but he doubted he would have enjoyed that. At least his present job was rarely dull.

Arthur Jamieson's office was on the top floor, along with the other Members and their assorted assistants. When dealing with Government, Le Fanu thought, much time was spent in waiting rooms, today no exception. Forty minutes later and with no offer of tea, he was shown into Jamieson's room, sure he was being taught his place.

"Good morning, Le Fanu."

No attempt at an apology for the delay, not a good start.

"Thank you for seeing me, Mr. Jamieson."

"Third Member, if you don't mind."

Definitely a poor start, and he could not imagine why anyone would want to style himself Third Penis. His old army pals would have enjoyed the laugh. The thought buoyed him; he could get through this.

"Of course, sir. I'll try not to waste your valuable time."

Jamieson looked suspicious, wondering if he was being mocked. Le Fanu tried not to notice and continued. "As you know, Miss Carstairs was found dead yesterday. We believe she was murdered. And, of course, she was last seen at a garden party at your house. Given that, we need to know everything you might have noticed, who else was there, who she might have been talking with. I'm sure you understand, Third Member."

Having articulated the ridiculous title Le Fanu was no longer sure he could keep this up, given what was in his mind, so looked earnestly at Jamieson in a futile attempt to keep that mind from straying.

Jamieson attempted anger. "You can't possibly expect I'd have spent every minute of that evening keeping watch over the activities of a fishing fleet member."

Well, she was not a Member, strictly speaking, Third or otherwise, was she, Le Fanu mused. He was now in trouble, his mind glued to the member theme, a belly laugh close to erupting.

"Of course not, sir! However, as a conscientious host, I'm sure you were aware of her movements from time to time."

"Well, yes, if you put it like that, one could see her moving about and enjoying herself, keeping her end up, as it were."

Or someone else's, Le Fanu thought, but berating himself silently. He was having trouble concentrating. "Third Member, that is very helpful, indeed. Were there any particular ends, ah, people, with whom she was mingling?"

"Let me see, that Billy Walsall chap was about but he took Miss Campbell home, I believe."

"Yes, Miss Campbell confirms that."

"Simon Lauder, from the Engineering Department, was hanging about, playing with himself and Miss Carstairs at one stage.

Odd turn of phrase, thought Le Fanu, perhaps the chap's Member was out of control?

"Sir, how many people were at this party, and how many were paying attention to Miss Carstairs?"

He put it that way, because it freed Jamieson to mention married Members. How long could this line of conversation go on?

"There were about seventy in total on the guest list. Of those, there were, perhaps, about twenty unattached men, mostly young but a couple of older chaps. Not sure the latter would have been interested."

Le Fanu was not convinced about that. "It will probably be better, Third Member, if we automatically put everyone on the list."

"Does that mean you'll speak with everyone who was at the show? Bit embarrassing for me if you do."

"Initially, we'll start with the unattached men. Then, as we get a better sense of things, we might better identify additional people we need to consult. How does that sound?"

"That sounds more or less acceptable. Can't have chaps swinging in the wind."

Or Members, for that matter. Le Fanu was ashamed of himself. But at least one Member was swinging somewhere with Miss Carstairs at some point. What about Miss Campbell, he wondered? Had she encountered a Member? The imagery was now too strong and it was all Jamieson's fault, Le Fanu reasoned.

He suggested the Third Member compile three lists to be collected later. The first would include all unattached men, the second unattached women, and the third whoever else was there. Jamieson agreed, reluctantly, protesting a work overload, though there was little evidence of that on his desk. Le Fanu thought the Third Member should be able to poke about with that in the next few hours, and point a stick at a few leads. This was getting out of hand. Damn Jamieson.

Tramping down the stairs, he wondered how he had become so different from other people, because he was. The war was partly but not wholly to blame. People like Jamieson were little older than him, but seemed infinitely older, almost belonging to a different race. Jamieson was a self-important buffoon, but held a position where his decisions affected the lives of millions of people. How could Jamieson's attitudes and outlooks possibly connect with those of the millions?

That was among the reasons Le Fanu ducked whenever promotion prospects arose. He did not fear command. Rather, he feared the soundness of his own judgment on matters bigger than a specific case.

The driver was waiting with a message that Wilson wanted to see him, soon.

Wilson was in his office. "We have the full autopsy report, LF, but it tells us little more than you told me yesterday. Ramachandran cannot be definite on the precise cause of death, but the morphine was a definite factor."

So why was he summoned, Le Fanu wondered.

"Meanwhile," the I-G continued, "two other matters have arisen. The first is trivial. No doubt prompted by this morning's hangover, Wark has lodged a complaint about you, but don't worry, that'll go away."

"Thank you, sir."

"The other one's more interesting. A report has been

lodged with the Adyar police that someone answering Miss Carstairs' description was seen out there at about eleven on the night she died."

"Adyar? But she must have been almost home. Well, Wark's place, that is. Given the time frames we have, it would have been difficult for her to get back from there to where the body was found, quite apart from the logic of going out to Adyar then back again."

"Exactly, LF. That's why I wanted you to know about it as soon as possible, because we need to fill those time gaps and we need to know who she spent time with at the garden party. Come to think of it, we also need to know about anyone who might have been upset because she did not spend time with him, or them."

"You think there might have been more than one involved, sir?"

"Right now, I suggest we assume nothing and expect everything."

"Fair point. I'll go and interview Miss Campbell again."

He was strangely unsettled by that prospect.

Thirteen

He retrieved the bike from the stables. A ride to Adyar might clear his thinking. It did not, but it was nice to feel the cool winter air, watch the Indian Ocean waves roll in, then ride along the northern bank of the Adyar River that, these days, was a more natural and unpolluted waterway than the Cooum. A rowing four cast elegant patterns across the placid waters.

As he turned the bike into Wark's driveway, he saw surprise hit the guard's face, and an unusually large number of servants just happened to be on the steps as he pulled up. A motorbike was not seen here normally, it seemed. He parked ostentatiously by the front door.

He asked for Virginia Campbell, and was shown into the same room as before, but with time now to view the photographs on the wall. Most featured Wark meeting dignitaries like the Secretary of State for India, Edwin Montagu, who visited Madras three years before. Neither he nor his hosts enjoyed the experience, the Madras reactionaries protesting Montagu's every reform proposal. Other photographs featured past Madras Governors as well as a couple of Viceroys including the present one, Lord Chelmsford.

This was an "official" India Le Fanu did not know, his lot was to maintain the peace and make it possible for people like Wark to do whatever it was they did, even if that sometimes appeared to be very little. Le Fanu avoided official functions as much as possible, especially the mass attendance garden parties at Government House where men still had to dress in tuxedos. It was all so incongruous, but was taken so seriously.

Virginia Campbell appeared, and Le Fanu wondered if she had dressed especially for him. For one thing, she was wearing trousers, expensive black silk ones, he thought, but trousers all the same. That was unusual here in Madras, especially ones that moulded to her body as tightly as these did. She perched on black high-heeled shoes, an unusual choice for morning, which added to her height and presence. Over the trousers she wore a long, cream coloured silk shirt, long sleeved and tailored, again, to emphasise her figure. A simple gold chain around her neck contrasted with the olive skin, and a slim gold linked bracelet on the right wrist completed a simple, but expensive look that was surely deliberate.

"Good morning Superintendent, very nice to see you again. You have caused quite a stir among the staff with your motorbike."

The tone was light, warm, engaging.

"I assume they don't see too many here," he replied.

"This is more of a car household, you might say." She smiled, then led the way out to the garden. As he followed, he could not help but watch the sway of the silk pants. She and the pants led the way to a table by the tennis court standing off to the side of the house and hosting large glasses of fresh lime soda.

"What can you tell us about Miss Carstairs, Miss Campbell?"

"Please, Virginia."

He was uncomfortable with that professionally, but would play along if it helped produce information. It did.

Over the next fifteen minutes he learned that Jane Carstairs was bright, intellectual ability elevating her from a lower middle class setting near Reading to Rodean near Brighton, then Cambridge, where she studied French and English. She worked as a translator in Paris before returning to a London publishing house that specialised in translating European fiction. She had been doing that for the past five years, lived in an apartment in Marylebone near the Baker Street tube station, and seemed content, though she remained unmarried.

"How did you come to know her?" he asked.

Virginia Campbell sipped at the fresh lime soda, dabbing her heavily lipsticked mouth with a napkin.

"We were at school together but a year apart, then in the same college at Cambridge, though never on the same floor. We had a couple of tutors in common and sometimes discussed work. For the first two years, that was all there was to it."

"You became closer, though?"

"At the end of second year, Jane was going to Paris over the holidays to improve her French. She asked if I would go along. Having nothing else planned, I did. We became good friends over those two months. She showed me the real Paris. When we came back we met up a lot both as friends and in a wider circle of people."

When Jane Carstairs returned to Paris to work, Virginia Campbell visited her there periodically.

"And the trip out here, how did that come about?"

Virginia Campbell looked as sheepish as a person of her background and position could ever be.

"Over dinner one night a few months ago, somehow the discussion arose about us both reaching thirty soon, and being left on the shelf. We were getting older, losing our looks."

He resisted the opportunity to be gallant.

"So we decided to come out to India. There was nothing to lose and a lot to see. The only reason we chose Madras was because I also had family connections to the Warks. Here we landed."

She reported that during the three weeks prior to Jane

Carstairs' death, the pair went out every day bar two, to dinners, lunches, balls, garden parties, soirees, drinks, sailing parties, riding parties, the races and even a local theatre production. They must have met every eligible bachelor in Madras.

He enquired, carefully, about the results of all this activity.

"As I said, we were relaxed about what might happen. If we found someone special that would be a bonus, but it was not vital we snare someone. We would have a good holiday, then, if nothing transpired, return to London and our comfortable lives."

"Was there anyone in particular Jane saw more of than others?"

"You mean as in frequency rather than physically?" The smirk revealed the deliberate tease.

"Yes," he smiled back.

"There were three chaps who took her out a few times. Sometimes I was with them, but mostly not."

She paused for another drink and, Le Fanu speculated, to gather her thoughts. He wondered what she was concealing.

"One was Charles Winstone."

Le Fanu knew him, a rising star Under Secretary at the Board of Revenue. Jamieson would have ensured he was to the fore.

"Then there was Jackson Caldicott, a junior man at one of the trading companies."

That would bear checking out, but why did he know the name already?

"The other was Preston Pyne. He's a junior doctor in the Indian Medical Service so is a Captain or something, all the ranks confuse me."

Le Fanu did not admit they confused him, too. The last two, he thought, might have possible access to morphine, especially Pyne. It would be more difficult, but not impossible for Winstone. They should all be interviewed. The list was growing.

The servant arrived with more drinks, and some vegetarian samosas that Le Fanu did not need but could not resist, especially with the tangy lime and mint sauce.

The silence here was deeper than in the city, and as they ate, he heard bird sounds and little else. A kingfisher flew onto a branch not too far away, and sat watching. They finished their snacks.

"What happens now, Superintendent?"

"I ask you some more questions about that night. With whom did Miss Carstairs spend the most time, and with whom did you see her last?"

"That second question is easier than the first. The last person I saw her with was Charlie."

"Mr. Winstone?"

"Yes, sorry."

Fishing fleeters rarely got the social nuances right in India. Winstone would squirm if he knew he was being described to a ranking officer as "Charlie".

"What is difficult about the first question?"

"Well, she was with Charlie, Mr. Winstone, a couple of times when I saw her, but for the rest of the evening she seemed to be in groups, and those groups kept changing, as they do on these occasions, as I'm sure you know."

"I get to very few of these things."

"That surprises me."

The tease had returned, but he deflected it. "Was there anyone she mentioned to you who might have been bothering her?"

"No, far from it, we were both having a wonderful time and everyone was so kind. That is why this has been such a shock."

For the first time, he realised, she looked distressed and shocked – well, the first time in his presence, at least. He wondered whether she had suppressed it all, or whether this was simply theatrics. Le Fanu thought that a really good friend might have been more overcome and a lot earlier.

"One last question. Is it possible she came back here after the party then went out again later?"

Virginia Campbell looked puzzled. "But why would she do that? It makes no sense. I'm sure she did not come in the house even if she did come back momentarily. We agreed that if we were in the house after one of these things we would look in on each other. I looked in her room just after midnight and there was no sign of her."

"But it is possible she might have returned to Adyar at some point?"

"Well, I suppose it's possible, but it seems unlikely and I certainly didn't see her if she did."

Le Fanu stood and began to make his goodbyes.

"I hope I've been helpful, Superintendent."

"Of course, Miss Campbell, every piece of information is vital, and you have connected some things for me. We may need to speak again, however."

"I look forward to that."

She stood closer to him than was necessary and he could smell the light touch of perfume. The look was almost challenging, and she smoothed the pants over her hips slowly, smiling. He left quickly.

Le Fanu rode back through some of his favourite haunts to lengthen the return journey to headquarters but it still ended too quickly, as did most enjoyable things, he thought. Now it was back to tediously piecing it all together with Habibullah who should have the Wark list, the Jamieson ones and, so, have a new set of people to be interviewed.

Fourteen

Le Fanu called Habi into his office, shut the door and they began sharing information. There was the guest list from Sir Roland Wark who was still uncooperative, according to Habi, and suffering from a headache. The more important list came from Jamieson who, again, was unhappy at having to name those present at his gathering.

That bothered Le Fanu. "Why should Jamieson be so difficult? A woman is murdered straight after being at his party, and he's reluctant to tell us who was there? What's he got to hide, I wonder?"

"Well, he did have some distinguished people there, so perhaps he doesn't want to embarrass them?" Habi offered.

"Even so, it's not normal for a garden party to result in guests being murdered, so surely he would want to be cooperative?"

Habi looked quizzical. "Sir, why does he necessarily have something to hide? He is a vain and pompous man, yes, but it's hard to see how he could be involved in this. He'll hate all the attention and gossip."

"Fair enough, but I still can't see why he would object."

They speculated further about Jamieson's behaviour, but soon moved on to other names on the list. The first three to be consulted, obviously, were Winstone, Caldicott and Pyne, the trio Virginia Campbell said spent time with Jane

Carstairs during the evening she died. However, there were another seventy-three people on the list. That shrank to fifty when they removed all married women. That became forty by removing all elderly men. There were twenty young single women, so that left twenty single young men including the three already identified.

"This is a starting point only, for the sake of convenience," Le Fanu said. "It makes them a priority, but others might still be investigated if their names come up for any reason once we get deeper."

Having recorded the results on the boards, they summarised other available information. According to Habi, closer inspection of Jane Carstairs' clothes had produced nothing new and nothing sensational. "What I am really saying, sir, is that if she did have sex, which Ramachandran says was the case, then it was consensual and probably somewhere civilized rather than in the back of a car, say, where her clothes might have been torn. She might have been at a house or an apartment where she could remove all her clothes."

Le Fanu was interested to see how straightforwardly Habi discussed all that. Sensing the question, Habi broke in. "Sir, I did a specialist course on these matters. The senior officers were trying to get Indians like me more trained in matters of sexual crime, especially assault. And, after all Indians invented the Kama Sutra, even if that was the Hindus – but you have seen some of those pornographic Mughal miniatures showing some of the Muslim rulers in action."

They both laughed. The humour was needed to help sustain them through these difficult early days, but even so, Le Fanu realised increasingly that Habi was a rare soul as well as an excellent policeman. The rare soul summarised the situation: Jane Carstairs left Wark's with Virginia Campbell, arrived at Jamieson's, was in the company of three specific men but possibly others, left at an uncertain time, had sex and took morphine at some point during the evening and probably not at Wark's, may or may not have returned to Adyar, was probably murdered somewhere between midnight and two am, then was found dead at dawn several miles away. There were too many holes in the story but it was more complete than twenty-four hours earlier, and they did have three specific people to interview. Le Fanu decided they should both conduct the interviews, so Habi went off to make arrangements.

Le Fanu retreated to the back of the building where a few benches under some trees stood on one side of a lane leading out to Edward Elliot's Road. The British did like to memorialise things: Edward Elliot was an early nineteenth century Governor whose name also graced a beach south of the Marina, down near Adyar. Who remembered him now? Le Fanu sat down and tried to order some thoughts.

Thinking of Adyar, though, had returned his mind to Virginia Campbell and what he still considered to be a cool reaction to the death of her friend. Perhaps the friend had not been all that much of a friend, or that Miss Campbell knew something she was not volunteering. There was a definable difference, he thought, between admirable sangfroid and questionable coolness.

Speaking of coolness, he should check with the I-G on the status of the Wark complaint. Wilson would protect him from the frivolous charge, but the best defence was to demonstrate it had no substance. It was unclear what Wark was trying to achieve, other than diverting attention from his behaviour over the identification of the body and his later drunken performance at the Club. Most people would see through that, but even so, Le Fanu reasoned, if Wark needed a distraction then a policeman many already mistrusted would be a good one.

The annoying aspect for Le Fanu was that it made him lose focus at a time when such a terrible crime in a small town like this needed a quick result. The longer the investigation continued, the greater the range of influences that came into play, and Le Fanu had to avoid that. Someone knew how Jane Carstairs died, and was probably connected to that death, and needed to be found quickly. And then there was Commissioner Jepson, and Le Fanu had no idea about his agenda.

He re-entered the building and asked Wilson's secretary if the I-G was in, and if so, available. Luckily, he was.

"Come in, LF, I'm just going over the autopsy report, as it happens."

Le Fanu summarised the analysis he and Habi had just done.

"As you say, LF," commented Wilson, "we are better covered than this time yesterday, but time is passing. Your biggest problem with that is not the witnesses, but the Commissioner. To be frank, he wants you off the case."

That was no surprise to Le Fanu, who made no comment.

"What is it about you that upsets him so much?"

"Perhaps you might ask him that, sir?"

"I have, and he just gives me this flannel about you not being a team player, and I know there's more to it than that."

"To be honest, sir, there's not that much more. A few years ago, before the war, we clashed over a small incident."

"Why do I not know about that?"

"Probably because it was so small it never went on record, but for some reason the now-Commissioner has never forgotten and, if anything, become more rather than less exercised about it."

"Well?"

"I was posted briefly to a station where Jepson had overall command, and he ran a flimsy disciplinary case against a constable. The evidence came from a local man whose cousin was also in the police and had disputes with the constable. This was a way to silence the constable, and Mr. Jepson couldn't see that. He disregarded my advice and disciplined the constable, who then left the police, which was a loss because he was very good."

"So you defended an Indian constable against an uniformed English officer?"

"Because the man was innocent."

"Say no more. Good for me to know. But we have to watch more than just this case, because Jepson's running a campaign against you, and will use everything he can. Mind how you go."

Le Fanu wondered if the I-G was referring to anything specific. And for some reason, he wondered if the relationship with Ro was known to someone. Jepson would use that mercilessly if he did know. "And what about Sir Roland, sir?"

"No difficulty there. He has been reminded, nicely, that he needs to behave at the Club, so that charge is withdrawn."

"Thank you, sir."

"Chap had it coming, and has no sympathy or support anywhere. But mind how you go."

There it was again, and the line was still in his head a few minutes later when he and Habibullah left to interview Charles Winstone.

Fifteen

Unfortunately, Winstone was the sort of ICS man who aggravated Le Fanu.

Sitting in the man's Secretariat office a few doors along from Jamieson's, Le Fanu felt that he and Habi were watching a future Third Member in morphosis. The room was set up so that Winstone was fully in charge, and Le Fanu even wondered if the guests' chairs were lower, or if Winstone somehow had his raised. Le Fanu had heard of people doing that but always thought it a myth. He was not so sure now.

The desk was scrupulously ordered, a fountain pen and blotter to one side of a leather writing base covered with blotting paper. Two files were stacked to one side on the front, another two to the left.

Winstone waited several deliberate seconds before rising to greet them. He was in his late twenties, slim with a foppish haircut, a blonde fringe falling towards his eyes. The expressionless face had a slightly receding chin, dimples just above each side of the mouth, and the top lip essayed a wispy blonde moustache. His suit was tailored, tan in colour, and Le Fanu noticed the two-tone brogue shoes. When he spoke, the ICS man had a pronounced public school accent delivered in a thin voice. Le Fanu took an instant dislike. This man annoyed him.

Inevitably, then, the conversation began badly.

"Thank you for seeing us, Mr. Winstone."

"I have absolutely no idea why you are here, interviewing me at my place of work."

"We could conduct it elsewhere, if you preferred, perhaps at police HQ," came Le Fanu's immediate retort.

Winstone railed immediately. "And I have no idea why both of you are here," he said, looking pointedly at Habi. "Why should a sergeant be here interviewing me?"

"Because he is an integral member of my team," Le Fanu responded, "with special knowledge of this case."

"You're wasting your time because there's nothing I can tell you."

"Mr Winstone, we know you spent a lot of time with Miss Carstairs at Jamieson's, and Miss Carstairs was found murdered the next morning. You must have expected we would question you."

"Not at all, quite the reverse. I go to many of these soirees and I talk to many people because they all want to spend time with me. That evening was no exception. The fact that Miss Carstairs was murdered is absolutely no concern of mine."

The policemen looked at each other, surprised.

"Did you really mean that, Mr. Winstone?" asked Le Fanu.

"What?"

"To suggest that Miss Carstairs' death was of no matter to you?"

"I didn't say that," Winstone said, retreating.

"We are investigating a murder," Le Fanu commented, "so I advise you to cooperate fully and carefully. If you do not straightforwardly tell us what we need to know, I'll speak with your superiors and I doubt that's something you desire."

Le Fanu glared at Winstone who broke eye contact quickly.

"I can assure you," he said, "I know nothing of value."

"We'll decide that," said Le Fanu, "now tell me about that night."

Winstone said he arrived at Wark's around seven fifteen,

approximately the same time as the women whom he had met at other functions during the previous three weeks.

Le Fanu wondered idly how much actual office work was occurring around Madras, because most of the workforce seemed preoccupied with after-hours activity.

Winstone reported that he spent several minutes with Jane Carstairs at the beginning of the evening, but in a group. Then he sat with Virginia Campbell at a table near the swimming pool where food was served. The discussion was mainly about how Miss Campbell was finding Madras and whether or not she missed England. She said she enjoyed Madras and did not miss England whatsoever. After that, Winstone encountered both women over the next hour or so, until around nine o'clock. He then asked Miss Campbell if she would accompany him elsewhere for a drink, but she was already booked by Billy Walsall.

"When you saw Miss Carstairs on those subsequent occasions, was she alone or in groups?" asked Le Fanu.

"Why is that relevant?"

"Mr. Winstone, just tell us what we need to know. We're not trying to trip you up, we simply need to know as much as possible about Miss Carstairs' final hours."

He emphasised the last two words, hoping Winstone would sense the seriousness. He did.

"Oh, alright. I saw her off in the distance with others throughout the evening, but also saw her directly at four other times. Three of those we were in groups and there was a general discussion. The other time we were alone, again over by the swimming pool where we had gone for snacks."

Le Fanu asked how she seemed at that point.

"She was enjoying the occasion, at least according to what she told me."

Habi broke in. "That seems an odd expression, sir. Could you expand it for us?"

Winstone was definitely displeased at being questioned by

an Indian.

"Are you questioning my grammar now? Because if you are…"

"Not at all, sir, "Habi continued, "I simply want to find out exactly what it is you are not saying."

"Well, she seemed preoccupied with something. On previous occasions she was a bright and outgoing person, ready to start a conversation or take up any opportunity." Winstone clearly hated saying all this.

"But?"

"That evening she was withdrawn. Very hard to get a conversation out of her. It was as if she was there physically but not mentally. She seemed miles away."

Le Fanu sensed something else. "Was there anything in particular to give you that impression?"

"Yes, I asked her if she wanted to go to the Connemara, before I asked Miss Campbell, actually. It was like she did not hear me, because she did not answer. Very rude, I thought."

So his attitude stemmed from the fact she declined an invitation or perhaps did not even hear it.

Habi was taking notes, knowing Le Fanu wanted him to watch how Winstone was coping with the questions. He interjected again. "Sir," he said, "would you say Miss Carstairs was calm or agitated?"

Again annoyed at being asked a question by a lowly Indian sergeant, Winstone struggled to conceal his contempt. "If I was to be doing that, I would be in the IPS and not the ICS. I much prefer to be where I am, thank you."

Le Fanu marvelled at Habi's sense of timing. Winstone was defensive again, and that was where Le Fanu wanted him.

"So you asked Miss Carstairs to accompany you, and she refused?"

"I told you, she hardly seemed to hear me."

"But that in itself was a refusal?"

"If you must put it that way, yes."

"Were you angry?"

If not then, he was now. Winstone's face was strained, along with the rest of his body. His elbows were on the desk, his face leaning on two clenched fists. He was flushed, eyes narrowed and darkening.

"Are you accusing me of murdering her because she refused to go for a drink?" The voice was strangled.

"Not at all, just trying to get a sense of how things were."

"She was an ungrateful woman out here on a last desperate mission, and she refused a perfectly reasonable invitation to have a drink. That does not mean I killed her. She was not worth it."

"In the circumstances, Mr. Winstone," Le Fanu continued, "that comment seems uncharitable."

"It is what I think."

"Then Miss Campbell declined your invitation?" Le Fanu resumed.

"As I said, she had already booked herself."

"Not a successful night for you, then."

Winstone was enraged by now. "This is outrageous. You are implying…."

"We are implying nothing, Mr. Winstone, just trying to determine what happened. You asked two women to go out with you and both turned you down. That would have been upsetting. Did it, I wonder, cloud your memory of what happened that evening?"

"Absolutely not, and I have told you everything I know. I will be complaining to my superiors about your attitude."

"Please do, Mr. Winstone, because we'll need to speak with you again, and we would not want any impediment to that."

Winstone saw them off in grim fashion, and they returned to the office in time for lunch.

Sixteen

The next task was to interview Captain Preston Pyne, Indian Medical Service, at the General Hospital where he was an assistant surgeon, just along from the central railway station. Habi's research had also discovered that Pyne lectured part-time in anatomy at the Madras Medical College right next door. He was a busy man.

Le Fanu's phobia for morgues extended to hospitals but he could not desert Habi, so went off reluctantly to the hospital, which they reached just after two. As usual in such a sprawling place, it took time to actually find Pyne. The hospital might run along military lines but that did not make it any the more efficient. They finally found their man in a small office at the back of the building, so had to traverse almost every hospital department and their smells and sounds. Le Fanu had already had enough.

Sensing his boss' disposition, Habi became mischievous. "Feeling alright there, sir?" he asked innocently.

Le Fanu shot him a glance that needed no interpretation.

"Always good to spend time in a hospital, I think," Habi continued, "gives one a sense of life's possibilities."

Le Fanu made it clear that those possibilities did not interest him.

Habi laughed, and they followed their guide through archways, corridors, doors, twists, turns and wards. Neither man was confident he could find his way back, and Le Fanu wondered if they should have employed the Hansel and Gretel method.

At last they squeezed into the cell that doubled as Pyne's office. Le Fanu was dismayed. The room featured a myriad of glass jars containing liquid, and worse according to his quick glance. There was just room for their two chairs on one side of a table overflowing with papers, one chair on the other side for Pyne, and two glass-fronted bookshelves so full of books and papers the doors splayed open. Wherever Le Fanu looked, some of those jars were in his sightline. A single light bulb swayed above their heads, and the interior was done out in the distinctive olive green of hospitals everywhere.

Preston Pyne was average height, thickset, dark, and looked like he needed to shave twice a day. Le Fanu had no idea what made men attractive to women, but he could not imagine those close set eyes in that pudgy face being considered attractive. Yet the man had spent good time with both Jane Carstairs and Virginia Campbell. Perhaps it was the medical background and the prospect of a solid career, he thought. Compared to his own salary of about one thousand rupees per month, Pyne must be on twice if not three times that.

"Captain Pyne," began Le Fanu, "thank you for seeing us, we know how busy you are."

"Only too happy to give you what little information I have," came back a rich, deep voice. Perhaps that was the attraction.

"Tell us about yourself and how long you have been here."

Pyne came from a Gloucestershire family, attended Cheltenham, studied medicine in London, did a residency at Guys, then joined the IMS in 1913. He came briefly to Madras but returned to England at the start of the war, and served on the Western Front almost continuously. What horrors had this man seen, then? When the war finished he returned to Madras and the hospital. He would be promoted to surgeon and major soon – and be paid even more, thought Le Fanu, enviously but simultaneously acknowledging that Pyne had paid his dues.

Habi asked Pyne if he had ever met Jane Carstairs before the evening at Wark's.

"Certainly. I received invitations to all the gatherings this season. Among other things, people are just glad the war is over, and having fun seems a good idea."

Le Fanu agreed, wishing he could adopt that approach more himself.

Pyne continued. "I met both Jane and Virginia as soon as they arrived in Madras, and we went out to dinner once during the first week, a rare free night for those on the circuit. They were wonderful company. Very bright, well informed. Looked good, too. Up until the other night, I probably saw them a dozen times."

Le Fanu was warming to him, despite the bottles and their contents. Habi was scribbling furiously in his notebook.

"How well did you get to know them, their thoughts, what was happening with them?" asked Le Fanu.

"Virginia was more open than Jane, but I got to know something about both of them. We had a lot of time to talk."

"And what were your impressions?"

"Virginia was here to have as good a time as possible and meet as many people as she could, women as well as men. It was like she was collecting character specimens or something."

Mention of "specimens" made Le Fanu lose his thread. Luckily, Pyne did not notice.

"In many ways," he continued, "Virginia was not, is not the typical fishing fleeter. Catching someone is neither here nor there to her. As a result, she can be her natural self and that makes her popular. She is warm, witty, outgoing."

"You like her, then?"

"Well, yes. It's always difficult in these situations where

most women are artificial and desperate, but Virginia is delightful."

So what was she doing with Winstone the evening Jane Carstairs died, Le Fanu wondered.

"Jane?"

"More difficult to judge."

Pyne met Jane twice at a Mount Road coffee shop. Run by an Italian, its coffee was Italian rather than south Indian which, though good, was simply too different for most newcomers, Pyne suggested. The shop made its own Italian biscuits and sweets whose reputation attracted Jane's attention. She asked Pyne if they could go there. That was two weeks before Jamieson's party.

"Did you have a decent conversation with her? More than just the normal pleasantries?" queried Le Fanu.

"It was more difficult than with Virginia but, yes, we did discuss some things."

Pyne thought Jane had not enjoyed Madras as much as Virginia, but could not explain why he thought that. There was an atmosphere, an attitude around her, he thought. She found people difficult to approach and deal with, and disliked the social ranking and pettiness of Madras. According to Pyne, she had not liked Charles Winstone at all.

She had some taste, then, but Le Fanu wondered exactly what it was she disliked about Winstone.

"Did she have any particular issue with Winstone?"

"Only that she thought him a pompous ass."

Good taste confirmed.

She also liked the Italian coffee shop because it stocked European rather than English newspapers and magazines. The proprietor attracted people from the small local French community, and the French in Pondicherry to the south made a pilgrimage to the shop whenever they visited Madras. He stocked French journals and newspapers as well as English ones so Jane caught up on those whenever possible, and Pyne enjoyed taking her there. She was one of those who found Madras too provincial, even by British India standards, but she was still a nice person.

Had Pyne noticed any change in her over those few weeks?

"Strange you should ask ," replied the doctor. "I saw her twice in the four days before the Wark party, then that evening at Wark's itself."

"Oh yes?"

"She was quieter, more withdrawn, and at Wark's she was positively sombre. I asked if there was anything the matter but, of course, she said no. And being a doctor, I wondered if it was her time of the month."

"She mentioned nothing at all?" Le Fanu asked.

"No."

"Captain, "Le Fanu continued, "do you have a supply of morphine here in the hospital?"

"Of course. We hold several different drugs, I suppose is the technically correct answer but, yes, we have morphine here. It is well locked away and accounted for. The eagle-eyed clerks and officers over at the Medical Stores keep close tabs on what they supply us, and in turn we keep good records concerning usage. Strange question. Any reason for asking?"

"Yes, but not one I can share, I regret." Le Fanu smiled as warmly as he could to help diffuse further curiosity. "But you do have access, I take it?"

"Comes with the job, Superintendent, people like me handle it all the time."

"Do you know if any has gone missing?"

"You could talk to our pharmacy people, they know more, but I haven't heard of any going astray."

Le Fanu took some pharmacy staff names from Pyne, to check on later if necessary. He doubted the hospital was the source, really.

As Pyne led them through the maze back to their car at the front entrance, Le Fanu was preoccupied with their slow progress on the case, so missed the additional humorous medical references offered up by Habi. Le Fanu pondered their next call, and wondered again why Caldicott's name seemed familiar.

Seventeen

Jackson Caldicott worked for Charles & Co., a shipping and trading rival of Sir Roland Wark's company. In reality there was little competition because there was plenty of work to share around, though conditions were tighter than before the war. The Government's mooted austerity program had yet to set in, and that worried some business leaders. The Charles & Co. offices were in First Line Beach, among all the other prominent trading houses. Given his office was up on the fifth floor, Caldicott was evidently a man with a future. This time Le Fanu took the lift, deferring to Habi who professed to not being a climber.

As soon as Le Fanu saw the face he knew why he should have recognised the name. Caldicott had been in Madras for three years and, more importantly, for three cricket seasons during which he had become a star all-rounder. His batting was excellent, bowling almost that, and fielding very good. He was a Cambridge blue, and Le Fanu had watched him help the club win significant fixtures against sides from Bombay and Ceylon.

The cricketer had an easy air, probably come from a life made easily successful as a good scholar and great sportsman, Le Fanu reckoned. He was Le Fanu's height, twenty-six, light framed but fit, brown hair cut closer than was now fashionable, a little angular in the face but with warm brown eyes. His dark Prince of Wales check suit jacket was hanging on a peg behind the door, and he was wearing a pale blue shirt with a darker blue tie, Cambridge cuff links and tie pin, plain black braces supporting the suit trousers, and smart black shoes. It was all highly fashionable for Madras, but Caldicott made it seem normal.

The cricketer shook Le Fanu's hand firmly, took their orders for tea and coffee, rang through to a secretary, and motioned them towards a table clearly used for conferences, or discussions with visiting policemen.

"I've seen you play," said Le Fanu, "you're very good. I suppose you would have been with a county had you stayed home?"

"Kent asked me to turn out, but I had a career out here potentially." The voice was light, modulated and pleasant. " I'd been in the War Office for the duration, felt I hadn't done much, and thought coming here might make up for that."

"And has it?"

"Madras has been kind. The cricket is good and the firm gives me full support, so I'll stay, I think."

Caldicott had not answered the question, Le Fanu thought, but he would be a partner and director inside two years because few like him came. Those who did were lionised. Within a few years Caldicott would be a business leader and on the Legislative Council. What possible reason would there be to go home, unless he got bored with the local cricket.

"We understand you spent some time with Jane Carstairs the evening before her death." Habi raised the real business.

"I still can't believe this, you know", Caldicott whispered, and Le Fanu believed him. The man was not acting.

"These things are always a shock, so your feeling is natural," Habi commented.

"I suppose so, but even then..." Caldicott did not complete the sentence, and looked close to tears. Things like this were not supposed to happen to the golden ones, Le Fanu realised, especially those who had not been on the front.

Caldicott's account was similar to Pyne's. He met the two women when they first arrived in the city, at a Governor's official residence function. Le Fanu had not been invited to, let alone attended that one, so Caldicott and the women were both well connected.

After that, Caldicott took them to the Madras Cricket Club on two Saturday match days. One of those visits transformed into a group dinner involving other players and additional members of the fishing fleet. The players escorted the women home from the dinner hotel with Caldicott responsible for getting Jane and Virginia back to Wark's in Adyar.

"Do you know if at any time either or both of the two women left the ground to explore the area?" asked Habi.

The same thought had occurred to Le Fanu – the MCC's Chepauk ground was a short distance from where Jane Carstairs' body was found. Perhaps she knew something about the area after all? The ground was a short walk from both the Chepauk Palace and the University of Madras, both of which might have interested them.

"I can't say for certain," Caldicott replied, "because I was either batting or fielding for most of both days."

Was there a flash of arrogance buried in there, a reference to his indispensability?

Caldicott continued. "I think they were there the whole time, from what I saw, but the servants at the club might be more helpful."

Habi scribbled in his notebook.

"So you saw a lot of the pair over the past three weeks, and of course, at Sir Roland Wark's from time to time?" Le Fanu asked.

"I was surprised at being invited there, because my senior partner and Sir Roland loathe each other. Wark tried to undercut us on a deal and that really is not done here, you know."

Interesting, Wark had critics in business as well as at the

Club.

"Anyway," continued Caldicott, "I saw both Virginia and Jane at Jamieson's that night. We were in the same groups on a couple of occasions, and I also spoke with both separately."

"How did Miss Carstairs seem to you?" asked Le Fanu.

"Unhappy, really, not at all like she was before."

Pyne had also reported Jane Carstairs as withdrawn in the days preceding her death, now Caldicott confirmed that. Something had upset her three to four days before she died. That something might well be a factor in her death.

"Did she mention if anything in particular was worrying her?" asked Habi.

"Nothing specific, but she mentioned a couple of people she was unsure about."

"Do you have any more detail?"

"On one occasion at Wark's she said she met an American at a party and he introduced her to a local friend of his. Both men are apparently in the movie industry."

Madrasis had watched films now for over twenty years. The movie tents that moved about the city were very popular. A few years earlier, a local wealthy enthusiast began producing his own films, mainly on grand classical themes that appealed to Hindus, but he also made local news reels and short films on Presidency tourist attractions. That petered out around the end of the war, and there had been no serious start-ups since.

"What were these two film people up to?" asked Le Fanu.

"I have no idea, but Jane was agitated about something. She said she had been asked to get involved, but I couldn't swear to that because another group of people came up to us and she stopped talking. I never got another chance to ask her, but she seemed uncomfortable with whatever they were up to."

Caldicott looked like he might break down again.

"I know this is hard, Mr. Caldicott, but did you see Jane Carstairs later that evening?"

"I certainly saw her at the party, mixing with other guests, but I left with a group at nine-thirty."

"You left with others?" asked Habi.

"Yes, I live in a chummery over in Kilpauk. Six of us share a house there, so we all left together, crammed into one car, I have to admit."

Others would likely corroborate that story, so Caldicott was out of the picture.

"Was Miss Carstairs still there when you left?" asked Le Fanu.

"Yes. I saw her in a small group of people, talking, a glass of champagne in hand."

"Did you recognise any of those others?"

"Yes." He gave Habi four new names.

"Mr Caldicott," asked Le Fanu, "are you sure there's nothing else you can recall Miss Carstairs saying about this American and his local ally?"

"I am afraid not, Superintendent, but they did unsettle her, I would say."

Encouraged by this new knowledge, Le Fanu thought it would be simple enough to track down an American. They stuck out around here and rarely used cheaper hotels, unlike the British and European vagrants who washed up. If they found the American, they would find the local movie mogul. Then there was Caldicott's information that Jane Carstairs was still at Jamieson's at nine-thirty, the best time confirmation so far. If Jamieson or his wife could remember any guests who left later, he and Habi could determine a precise time for Jane Carstairs' departure, and with whom.

One thing troubled him. If the American and his accomplice were a factor, why had Virginia Campbell not mentioned them? Perhaps she thought it not worth mentioning, or had simply forgotten, or had deliberately avoided the point. If the latter, why did she do that?

Caldicott, still shaken, saw them off the premises, but not

before having invited Le Fanu to the next home cricket match a couple of weeks away. They exchanged telephone numbers and agreed to keep in touch on both the case and the game.

As they were driven back towards the office, past the High Court and its domes, dodging bullock carts in turn trying to dodge cars and trucks driven by learning drivers, Le Fanu felt better than at the beginning of the day. Progress was slow, but it was occurring. There were more questions to ask of people already interviewed, and new names to follow up. Above all, he must speak with Virginia Campbell again tomorrow.

When they reached headquarters, the I-G had his doors open allowing in a light sea breeze. They sat out there while Le Fanu provided an update. Wilson was also happy, so by the time Le Fanu wheeled his bike out of the stables, he felt almost satisfied for the first time since this affair began. He was now more confident they would find the killer, but the time taken to achieve that was still critical because, according to Wilson, Olli was still after him.

Eighteen

The sea breeze was cool and strong, so the bike ride home was exhilarating. He flew past carts, pony traps, bullock drays, cars, bicycles and pedestrians with much less irritation than normal for him at this time of the day, then roared through the tree-lined streets to the house and calm. He was smiling, for the first time in a while, a good sign. He found his golf bag, pulled out the putter and a few balls and headed to his practice green. Even missing a few putts did not blight his optimism, and he anticipated a breakthrough in the case.

He took dinner on the verandah, reluctant to leave either garden or good mood. The food added to his pleasure, an excellent mutton curry with the right south Indian accompaniments and a fruity white wine kept for a good moment. This sort of moment was increasingly rare in his life, one when he knew why he stayed in India, so he stretched it out as long as possible.

As he finished eating, Ro sat down with him – another rare moment, because the other servants were absent from the house. But she was preoccupied.

"Are you alright?" he asked.

"There was a phone call for you this afternoon," she replied, "a woman."

"Did she have a name?"

"Miss Campbell."

Why would Virginia Campbell call him at home and, for that matter, how did she get his number? Wark, probably, he had access to all sorts of information. But why was Ro so upset?

"What did she want, or have to say?" he continued.

"She wanted to know where you were. What's going on here, Chris?"

This was very odd. Virginia Campbell called at about two in the afternoon, asking where he was. She had to have known he would be working, so what was she up to? And how was he to deal with Ro, who was visibly upset?

Ro had no doubt about the reason for the call. "She was checking if you have a wife."

"What?"

"She didn't ask directly, but when I said you were not here, she asked who I was, and if there was anyone else she might speak with. That was code for is Mrs Le Fanu home?" Ro looked reproachful. "Are you just interviewing her, or is something else happening?"

"Ro, she's a suspect in a murder case. Of course I'm just interviewing her. What on earth else could I do?"

Le Fanu thought back to the first interview when he told Virginia Campbell about Jane Carstairs' death. She took it well, almost too well. And then there were those moments when he wondered if she was flirting with him. He continued his faltering attempt to placate Ro.

"Miss Campbell took the news about Jane Carstairs' death calmly, and the rest of the interview was routinely straightforward." He did not want this to get complicated.

"What does 'routinely straightforward' mean?" Her voice was taut. She really was distressed.

"Ro, she was the best friend of the murdered woman, and she's important to the inquiry. When I questioned her, she replied straightforwardly and with no surprises. That's all. Are you upset?"

"She's a fishing fleeter, and she wants to hook you, and you can take the word hook any way you want."

"But that's ridiculous," he responded. "Why would she think about me? I'm investigating a case in which she's involved. That's where it starts and ends"

"Police, ICS, Army, all the same to her. She might consider a company director if pushed, but nothing lower. If there's no Mrs. Le Fanu, you're a candidate."

"That's just not possible." His voice wavered, he hated these conversations because he could never predict their end point. He had never known how to deal with them.

"Why not? You're a good catch: senior policeman, important job, good war. And you are half good looking. Any fisherwoman would be happy."

Le Fanu had no idea where this was going. "Ro, even if she was interested, what difference does it make? I'm not, because you are here"

"So you think she might be interested?"

How had she concluded that from what he had just said? He really didn't know what to say in these situations. He was more comfortable at a scene of offence. That was probably not to his credit, he thought.

"No, Ro, I didn't say that, or mean to say that. I'm just saying that even if she did think about it, I'm still just the investigating police officer on a case in which she's directly involved."

"That gives her even more opportunity to cast a line."

Dangerous waters, Le Fanu. "No. Besides, I have you."

She viewed him like a raptor about to snatch a rodent. "Yes, you do, but that's hardly public or permanent, is it?"

Le Fanu recognised, too late, that what he considered a clever debating switch was exactly the change Ro was seeking. And he was supposed to be the interrogator? At this rate he might have to get her a job at HQ.

Their relationship had begun accidentally but inevitably

months earlier. She was magnetic, the sort of woman to whom he was always attracted. He realised that the moment she turned up and, in fact, considered not employing her for that reason. He still thought vaguely then that his wife might return, but as time disappeared so did that idea. That memory reminded him of the letter he had now been carrying around unopened for two days. Ro's references were excellent, she came recommended by a friend, and despite the hesitation he hired her immediately and she began the following day, shifting into the servant's quarters.

About a month later he was up late one night, trying to draft an answer to his wife's latest mad demands. He had a couple of whiskeys and was feeling sorry for himself when Ro appeared at the door. She asked why he was down, they swapped life stories, she took a whiskey, and opened his door for the first time a couple of hours later. He did not send her away.

She was realistic about the relationship, he thought, and about her being Anglo-Indian and him still being married. They were both lonely, attracted to each other, so why not spend some time together? If they kept it quiet, it would serve both their purposes. He was not convinced about it being so straightforward, because he actually liked her. She was smart, funny, very attractive, and wonderful in bed. She was far better for him than his wife had ever been. They had carried on in relaxed fashion, until now.

"Ro, I really like you, and I'm lucky you're in my life. Yes, it would be awkward for us now if it got out, but at some point there's no reason it shouldn't become public."

He had not meant it to come out quite that way but now it had, he did not mind. He liked her a lot.

"What, you mean if you got a divorce it might all work out for us?"

"Why not? I'd be delighted if we could fix that. But I thought your idea was to keep it at the same level as before."

"I might just have changed my mind. Especially now that woman called, and she's after you." She smiled, but he was not sure the remark was meant to be funny.

He poured them another drink, and they sat silently for a while, listening to the insects and the other night sounds.

"Well," he said, "if you think you're in danger from her, think again."

"You just watch out for her."

She looked stern but he caught the faintest touch of a smile she tried to cover with her glass.

"I will, promise."

"And Chris, I'm flattered by the idea we might be together permanently, but you and I both know that's no easy matter. We can take our time on that. Meanwhile…"

He smiled, crisis averted. All the same, what was Virginia Campbell trying to achieve? Was she trying to distract him? Surely she had nothing to do with her friend's death? She was cool on receiving the news, practically detached, and that bothered him. He would get Habi to check her background in the morning, before he interviewed her again.

Thinking back over the evening which he had started in such good spirits, he thought he far preferred police work to sorting out relationships, present or past.

Later, his door opened quietly, as usual, and he got little sleep.

Nineteen

Habi was already in the office, reviewing notes and amending the boards, when Le Fanu arrived.

"Good morning, sir. You know we haven't spoken with Billy Walsall yet, the one who apparently drove Virginia Campbell back to Adyar after the Jamieson party."

After the previous evening's conversation with Ro and his own thoughts about Virginia Campbell, Le Fanu could only nod at first. "What do we know about him?" he managed finally.

Habi had checked. Walsall was twenty seven, an artillery lieutenant. He did the usual training in England and arrived in Madras at the end of the war during which he served mostly on the Western Front. His army records were fine, and local police checks revealed nothing.

"Where is he?" asked Le Fanu, "Not all the way out at St. Thomas Mount, I hope?"

Habi laughed. Dealings with the military annoyed the police because the main quarters were well out beyond Adyar, the artillery especially distant at the foot of the little hill where St. Thomas was said to have met his end several hundred years earlier. It was pleasant enough for a Sunday excursion, despite its grim heritage, but inconvenient for a week day investigation.

"Luckily," Habi replied, "he is currently posted to

Poonamallee High Road in an office at the Reserves. He's doing some training for them or something. Has a little cottage there, been in it for the past few months."

"No doubt he's as cocky as the rest of them, now they are 'The Duke's Own'."

A month before, the Duke of Connaught came to Madras to promote the constitutional reforms local Europeans hated so passionately. As part of the flattery, he announced that the artillery would now be known as the Madras Field Brigade "The Duke's Own". It was a mouthful that, in Le Fanu's view, did little more than boost several egos. If nothing else, it suggested that the conservatism in Madras really worried the India Office and the government in the United Kingdom, as well as the British India leadership in New Delhi.

Habi had telephoned the Reserves office, spoken with Walsall and they were expected. Before they left, he reminded Le Fanu of several other tasks listed on the boards, among them tracking down the mysterious American and his local partner in film.

Twenty minutes later, they stood in front of a stocky, dark haired individual with an enormous handlebar moustache, regulation army haircut, sallow skin and dark eyes with bags under them. He was also slightly deaf, a result of all those years at the front. Walsall had tea fetched, and insisted they call him Billy.

"Billy," began Le Fanu, "you drove Virginia Campbell to the Connemara then back out to Adyar the night of Jamieson's garden party. Can you give us some timings on that?"

"Surely. We left Nungambakkam about nine, took about ten or fifteen minutes to get to the Connemara so got there about, say, nine-fifteen. Stayed there until about eleven-thirty, and went back to Wark's about midnight, I should think."

That was close to Virginia's Campbell's account, so it was either correct, or rehearsed. Le Fanu wondered why that last thought arose, it had not crossed his mind previously. Was he beginning to suspect Virginia Campbell?

"What time did you arrive at Jamieson's?" asked Habi.

"Oh, good question." Walsall's undistinguished, weak voice seemed odd in an artillery officer. "Probably about seven, I would reckon."

"Were you there when the Misses Campbell and Carstairs arrived?"

"Not sure. There were already a lot of people there, but I was among the first to arrive."

Le Fanu was annoyed that, after two days, they were still hazy on the timing of people arriving at then leaving Jamieson's. Caldicott had helped, but otherwise they had had little assistance. He asked Walsall about the two women at Jamieson's and their movements.

"Saw them both several times and spent a lot of time talking with them together, individually, and in bigger groups."

"Sounds like you might have talked to them more than anybody else present?"

"Possibly so, they were good company."

"And when did you ask Miss Campbell to go to the Connemara?"

"About eight-forty-five."

"And you left soon afterwards?"

"Yes."

"When did you last speak with Miss Carstairs before leaving?"

"About eight-thirty."

"How did she seem?"

Walsall looked awkward, shifting in his chair and running fingers inside his collar as if it and the regimental tie were too tight.

Habi picked that up and rephrased the question. "Was Miss Carstairs upset about anything, do you know?"

"She was upset with me."

"Why was that?" Habi asked.

Walsall flushed, and looked away. "She didn't welcome my approach."

Interesting, Le Fanu thought, Walsall was now hesitant.

"What approach was that?" Le Fanu asked.

"I asked her for a drink at the Connemara, and if, well, er, um, she'd be interested in staying there the night."

Clumsy, thought Le Fanu, not to mention presumptuous. "What made you ask that?"

"She was in the fishing fleet, never know your luck. But she turned me down flat on both counts."

Walsall claimed there were no hard feelings over the refusal and insisted that he and Jane Carstairs parted on good terms. He saw her again in the minutes before he left, and she had greeted him well enough.

Le Fanu was curious. "Tell me, did you put the same proposition to Miss Campbell?"

Walsall blushed. "Ah, well, now you ask, yes. She accepted the first part and not the second. She was a good sport."

Incorrigible, thought Le Fanu, 'The Duke's Own' elevation had gone to their collective artillery heads. Importantly, though, this background made Walsall more interesting. He propositioned both women, was refused totally by one and partially by the other. He took one back to Adyar, and there was a distinct possibility his first target, who turned up dead next morning, was around Adyar at the time he dropped off Virginia Campbell.

Habi got in ahead of him. "Lieutenant Walsall, what time did you return to Poonamallee High Road, and can anyone else confirm that time?"

Le Fanu watched Walsall closely. The man was edgy, nervous.

"It's a trek from Adyar, of course. I think I got in about one."

It was a trek, yes, but did not take an hour, especially at that time of night/morning. Thirty minutes at best, Le Fanu thought, so what happened during the rest of that time, he wondered.

Walsall was equivocal, saying first he was unsure of the time, then that he lost his way on the return journey. Neither option seemed credible.

"Not a strong story, Lieutenant," commented Le Fanu. "You didn't happen to bump into Miss Carstairs after you left Miss Campbell?"

"In Adyar, you mean? I was unaware she'd gone back, so…"

"Where else was she going to go? She refused your kind offer of looking after her for the night, after all."

"Ah yes, no, I meant that I was not sure…"

Habi chimed in. "Lieutenant Walsall, the longer you keep this up the more complicated it becomes and the worse for you, so tell us what you know."

Walsall looked troubled. "I dropped Miss Campbell at Wark's at twelve, and turned back into Chamier's Road to see Miss Carstairs walking towards Boat Club Road. This was, say, five or ten minutes after midnight."

So Jane Carstairs made it back to Adyar, but how? Walsall had a partial answer.

"I stopped to ask if I could help, or drive her to Wark's. She said no, she wanted to walk. I asked how she got there. Someone else had given her a ride to the Chamier's Road corner. I asked who, but she wouldn't say. I tried to persuade her to get in my car, but she wouldn't. Maybe it was because of my earlier invitation, I don't know, but you can imagine how I feel now."

Perhaps so, perhaps not, thought Le Fanu, but her reluctance to accept the offer resulted in her death. However, she was still alive and in Adyar a few minutes after midnight. It took at least half an hour or so to get to there from where she was found, but they knew from the autopsy that she was killed elsewhere. That all suggested time of death was between one and two in the morning, the big question now being where she was murdered. And Walsall, the last person to see her alive, so far as they knew at this point, was a suspect.

"You still maintain she didn't get in your car?" Le Fanu asked him.

"Yes, no. I mean, she did not get in my car. She walked off down Boat Club Road towards Wark's. I was worried about her. It is a safe enough area but, even so, I would have preferred her to accept my offer."

"But she did not, and you drove off."

"Yes."

Le Fanu thought Walsall's confusion and lack of clarity might spring from his guilt at not having accompanied Jane Carstairs to the Wark mansion. He understood that, remembering the guilt he still carried for those who died under his command. Even so, Walsall deserved deeper investigation.

As the car carried them back towards the city centre before turning towards HQ, Le Fanu and Habi agreed on Walsall as their current leading suspect, though neither really believed him to be the killer.

"We are answering some of those Gross questions, Habi?"

"Sorry sir, I do not understand?"

"I should have said the Hans Gross questions, the ones Wilson makes us put on the wall sometimes:

"What was the crime, who did it, when was it done, and where, how done, and with what motive, who in the deed did share?"

"If you ask me, sir, we have too few answers for those questions. We know who died, and more or less how, but as for the rest, not much."

Twenty

They sat around the office table, reviewing progress in the short time left before Habi left for lunch at home. He tried to do this every day. Habi's home life was strong, but unusual and well known in the force— he was a Muslim married to a Hindu woman who had converted to Christianity. The marriage challenged both families involved, but was very successful. They had a young son and a younger daughter, and Habi liked to be at home for lunch to see them. Le Fanu happily supported him, sensing a kindred spirit and, deep down, envying his sergeant's rich home life. It was a deep contrast to his own.

Now they had the probable time of Jane Carstairs' death, and could place her back in Adyar near Wark's house before that death, Le Fanu was satisfied with progress if still bothered by the gaps in their knowledge.

"We still have no idea how she got morphine in her system," he commented aloud, more for himself than Habi, already well used to his superior's musing.

"We don't really know it was the morphine that killed her, do we?" Habi commented. The morphine issue centred on two main questions, he continued: how Jane Carstairs got and consumed the stuff. And that prompted another question: who gave her the drug?

"Habi," Le Fanu asked, "do we have any more information

on obvious Americans currently in Madras we might go and interview?"

Habi did. He could identify all Americans known to have been or still resident in the city over the past two months. It had taken him a day's work in total, peering through port landing records and checking with the American consulate, as well as local firms with strong American connections. Most of those firms traded in tobacco, though a few motorcar traders were appearing, too. Given the movie connection, Habi could also now identify several Madrasis involved in film activities, either past or present. He had also linked any obvious names appearing on each list. That produced a preliminary shortlist, and Habi told Le Fanu he would finalise the connections – after lunch. He entered his preliminary findings on the board before racing to the door as quickly as his body would allow.

Le Fanu himself ignored lunch and created a priority list based around his sergeant's research. Getting further information about Billy Walsall was a priority, as it was for all the others interviewed so far. Le Fanu paused, then muttered aloud:

"We need more background research on Virgina Campbell, too."

He was admitting to himself she was a suspect. Yes, she was Jane Carstairs' best friend. And, yes, Wark said she was in by midnight, but there were oddities in her story and behaviour. Wark had not actually seen her, she told him she was home by midnight and Lady Wark saw her only at breakfast the next morning. Then, she and Walsall said they were at the Connemara but there was no confirmation yet. The bar staff must be interviewed.

Wark required more investigation, too. What time had his dinner party ended, and had he gone out following that? Given his recent behaviour, he might well have been too drunk to go anywhere after dinner, but it needed checking. He might not have killed Jane Carstairs himself, but he might have arranged for others to do so.

Le Fanu wondered where that line of thinking came from. At this point in any investigation, his suspects list was always wide-ranging, even fanciful. But even by his standards, that last Wark option looked far-fetched.

He knew he needed to meet Virginia Campbell again later, and that dredged up Ro's comments. Caution was required. Le Fanu was apprehensive, though. He was attracted to the woman, and he now thought she was dangerous.

A constable arrived with a message. The I-G wanted to see Le Fanu as soon as possible. Le Fanu left a message for Habi, saying they should meet up sometime after five, and he went across to the I-G's office.

Wilson was worried. A series of strikes had broken out at the Buckingham and Carnatic Mills in Perambur, close to the railway system's nerve centre. The mill owners were insisting on additional police being posted. That aggravated the strikers, clashes resulted and shots were fired. There was no news of casualties but the situation was threatening.

"Dammit, LF, the timing's dreadful. Wark and his commercial friends are demanding the military be called out. And Special Branch tells me that some of the strikers are Congress party members, so this is fast becoming a serious mess. Do you have any good news?"

Le Fanu updated him, especially on the need for additional inquiries into Virginia Campbell and Wark.

Wilson groaned. "Go carefully, LF, Wark is trouble and well connected, always a rotten combination here. He has us both down as pro-Indian liberals. Mind how you go. I may have to rope you in if this mill strike gets worse, but I'll try to avoid doing so. Getting this case settled would allay a few European fears, at least. Only a return to the eighteenth century would satisfy most of them, though."

Le Fanu was about to leave when Wilson stopped him.

"One more thing. I hear you've not seen Jepson for thirty

six hours. You do report direct to me, true, but keep him onside as well, can you? Call in there this afternoon before you do anything else."

Returning unhappily to his office, Le Fanu called the Commissioner's secretary and arranged to go straight over. Jepson would go to the mills after the meeting to see things for himself.

The driver took Le Fanu down the Marina, into Walajah's Road, across Mount Road into Blacker's Road then Cooum Road before reaching Police Commissioner's Road in Egmore. It was another journey Le Fanu usually enjoyed, but he hated the destination. Who was the writer, he wondered, who argued it was always better to travel than to arrive?

The trip touched the edge of Triplicane and older Madras, then reached the magnificence of Egmore with its ornate railway station and the even grander Museum - Connemara Library complex. Today he did not savour those buildings as he did normally. It was not so much the building and office that bothered him as the present occupant. Le Fanu marvelled again how great buildings could be transformed atmospherically by the mood and outlook of their commanders.

Jepson darkened his building, certainly, and was already in high fury when Le Fanu entered.

"Good God, man, two days and you've not bothered to give me any information at all. Disgraceful. I'd have you removed except the I-G won't have it. Not sure what hold you have there but I'll break it, and you."

Le Fanu wavered under this direct attack.

"My apologies, sir, it's been busy and…."

"Too busy to report to your superior officer? Since when was that acceptable police behaviour?"

"Sorry sir, all I meant was…."

"No more excuses, do you hear? What results do you have?"

As best he could, amidst constant interruptions and

exclamations from across the desk, Le Fanu summarised progress and repeated what he had told Wilson.

"Is that all you have?" shouted Jepson, now stomping around the office and lacerating a boot with the riding crop. "Two days and this is all? This is why I didn't want you in the first place. How on earth could you have Wark as a possible suspect, let alone that young woman Campbell? You're mad. All these mad detection theories the I-G spouts and you aid and abet, that's the problem. We need action, you damned slacker, not more damned Austrian theory."

Le Fanu knew Gross was part of the problem for Jepson, who brewed a potent mix of personal animosity, vanity, conservatism and suspicion. That made for a larger problem than Le Fanu had counted on. Jepson was stalking the Commissioner as well, supported no doubt by the local conservative establishment. There was now no chance of concentrating solely on this case. Local politics were fully in play.

He left the Police Commissioner's compound a deflated man, steeling himself for the appointment with Virginia Campbell.

Twenty-one

He would meet her at his office rather than Wark's house, an old trick that always worked. Get the subject off familiar territory and escape routes and into an unknown, uncertain site. He had no qualms treating her this way. Just two days ago he would have thought differently.

She appeared in the outer office promptly at four pm and he had her shown in immediately.

"Thank you for coming Miss Campbell, and I apologise for bringing you here. My busy schedule today does not allow me time to go to Adyar."

She was dressed more strikingly than ever, if that was possible. The soft linen dress was short sleeved with a high neckline, cut straight and long to just above the ankles. Virginia Campbell made an excellent clothes horse, especially wearing this deep lilac colour repeated in shoes, gloves, small clutch bag, and sweeping hat worn at a low angle over her right eye.

"That's quite alright Superintendent, thank you, I'm happy to meet you anywhere." She emphasised the you.

Her textured, inviting voice was accompanied by a smile flaring out from beneath the hat brim. She did not repeat the "please call me Virginia" approach, so he wondered how she was approaching this meeting. She was toying with him, he thought, remembering Ro's warning.

He opened aggressively. "Miss Campbell, apart from

Lieutenant Walsall, is there anyone who can prove you arrived back at Wark's house at midnight?"

She looked up, concerned.

"Are you saying I'm a suspect, because if…"

"Miss Campbell, detectives ask the questions and those being interviewed answer them, so please just tell me."

She was off stride now, he thought.

"Well, Superintendent, as you say, there is Lieutenant Walsall's word. Surely that's enough? He is an officer and a gentleman, after all."

"I did say in addition to him, but we can get to that. How reliant do you want to be on Walsall, given his real intentions towards you?"

"Did he tell you? How funny, he'd no chance there, I assure you." Her voice was lowered, suggestive and devoid of embarrassment.

"Yet you still went to the Connemara with him."

"For a drink, only."

"You were trusting. Did he tell you he offered Miss Carstairs the same opportunity fifteen minutes earlier?"

"No, he didn't. Desperate little blighter, isn't he?" The frivolity resurfaced, the voice lowered even further. She was teasing, but stalling, and Le Fanu had to prevent her regaining balance.

"Why did you trust him to take you home?" he asked.

"Well, by then I'd no alternative and no idea where Jane was. I doubted he would attack me."

"When you reached Wark's, did anyone else see you?"

"No, I went straight to my room."

"We have only your word for that." He stared at her.

She was worried. Was she was hiding something, or worried nobody could vouch for her?

"Did Walsall later mention that after dropping you, he saw Jane Carstairs at the corner of Chamiers Road and Boat Club Road?" Le Fanu wanted to see her reaction.

Her expression told him the answer was no. She was shocked, and the most uncontrolled he had seen her so far.

"Were you still with him when he saw her?" Le Fanu didn't think so, but it was worth the try.

Her eyes widened, tears trickled, scarring the makeup. That was unexpected.

"Superintendent, I have told you that I went to my…"

"I know what you told me. What I want to know is what happened."

"Do you think I might have a drink?"

"Coffee, or water?"

"I was thinking something stronger."

She was genuinely stressed, Le Fanu thought. He did have something stronger hidden away. Perhaps the single malt might serve a purpose here. She appeared anxious to say more, and if it was this difficult for her to do so, it might be significant. He was prepared to waste some whiskey for that. He left his desk, went to a corner book case, opened the lower cupboard door, reached in towards the back and retrieved the Lagavulin along with two glasses kept for special occasions, usually to celebrate the end of difficult cases with the Inspector-General rather than reassure beautiful women. Yes, he acknowledged, he did think her beautiful.

"You have excellent taste in whiskey," she said, a small shade of the smile returning. Was this part of the game, he wondered.

He poured two strong measures. She refused water, another surprise, but she was a Scot. He carried the tumblers back, handed her one.

"Sleinte," he said, raising his glass. "What do you want to say that warrants a raid on my secret supply?"

Virginia Campbell acknowledged the toast and drew hard on the malt.

"I did go out again after Walsall dropped me off, and returned only at about five am That was why I was late for breakfast the next morning, or that morning, rather."

She fiddled with the glass, tears still in her eyes, hands shaking so much the whiskey was like a dark sea in the glass.

"But that's not all," she continued. "I also saw Jane, but later than Billy did, and she was walking away from the house, not towards it."

"What time was that?" asked Le Fanu.

She thought it was about twelve-thirty because she waited a few minutes after Walsall left before venturing out again. A car awaited her and she was driven away along Chamier's Road, and she noticed Jane walking back towards Mount Road. She asked the driver to stop but he refused, saying he had a strict timetable and his employer did not like him being late.

Le Fanu thought the story far-fetched. A woman gets dropped at midnight at a house where she is staying as a guest, then slips out again to be picked up by a car and driver on behalf of an "employer". This sort of thing never happened in Madras. It had to be a fabrication, so the obvious questions were "who" and "why?"

"Miss Campbell, that story is incredible, in the purest sense of that word. Why would you go out again and why would the driver not stop when you asked, especially when your friend was walking about Adyar in the dead of night?"

"I know it sounds dubious." Tired and disconsolate, she was now far from the self-assured woman who walked in half an hour earlier. "But that is what happened."

She claimed that, before the Jamieson party, she arranged to be collected from Wark's at twelve thirty, so nobody would know she was going out again. The secrecy unravelled when she saw Jane Carstairs walking, and especially when Jane saw her and began waving. Virginia Campbell looked back through the rear window at Jane waving, then looking puzzled when her friend did not stop to pick her up.

That was the last time Virginia saw Jane Carstairs alive.

"My next question, obviously, Miss Campbell, is who provided the car, and where did you go?"

"I can't tell you that."

"Miss Campbell, your friend is dead, and right now you're the last person to see her alive. You have no choice but to tell me. Otherwise I'll arrest and detain you here, and you are hardly dressed for some time in our cells that are far from comfortable."

She finished her whiskey, pushed the glass across. He hesitated before pouring more for them both.

"Can we come to an agreement on this?" she whispered.

"None whatsoever, your friend was murdered. What possible sort of agreement could there be? Tell me, who were you with, and where?"

She gulped half the new measure, looking flushed and anxious.

"I was taken to Government House at Adyar."

Le Fanu was stunned. She had gone to the Governor's edge of town house, Raj Bhavan, a prized address on the fishing fleet circuit and for all Madras society, second only to his town address that, ironically, was not that far from where Jane Carstairs was found. Moreover, Virginia Campbell had done so after midnight, leaving her friend to walk about Adyar alone. A few hours later, that friend was found murdered. If this news leaked, the consequences were incalculable.

He topped up her whiskey again, and his own, because there was obviously more news to come.

Her story now was that, at an earlier function, she met a senior member of the Governor's household. They had dinner on two occasions. On the second, her host asked if she would like to see Raj Bhavan and she said yes. However, he said that it had to be after the Wark garden party, and late, because it was difficult to get her in otherwise.

"You didn't think this strange?" asked Le Fanu.

"Yes, but it was the Governor's house so I thought it

would be alright."

She reached the house just before one in the morning, and returned to Wark's at five.

"You know I have to ask what you did during those hours?"

"Yes," she replied, "but you also know you really don't have to ask because I'm sure you know." She stared him down, defiantly. He looked away, unsure whether his feelings were shock, envy or disappointment.

"And the name of the man?"

"Do I really have to say?"

"Of course."

"The Governor's Private Secretary, James Winterton."

His earlier optimism about making progress on this case dissipated directly. This turn meant more trouble, and he'd had enough of that already.

Twenty-two

Early next morning, eight thousand newly politicised Buckingham and Carnatic Mills textile workers struck to demand higher wages, and joined local Congress Party leaders to link that claim to demands for political reform. By nine o'clock, over thirty thousand demonstrators thronged Marina Beach between the Secretariat and Police HQ.

Wilson relayed this to Le Fanu in a rare personal telephone call. He wanted Le Fanu at the scene immediately, no matter the state of investigations into Jane Carstairs' death.

Le Fanu had slept little anyway, wondering how he could possibly investigate the Governor's Private Secretary who was among the most protected of Europeans in Madras. Simply because Winterton and Virginia Campbell had apparently spent the night together, that did not mean the Secretary was automatically a suspect. That meant getting permission to interview the man might be difficult. On the other hand, it was obvious Winterton had to be questioned, if only to corroborate Virginia Campbell's story because, now, she was even more of a suspect having seen her friend even later than Billy Walsall's reported sighting.

And, he admitted to himself, he was wondering about Virginia Campbell and Winterton. Was he jealous? How could he avoid discussions about the case with Ro, because her instincts would pick up all this directly.

Sitting over early coffee and breakfast, watching and listening to the morning's first birds, Le Fanu observed ruefully that each day on this case added another layer of muck to an already grubby mess. He shivered as he recalled Jane Carstairs' head leaving the mud. That should not happen to any human being, let alone a woman come to Madras in search of fun and opportunity. It was just a couple of days ago, but already seemed far in the past as the complexities built.

His two months old Times gave no relief, being full of dismal stories about post-war change in Britain. Le Fanu was last back there in 1913 and had no idea when his next visit might be. England held no attraction now, especially given his wife's presence there, and the country promised him no future anyway. That was clear enough, but his dilemma was that currently India was none too promising, either. Where else could he go if he had to leave? Another coffee helped, as did an affectionate brush of his arm from Ro.

"This could be a really long day," he murmured.

"I know – but I'll wait up so there is food for you at any time."

"Really?" he said. "That might be too long a wait. Just leave something somewhere and I'll find it if I am desperate."

"No, I'll be here, otherwise who knows when I'll see you next?"

He stood, looked about and, seeing no one, gave her arm a warm squeeze.

"I'll see you later, then."

He gathered his bag, left by the front door, climbed into the back seat of a car sent by Wilson, and set off on the familiar journey. The driver followed a more direct route than Le Fanu's normal motorbike ride.

All the senior officers were to meet first at Wilson's office, receive orders and operating plans, then disperse to lead their assigned armed police detachments to the beach. The office was filling when Le Fanu arrived, Commissioner Jepson planted strategically near the I-G's desk, though Wilson was in deep conversation with another officer. Le Fanu thought Wilson was ignoring Jepson, but wondered if that was just wishful thinking.

Wilson called the room to order. "Right. You know the basics. At latest count, the numbers are now around thirty-five thousand and growing."

That caused a stir. It had been years since a political crowd that big had gathered in Madras.

"Concentrate," Wilson ordered. "Yes, the numbers are big, but that's not the main problem. We have a couple of our Special Branch chaps in the crowd under cover, and they report the presence of some serious troublemakers. Those characters are small in number but determined and aggressive. We are checking, but it seems that at least a couple of them are members of the new local revolutionary party inspired by our new friend, Mr. Marx."

The Russian Revolution alarmed the city's Europeans, coming as it did near the end of a war that had seen a German ship shell Madras. Policemen were not exempt from the fear. Several officers now ranted about the imagined horde assembled on the nearby sands, and Le Fanu feared discipline was slipping.

So did Wilson. "Don't turn this into an anti-Red campaign," he said. "We treat it just like any other political disturbance. And remember that the press will be there, along with all the other usual do-gooders, like Forrester Paton."

Suppressed laughter broke the tension, and Le Fanu joined in. A well-intentioned Scottish missionary doctor, Paton ran a clinic up-country but materialised in Madras whenever an opportunity arose to demonstrate against British rule. His work was appreciated but he cut a comical figure, dressed always in the rough hand-spun cotton garments championed by Mahatma Gandhi as part of the nationalist campaign.

"He's a Red alright," declared one officer, "never seen a

man so perpetually sunburned."

The laughter pitched higher.

"Alright, alright," said Wilson. "He is a bit of a joke, yes, but his brother is well placed back home, so the newspaper types will watch what happens to him. If one of you or your men give him the lathi, it will go around the world in twenty-four hours."

Le Fanu immediately registered just how serious this was. The war over, India was pushing for political change and had friends around the globe. People like Paton built publicity. That fuelled the local politicians, and protest developed a momentum of its own. This was so different from just six years earlier, and even Jane Carstairs must wait while he reluctantly joined this struggle.

Orders given and received, they dispersed to meet in ten minutes at the side gate where a fleet of bone-shaking trucks would carry them to the demonstration. The rumour was that some elements in the crowd wanted to march on police HQ, but Wilson decided to get in first, so ordered up the transport to deploy his forces quickly.

Le Fanu found Habi, and walked towards a group of twenty uniformed constables all armed with the lathi, the long wooden baton forever the mainstay of Indian policemen on the ground. It looked innocent enough but a well swung lathi could split a skull. They boarded a lorry, three behind the I-G's and two behind Jepson's. Wilson always led from the front.

The convoy turned right out onto Elliots Road, then immediately left into the Marina and past St. Mary's College. Le Fanu counted sixty trucks, which meant twelve hundred police officers. This was a big force, leaving precious few officers to cover the routine, mundane developments of the average Madras day. He hoped, perversely, that the smarter criminal minds were involved with politics, because if they were not, then Madras today would become one giant scene of offence, the thief's delight.

As they neared the demonstration, even above the lorry engines Le Fanu heard the crowd noise that suggested a rowdy atmosphere. The mill workers, with a longstanding wages and conditions cause, now had the perfect opportunity to voice that cause. Tempers were up, and the slogans abroad:

"Down with capitalism."

"Gandhi ki jai!"

"No police here."

"British go home!"

"Britain is draining India's money."

"Montagu must go."

"Pay us more."

"Stop exploitation."

"Freedom for India."

"Jepson out!"

At least there was something with which Le Fanu could agree.

Reaching the sands, the police realised they were confronting a serious demonstration. Hammer and sickle flags fluttered everywhere, contrasting with the Indian National Congress ones. Other flags represented the myriad of political bodies that had mushroomed since 1918, ranging from anarchists to syndicalists and everything in between. The noise deafened the police ranks as they got closer and that, thought Le Fanu, made control and communication more difficult.

The speeches were done, the crowd was ready to move anywhere, to do anything, now. The ringleaders stood on the stage down near the surf, using microphones to make themselves heard. Le Fanu checked his own loud hailer. It seemed inadequate to deal with this crowd. A crush of bodies surged on all sides, hurtling forward as the trucks neared, demonstrators confronting police before they could even alight.

At these moments, Le Fanu thought, India defied logic. Individually, the crowd members looked threadbare, ill-nourished, guileless, directionless and pliable. Collectively, though, they were none of those, as he knew from direct experience. Combined, they made a wall of aggrieved and determined citizens. This crowd was determined, and purposeful. It must have been like this in Paris in 1789.

Climbing down from the truck with his squad, Le Fanu noticed all the other Raj support units moving into position. The military was out, a sure sign of how seriously Wilson was taking this. Half a dozen armoured cars were lined up, and additional army officers on horseback waited off in a side street. Thinking back to wartime battles, Le Fanu knew that this situation could become uncontrollable very quickly.

He noticed Billy Walsall standing near one of the armoured cars, kitted out ready for action, but talking to a civilian who had his back to Le Fanu. A few seconds later the figure turned. It was James Winterton.

What was he doing here?

Twenty-three

The noise increased and the edginess became more manifest as the police contingent moved towards the crowd. Le Fanu hoped the days of violence were behind him when he joined the detective ranks but here he was again, eight years since his last riot. He hated the confrontation. Back then it was over grain prices. Now, it was supposedly about mill wages but the real cause was Congress and its political ambitions. This was new territory for him but not for his colleagues. Political change was detested and contested throughout the European and Indian ranks of the Madras police because it threatened job security. For many of them here now, then, the struggle was personal, and that transformed a difficult situation into a volatile one. Especially so because Wilson, at Jepson's request, had requested the military back up. Armed troops waited in lorries a few hundred yards away, along one of the blocked-off side roads.

Le Fanu could literally "see" the political side to this demonstration. Mahatma Gandhi captured the popular imagination by insisting that Indians use homespun fabric for clothing and that they live simply. His Madras followers seized on those aims so most people in this huge, heaving crowd were wearing the rough, off-white khaddar painstakingly spun on home wheels. The long shirts fell over the lunghis, the uniform completed by the now familiar Gandhi caps along with the simple sandals or even bare feet. Protestors held placards that demanded the British leave India, supported Gandhi, denounced British politicians, or sought home rule for India. Here and there among this sea of signs were a few supporting a wage increase for mill workers. The crowd chanted anti-British slogans, urged on by khaddar-clad leaders speaking into microphones arranged on a stage around which thousands of protesters gathered.

The crowd surged forward to meet the police lines, then fell back to avoid conflict. That was a danger sign. Le Fanu remembered similar patterns from past demonstrations gone bad. Those crowd swells created momentum, and if a surge kept advancing and crashed into the police lines then anything might happen. Chants were increasing, placard waving became more energetic. The faces of frontline protesters confronting police were strained, flushed and intent. Those lined up behind urged on those in front who had no control over what might happen.

Le Fanu sensed anxiety rising in the police ranks. Strong leadership was critical now but Wilson had delegated command to Jepson because, technically, this was a city and therefore the Commissioner's problem. Jepson had first call on the armed troops, and if he ordered them into action, then Wilson would have to be quick to rescind the order. If the troops were called in, deaths would follow and Wilson could not afford that.

Le Fanu realised he was in the first echelon of officers rowed behind several lines of lathi-carrying constabulary. He had command of fifty constables immediately in front of him, and had to coordinate with the officers on either side of him. He knew both to be reliable. Behind him, a reserve constabulary would move forward if the front lines faltered, and behind them was the command group, complete with vehicles ready to evacuate everyone if the demonstration went seriously wrong.

He saw Winterton and Walsall standing with the command group. Le Fanu rationalised a case for Winterton being there: to gather a first-hand account for the Governor and provide intelligence to inform later policies and strategies. But Walsall was an engineers' junior officer and only infantry units were on hand here. So what was Walsall doing and why was he here? Winterton had probably engineered his presence, but why? The pair was still deep in conversation, oblivious to the situation and to the senior officers around them. Surely they were discussing Jane Carstairs?

The crowd noise escalated sharply. A popular local political figure took to the stage, urging the crowd to confront the police. Looking back again, Le Fanu saw Jepson reddening in the face, another bad sign. Through a loud hailer, Jepson ordered the front row constabulary to raise their lathis ready for a charge. Le Fanu cursed silently. Jepson was relinquishing initial advantage, his only choice now being to proceed with or withdraw from the charge. Whatever the decision, the crowd would sense weakness. An even bigger roar escaped, and protestors surged towards the police. By now it was hot, radiated heat from the sand combining with direct sunshine to make conditions unpleasant. Neither side had water supplies, and everyone was sweating profusely. Tension was rising, rapidly. Le Fanu watched his men clutch their lathis more tightly, essaying practice swings. They were nervous. The biggest surge yet pitched front row protesters straight into the police lines, with scuffles breaking out along the whole distance.

"Charge," roared Jepson into his megaphone.

Constables swung their lathis wildly, and Le Fanu heard the bash of stout stick on brittle bone as lathis connected with heads and shoulders. Some policemen went for legs and knees to restrict further movement or escape. Some demonstrators suffered immediate injuries with blood flowing from head and face cuts. Other protesters were on the ground, the crowds behind trampling on them and adding further injuries.

Le Fanu shouted at his men to protect those grounded, but there was little they could do other than watch the waves of oncoming protesters. The only way to save those fallen was for the police to withdraw and regroup. Otherwise people would die.

"Charge!" came the repeated roar from behind.

Le Fanu swore. The police lines faltered, experienced officers and men knowing disaster was imminent.

"Charge, damn you," Jepson snarled.

The constables could not charge because the crowd was immediately on them. Le Fanu and the officers either side of him coordinated their men to stop the surge, but the police line elsewhere broke under the pressure. Small bands of protesters charged towards the command group or attacked police units from behind. Surrounded, the police organisation disintegrated. Le Fanu had half his men turn around so that they were back to back with their colleagues, but it halved their strength on both flanks. Shouting protesters were in his face wherever he looked. They were unarmed, but many carried large stones, pieces of masonry or lumps of wood, anything they could throw. Some of those racing towards the command group carried rocks that Le Fanu then saw hail down on the I-G who instinctively hunched up. Jepson was puce, incapable of saying or doing anything. A rock struck Le Fanu on the shoulder, and he noticed a few of his men bleeding from similar strikes.

He looked to the officers either side, raised his eyebrows, and they nodded.

"Alright, men," Le Fanu shouted. "We must retreat towards the command group to protect them. Hold your lathis high, but use them as protection. Get together now. Move."

The combined one hundred and fifty strong police group moved slowly back towards the I-G to surround him and the other officers, including Winterton who looked terrible and Walsall, who seemed composed. Winterton had sat out the war at a Madras desk so this was all new to him. He looked pale and rattled.

The rescue squad formed a square around the senior officers, lathis held horizontally to form a protective wall. Other police groups were involved in skirmishes across the beach, and much of the crowd surrounded Le Fanu's protection squad.

Stones and other missiles sailed in from all sides, and the I-G fell having taken a bloody blow to the head from a brick. He was unconscious.

"Walsall!" The shout came from Jepson.

"Yes, sir?"

"Get out and bring in the troops."

"Sir."

Le Fanu protested. "Commissioner, he might not get through. Even if he does the troops won't be able to control this. Better for us to withdraw and let the steam run out of this thing."

"We all know your cowardly reputation, Le Fanu, I'm running this."

"But Commissioner…"

"Fuck, Le Fanu, just shut up. Walsall, get going."

Walsall dropped on his hands and knees and disappeared into the crowd.

Le Fanu wanted his men out of there, because with the police personnel so dispersed across the beach, the troops would be hard put to distinguish friend from alleged foe. One of his men picked up the I-G who was drifting in and out of consciousness. With the man carrying Wilson in the middle of the group, they retreated, accompanied by the neighbouring officers and men. This was a dangerous move because Jepson could accuse him of disobeying orders, but he had to save his men. They reached the road and formed up, demonstrators drifting away to resume the contest with other police groups.

The troop lorries arrived, so Walsall had found them, obviously. The soldiers got down, lined up, and advanced on to the sands, rifles at the ready. A lieutenant took charge and led a small group through the throng to reach Jepson. Le Fanu watched the discussion from afar, and registered the officer's alarmed look. More discussion followed, Jepson waving his riding crop about. The lieutenant looked increasingly worried but withdrew, lined up his men, and issued orders.

Le Fanu watched the front line of men drop to one knee, and raise rifles. The men standing in the line behind raised theirs, too. All rifles were aimed above the heads of the crowd.

A volley followed. The crowd stopped, then surged towards the soldiers and Le Fanu heard Jepson on his loud hailer.

"Direct fire."

The lieutenant could but obey the officer in charge. A second volley erupted, and several oncoming protesters fell. Le Fanu heard the screams before he saw the blood, but he was back in Shaiba. Demonstrators were calling for help. Most had taken stomach shots but some were bleeding from head wounds, others from leg injuries. Somehow, someone had forgotten to have ambulances on standby, and a couple of soldiers were now screaming into field telephones to get assistance. A few soldiers were applying basic first aid but there were no trained medics on hand, either.

Those demonstrators still standing ran for cover. The remaining sporadic fights stopped immediately, allowing police to regroup.

Le Fanu left his men, but ordered two to commandeer a vehicle and take the I-G to hospital. He then returned to the beach, reckoning the hospitals would receive many casualties this day. As he walked by, Le Fanu watched two people die from their wounds, something he had hoped never to see again. He was dazed, and despondent.

A □ ADRAS □ IAS □ A

Some police were already checking on the fallen protesters and in a couple of minutes the tally was back: twenty-three dead and eighty-five injured.

And among the dead, somehow, was Billy Walsall.

Twenty-four

A sombre group met in the I-G's office an hour later. Wilson, still groggy from his now-bandaged temple wound, had rearranged his room. Now he sat facing away from the sea view he loved, the desk between him and his officers. A bad sign, thought Le Fanu, this will be rough.

"Right," said Wilson, harshly. "Where do we start with this fiasco? I'm getting savage telephone calls from just about everyone with an interest, from the Governor down. I need answers, gentlemen. What the hell happened here?"

Winterton had telephoned the Governor immediately, thought Le Fanu.

No one responded, all eyes inspecting the floor.

"Fuck it," exploded Wilson, "twenty-three dead and eighty-five injured on my watch and none of you has anything to say?"

Le Fanu was one of six present. Jepson looked drained and his Deputy Commissioner even worse, no doubt from being blamed by his boss. There were two from the I-G's office, who had handled liaison with the Commissioner. The other was a junior European whom Wilson trusted to be scribe, knowing nothing would leak.

Jepson was the target of this rare and significant I-G profanity. The Commissioner knew it. His career was teetering.

"Sir, this is regrettable but I believe we…"

"Jepson," cut in the I-G, menacingly, "I'm not interested in what you believe. You were in charge, as you insisted because it was in your jurisdiction. I doubted the sense of putting you in charge, but you pushed. Now it has all gone very, very wrong. Explain yourself now, dammit."

"Sir, that might take time to ascertain …"

"Jesus Christ, man, do you have absolutely no idea? Are you completely stupid, or just doing a clever impression of being as thick as a fucking brick?"

Jepson wilted under the barrage. Le Fanu had never seen Wilson this animated, or angry.

"Sir," the Commissioner stumbled, "I, ah, er, do not, ah, think…"

"There's the problem, Jepson, you just don't think. If you were thinking you would have pulled the men back when it was blindingly bloody obvious to do so. But not you. You ordered another charge that was physically impossible and tactically bloody insane. That's why we're here now – because twenty three people are dead and the Secretariat wants to know why. And so do I."

Le Fanu wondered if Wilson simply wanted the rest of them to be there as witnesses to this ferocious dressing down. If so, his admiration for the I-G rose higher. Jepson would escape serious public reprimand because the administration could not afford a spectacle at this point. Wilson was ensuring word would spread inside the force that Jepson was on the skids.

As if reading Le Fanu's mind, Wilson continued relentlessly.

"In all my now too many days in this force, I've never seen a worse piece of command. The strategy was wrong, the tactics worse. You exposed our front line constables and endangered their lives unnecessarily. Then, having already made a complete balls of it, you called in the troops. In the circumstances that almost guaranteed a bloody result. And we now have that bloody result, literally. The miracle is that there was not even more blood on the sand. You are a fucking disaster."

Even during his most stressful wartime experiences, Le Fanu had never witnessed such an attack on an officer. Jepson was speechless. The uniform, shoes and riding whip were spruce, but their owner half his previous blustering size, it seemed.

"I'll deal with you later, Jepson," continued the I-G, Le Fanu wondering how much worse the private conversation could be after this volcanic spray.

"Now," said Wilson, "what about the rest of it? Le Fanu, you have a line of inquiry to follow, I gather?"

"Yes, sir, Billy Walsall's death bothers me, because it seems to link this episode to Jane Carstairs' death."

The others looked at him curiously.

"Before the incident," he continued, "Walsall was in deep conversation with Winterton, right up to the moment of the firing." He sensed Jepson's eyes attempting to melt his face.

"Why is that curious?" asked the I-G. "Winterton was there on behalf of the Governor, and I suppose Walsall was there as military liaison. Perfectly reasonable for them to be talking."

"Sir, Walsall was an engineer, all the troops were infantry. Wouldn't a liaison officer normally be from infantry in that situation? Do we know if Walsall was there officially as liaison?"

Wilson ordered an assistant out to question the military as to why Walsall was there.

"Sir," asked Le Fanu, "do you have a report on how he died?"

Wilson retrieved a folder from his desk and flipped through the papers.

"Yes," he said, "and looking at this, you might just have a point: he was shot twice. In the back."

The room went even quieter.

"Sir," Le Fanu continued, "the bodies will be on their way to the morgue and the staff there will be overwhelmed." He thought of Ramachandran. The doctor had plenty of opportunity to serve the dead today. "Could we ask for the Walsall autopsy to be done first?

Wilson signalled his remaining staff officer to lodge the request.

"What's your thinking, Le Fanu?" the I-G asked. "This Carstairs case is important, certainly. Right now, though, twenty-three dead take priority over one." He glared at Jepson. "I need all your ideas before I release you back to that investigation. My very best people have to be concentrated on this current heap of shit." Another venomous look went in Jepson's direction, the others present shuffling awkwardly, increasingly aware of their spectator roles.

The first staff officer returned. According to the infantry commander, Walsall was not at the beach as official liaison. Furthermore, the engineers reported Walsall was not authorised by them to be there, or even to be off their base.

"That," said Le Fanu, "suggests we need to find out what he was doing at the beach, and why. And that means an immediate discussion with Winterton."

Wilson did not relish the prospect of Le Fanu's departure but knew it was inevitable given this news.

"Could it wait, LF, at least until we get together a coherent story we can give the Governor and the Chief Secretary on the shooting? These dead demonstrators are the priority, and if we go bothering the Private Secretary right now the Governor will wonder what the hell we're doing."

Le Fanu saw a solution. "Sir, if I can help your team assemble that story, it should also involve Walsall's movements and fate, anyway, so we'll advance both matters. Then you can give the Governor a presentation that covers all relevant matters."

"Good man, excellent approach."

Jepson sat uncomfortably, as if his arse was alight, his complexion at least blazing. He knew more was to come after the others left, and Le Fanu gaining open praise aggravated his agitation. He's desperate now, Le Fanu thought, and even more poisonous. If Jepson had not hated Wilson before, he certainly would now, and that meant even more attacks on Le Fanu himself. Again, Le Fanu wondered where he might possibly go if he had to leave India.

Wilson ended the meeting, Jepson stayed behind, Le Fanu left with the staff officers to assemble the shooting story, but not before going to his office to find Habi. He asked his sergeant to review Chapter XI in Gross, on firearms and ammunition, then return to the beach and search the site, especially near where Walsall's body was found. They would then match any evidence found there with that found where the other victims died. If Le Fanu was guessing right, Walsall's death would not be like those others.

For the next three hours, Le Fanu worked with the I-G's staff, compiling the report for the Governor. Mostly, though, he wondered why Walsall was at the beach, what he had discussed with Winterton, and how he had died. Le Fanu was convinced the answers to those questions related to Jane Carstairs' death. Today's events meant her case might be sidetracked for a couple of days, allowing more time for the killer to further blur the trail.

Right now, however, that trail, marked with danger flags, led towards Government House.

Twenty-five

Le Fanu hit that trail sooner than he had imagined. Wilson asked him along on the drive out to Government house to present the report on the shooting. That further slight would be noted and remembered by Jepson, but with luck might not matter – surely he could not survive this disaster? During the ride up the coast road and along the Adyar River the I-G did not mention the discussion with the Commissioner, but Le Fanu knew Jepson was insecure and even more intent on shifting blame.

As they travelled through the leafy suburbs, passing the usual posse of bullock carts, horse-drawn buggies, handcarts, wandering cows and pedestrians, they did discuss the morning's disaster.

"Bloody hell, LF. It's not like we haven't dealt with these things before. The political twist is new, but the basics of crowd management remain, surely? And don't give me your usual loyal to colleagues routine, I know there's little love lost between you and Jepson."

"Sir, it was handled badly, as you made clear in the meeting. After the first charge, we should have withdrawn and let things cool down. We couldn't advance, so another charge was futile. And there were already demonstrators underfoot, so even if we'd been able to move forward, we would only have made that worse, and it was dangerous enough already."

Wilson shook his head, ruefully. "What was he thinking?"

"Whatever the thinking, sir, it was based on too little knowledge of the circumstances."

"What are you trying to say, LF?"

"Sir, our line was fragmented. The three of us towards the centre could link and hold, but the units next along broke, and that allowed demonstrators to get in behind us. When the Commissioner ordered the second charge, we were too disorganised to respond adequately. He didn't realise that, I think. The textbook move would have us withdraw, regroup, and assess from there."

"So you're saying that as a field officer he's inadequate?"

"Well, yes, if you want a direct answer. You and I have military backgrounds that allow us to see patterns in the middle of a struggle, but I don't think the Commissioner does. You want me to be honest: if there are any more of these demonstrations, then the Commissioner needs to learn those skills, or…"

"…be reassigned?" Wilson finished the sentence.

There was no further discussion. They knew the possible consequences of that line of thinking. Jepson would gather all his conservative supporters to undermine them and to shore up his own position.

The larger southern suburbs mansions were now slipping by, houses like Wark's set in several acres of grounds. Some Madras people had become extremely wealthy in recent years and more of these grand country houses were appearing, defying the north India view of Madras as an undeveloped wilderness. These houses were several miles, even galaxies away from the morning's beach events, and their inhabitants would criticise those developments, imagining that their newly enriched positions were at risk. That was why Wilson was under pressure from the official and non-official European community, and why the Governor would have some probing questions.

Wilson returned to the Jepson theme. "I agree, LF, " he said, " but you know as well as I do that shifting Jepson so soon after his appointment will be an admission of failure. I can tell you the Governor dislikes many things, but admitting an official failure tops his list. He takes these things personally even though, really, these days his contribution to senior appointments is more ceremonial than substantive. If I switch Jepson now, His Excellency will see it as a personal affront."

"Perhaps you could create a small designated riot control group that reports directly to you, and is available for deployment all over the Presidency? With authorised powers to interact directly with local military units, but only at your say so?"

The I-G smiled. "You always were smart. I've had that exact idea under discussion with HE and the Chief Secretary, and this morning's incompetence has accelerated my thinking. You interested in running it, if it transpires?"

"Honestly, sir, not really. I'll do it if you ask, but I'd prefer to stay where I am."

"Fair enough, but I'll keep you advised on how it develops, and should you change your mind…"

They reached the guard box marking the main entrance gates to Government House and its parklands. They set off down the long driveway to finally reach the impressive if simple mansion facade, all white Palladian style and deep verandahs. The Governor spent a lot of time out here now, instead of in the more convenient house near Fort St. George. There was no apparent reason for that, but it caused a lot of chatter.

The driver pulled up at the main entrance where uniformed soldiers sprang forward to open the car doors. A house servant showed them into a small waiting room where they spent a couple of minutes before being shown upstairs and into the Governor's cavernous study. It was full of bookcases and display cabinets that recalled service to the Empire in many locations. There were artefacts from the Pacific and Asia, and photographs of the Governor with several luminaries.

Lord Willingdon was tall and slim, now in his mid-fifties, high browed, angular in the face with a prominently long nose set below strong cheekbones and deep set eyes. He had played cricket for Eton, Sussex, Cambridge and the MCC, and established the Cricket Club of India in Bombay, where he was Governor immediately before coming to Madras. Rumour had it that he and especially his wife, the former Lady Brassey, were unhappy at his not being appointed Viceroy. He openly despised the Madras ICS, considering it reactionary, and he and his wife were energetic social reformers. She was renowned for an addiction to the colour purple and for having buildings named after her. The pair were popular though, and the loss of their eldest son in the war won them sympathy.

Willingdon stood up to shake hands with Wilson.

"Good to see you, Wilson, though the occasion is regrettable. I take it this is Le Fanu?"

He was taller than Le Fanu and gripped his hand strongly.

"Golfer's hand there, I'd wager," Willingdon said with a smile. Did he guess or was he advised? Le Fanu thought the latter.

"Yes, Your Excellency."

"Plain 'Sir' will be just fine in here, for now."

"Thank you, sir."

Willingdon had coffee brought in and steered them towards a small, round table over in one corner near a door onto the verandah, and a view out to a small oval with a cricket net set up at one side.

"Do you still practice, sir?" asked Le Fanu.

"Of course, helps keep my mind off things like this mess."

They sat, Wilson handed over the report, summarised the main points, and awaited comment.

The Governor flicked through the pages, scribbling notes with a gold banded fountain pen. "What do you think, Le Fanu?" he asked as he turned over the last page.

Wilson intervened, indicating Le Fanu had overseen compilation of the report and that much of the analysis was his.

"I see," said Willingdon, "so, my question is even more apposite. Le Fanu?"

Le Fanu spoke for five minutes, indicating where he thought crowd management had failed, the consequences of that, and how matters might be improved.

"Any thoughts how we might best handle this publicly?" asked the Governor.

"Best be as straightforward as possible, sir. There were multiple witnesses to the events, so trying to counteract their reports to newspapers is futile. We might just say a regrettable result followed a failure to discuss and negotiate adequately, and that breakdowns in communication made handling the matter more difficult."

The Governor nodded, asked Le Fanu to draft a statement before he and Wilson left, then hand it to a Government House officer.

"Sir, who would be that officer?"

"My Private Secretary, James Winterton."

Le Fanu glanced at Wilson, who asked, quietly, "Your Excellency, may we have your permission to speak officially with Winterton while we are here?"

The Governor looked up, surprised.

"Winterton? Why?"

"Sir," replied Le Fanu, "Mr. Winterton entertained a guest here after Mr. Jamieson's garden party. That guest was the friend of Miss Jane Carstairs, the woman whose body was found in the Buckingham Canal and whose death we are treating as a murder."

If Willingdon was surprised he did not show it. "Well, of course you must speak with him if it is necessary."

"There is more, sir. One of the last people to see Miss Carstairs alive was Lieutenant Billy Walsall who appeared at the demonstration this morning. After the shootings he was found dead, two bullets, in his back. We are suspicious about that, too. We don't know why he was there, and his regiment had neither rostered him there nor signed him out. However, he was in deep conversation with Mr. Winterton whom we are assuming was there to keep you informed."

Willingdon looked puzzled, some of the imperturbability slipped.

"I rarely do this, but it is late in the afternoon and I need something strong. Will you join me?"

He poured three good measures of Glenmorangie into crystal whisky glasses. None of them took ice or soda, and they raised glasses towards each other. The Governor stood by the door, looking longingly out to the nets.

"There was some suggestion Winterton go along and watch for me, but he was asked to clear that formally with you at police HQ. It sounds like he didn't do that."

Wilson and Le Fanu confirmed there was no clearance.

"He said he was going into town anyway," Willingdon continued, "so could look in on things if I needed. At that stage I was happy you had it under control, so said if he was passing he might look in, but there was no specific plan for him to be there."

He sipped the whiskey.

"I don't think I know Walsall," he said, "so why Winterton would be in discussion with him is a mystery to me. What regiment was he in?"

They told him the engineers, and the Governor became more puzzled. As a former military officer, he saw no reason for Walsall to be at the demonstration, confirming Le Fanu's earlier thoughts.

"You'd better have a chat with him now. I'll tell him I've authorised the discussion. He's a good PS, for the most part, but there've been some oddities of late."

"Anything specific that might be relevant, sir?" asked Le Fanu.

"Not really. Some unexplained absences, the odd disappearance for an hour or two, one or two slips in work. Nothing major, but out of character, if you know what I mean."

He was remembering those episodes and putting them in sequence. He refilled his whiskey.

"Gentlemen, thank you. I'll have someone take you to Winterton and I'll pass on anything that occurs to me. Call my direct telephone number here if anything at all comes up you think I can help with." He gave them both the number, which Le Fanu doubted he would ever use. He could not imagine dialling a number and having the Governor answer.

Even so, he thought, very few people in Madras had that number. This case was taking him to rarefied places.

They returned to the small room downstairs, and awaited Winterton.

Twenty-six

James Winterton entered the room with less assurance than he showed at the crowd scene earlier. There was a pallor in the otherwise flawless face of the mid-thirties man with a future, the rimless glasses not disguising bloodshot eyes, the elegant grey suit hanging loose on the slender frame. He was uneasy, apprehensive and bothered by the I-G's presence alongside the city's leading crime investigator.

"You wanted to see me?" The voice was strained.

Wilson bounced in fast. "Of course we do, man. You were the last person seen talking to Walsall at the beach. A few minutes later he's dead, shot in the back, and you've disappeared. So, yes, we are very interested in your story. And that's even before we start discussing your activities with Miss Campbell here in the Governor's house the night Miss Carstairs was murdered."

Le Fanu was fascinated. The I-G was usually more measured in interviews, but this time the aggression he used against Jepson earlier remained. And Winterton's reaction was physical because he literally reeled back as if struck. He was not usually subjected to such confrontation.

"I, ah, I, well, do not appreciate your approach…"

"I don't care," Wilson shot back, "I've too many dead people to account for and if you're responsible I'll find out."

Le Fanu fancied Wilson disliked Winterton, giving the

interrogation an intensity when really, Winterton was no more a suspect than anyone else present at the disturbances.

"I don't know about any deaths!" Standing up, but gripping the edge of a small table so hard with both hands that a bowl of flowers was shaking violently, Winterton was shrieking.

"Perhaps you might sit down, Mr. Winterton," Le Fanu slid in softly, "It will take a little while to get through some of the questions we must ask, and it's always easier to deal with them if you're comfortable."

Le Fanu caught Wilson's acknowledgment as Winterton fell into an armchair. The two policemen took the high-backed chairs either side of the small table, ensuring the sunlight speared over their shoulders into Winterton's eyes as he looked slightly up at his interrogators. Too late, he realised he'd selected the wrong chair.

"Now, sir," continued Le Fanu, "can we start at the end and work backwards? Why were you at the demonstration this morning, and I should say that the Governor tells us there was no formal instruction for you to be there."

Winterton spluttered. "But he said I could drop by…"

"Yes, because you were already going into town, was what he told us. What was the real purpose of your visit? To see Walsall?"

"No, well, I mean, I was to see Billy but I was…"

"Why were you meeting Lieutenant Walsall?"

"There were some issues we needed to discuss…"

"Well obviously," interjected Wilson, maintaining the rage.

Winterton was squinting against the bright sunlight streaming through the window. "Do you think I might have some water?" he asked

"No," said Wilson, "we need to get this done. Tell us the purpose of your meeting with Walsall."

"If you insist, though I must say as a senior ICS officer I object to this badgering."

"Mr. Winterton." Wilson was grim. "If you persist in trying to avoid answering questions, I'll have Superintendent Le Fanu here arrest you, so that we can continue the discussion at Police HQ. Your superiors will not welcome that development, I think. So stop wasting our time."

"Walsall and I were at the Jamieson party the other night, and spent time with Misses Carstairs and Campbell."

"We know that," said Le Fanu, "what we want to know is what those discussions were about."

"This is embarrassing. We agreed to try and have the women accompany us after the party…"

"With a view to tupping them," Wilson added.

Winterton nodded, reddening spectacularly from the neck up.

"You succeeded, it appears," Le Fanu added, earning a glance from Wilson, "but Billy Walsall did not."

"That was what I was trying to ask him at the demonstration."

"But that was two days later," commented Le Fanu, "surely you exchanged notes the following day, especially given Miss Carstairs' death?"

"I was too stunned to ask then. I assumed Billy took her home from Jamieson's, that he was the last person to see her…"

"And that he killed her," said Wilson.

"Well, I had to consider it a possibility."

"And what did he tell you at the demonstration?" asked Le Fanu.

"We did not finish the discussion."

"You were with him for several minutes before the clashes began, and I saw you still with him when the struggle started."

"Alright, he said he had seen her, but she was walking away from Wark's house in Adyar at the time."

At least that was consistent, thought Le Fanu.

"Did you discuss the morphine?"

If Winterton was pale before, he was translucent now.

"How did you know…?"

"The medical report on Jane Carstairs revealed morphine, so given you and Walsall had designs on the women, it seems likely you were involved in the drugs as well. Which of you two obtained the morphine and from whom? You do understand, of course, that for you the drug use matters stand separately from the murder of Miss Carstairs, even if the two things are related."

Winterton folded. He claimed Walsall got the drugs from a medical stores employee – Le Fanu reminded himself to check how that was possible, because Ramachandran suggested security on the morphine was stringent. Walsall brought it to the garden party, told Winterton, and suggested the women would be more compliant if they could be persuaded to take some.

"So you targeted these women before the party?" Wilson asked.

"Yes, and we arranged the transport in case things went to plan," replied Winterton.

"Did you ask Miss Campbell to take opium at that garden party?" Le Fanu queried.

"Yes, but she refused."

"And Walsall asked Miss Carstairs and it seems she did."

Winterton hesitated. "When we were talking at the demonstration he said he had asked her to but that she refused."

"Was he telling the truth, do you think?" Wilson demanded.

The Governor's Private Secretary was now slumped deep in the chair, making himself as invisible as possible. "I have no idea," he said, "by then I didn't know what to believe."

"When you brought Miss Campbell back here, did you see Miss Carstairs at any point?"

"No."

"Very well. How did you kill Billy Walsall?" asked Le Fanu.

"I didn't kill him!" Winterton screeched.

"So you say," replied Wilson, "but we've no proof of that, and neither do you given what you've said, or not said so far."

"We'll leave it there for the moment, Mr. Winterton," Le Fanu said, "but we'll continue the discussion soon. You don't need me to tell you your career is in jeopardy."

Winterton nodded, prised himself from the chair and shuffled towards the door.

"There's a lot he's not telling us, LF," said Wilson. "And he knows a lot more about this whole mess than we do right now. That bothers me."

Le Fanu nodded, but he was really thinking about Virginia Campbell. Had she really slept with Winterton? Somehow that did not fit, but he wondered again if that was jealousy rather than an investigative hunch.

As they drove back towards HQ, Wilson and Le Fanu remained silent for some minutes, assessing what they had heard. Wilson broke the silence.

"LF, when we get back, call in your chap for a discussion because there are several aspects of this we need to understand and agree on how to handle," said the I-G, looking out the car window. "The newspaper hounds will devour this, and us, if they hear about it, so we must avoid any leaks."

"Yes, sir. We should also brief the Governor. He won't be pleased to hear his PS has been dealing with drugs as a way to seduce visiting women."

"Oh God, LF, why is this happening here, and now?"

Twenty-seven

As people assembled in the I-G's room, two things happened.

First, Habi produced a report on the Walsall examination conducted by Dr. Ramachandran who retrieved two bullets from the body. They had entered through the back and lodged behind the rib cage. The bullets were fired from close range. Someone standing close behind Walsall had shot him. Given the artillerymen were near the back of the group and did not move forward when the struggles began, that reduced the number of suspects considerably. It also made Winterton even more of a suspect but, it occurred to Le Fanu, they still had no real idea why the ICS man would have shot Walsall.

Dr. Ramachandran also reported that the bullets were not standard issue and matched no known military firearm, nor any of the standard manufacturers' products. Purchase of standard ammunition was tightly controlled in British India, especially after the armed terrorist episodes before and after the war. That control, Le Fanu and all other policemen knew, encouraged clever alternatives called "country weapons", manufactured in backyards to help settle local disputes and faction fights, scare off jealous husbands and occasionally wives, add weight to robbery attempts on gold and gem dealers, or simply provide entertainment on dull afternoons. According to Ramachandran, such a weapon killed Walsall.

What they now knew, Le Fanu suggested to the group, was that Walsall and Winterton were both at the demonstration with neither good nor authorised reason. They discussed Misses Carstairs and Campbell, and probably morphine and the person or persons who supplied it to them. The drug purchaser was allegedly Walsall, but he was dead and the evidence came only from Winterton. Morphine was a direct factor in Jane Carstairs' death, and most likely an indirect one in Walsall's. Additionally, whoever killed Walsall arrived at the demonstration with an unauthorised gun, probably a pistol, and ammunition, and that suggested premeditation. The central question was whether or not that person was James Winterton.

"Habi," said Le Fanu, "could you check if Winterton has permits for firearms? That won't help us directly because the weapon used was unauthorised, but it might give us a lead on his familiarity with firearms."

"Sir," replied Habi, not really concealing a smile, "he has permits for two rifles, both of the hunting kind, and a permit for a revolver. Furthermore, he has an Oxford Blue for shooting."

"Brilliant work, Habi. We now have Winterton on the scene and among the few who might have shot Walsall. We have him with a weaponry background though he did not serve in the war, and we have him still hiding something he and Walsall discussed just before Walsall died."

Wilson broke in. "LF, that's good enough for me. If he used an unauthorised gun, he would have got rid of it. However, we should search his rooms at Government House. I'll ring the Governor to clear things, but you get some chaps out there immediately."

Habi took that task, along with some constables, and looked pleased at the prospect. It was not every day someone like him got to search the Governor's house.

The second development arrived at that point. Wilson's

principal secretary knocked and entered, looking worried and uncertain about whether he should speak freely. Wilson waved him to do so.

"Sir, the editor of the Madras Mail is outside, and says he'll remain there until you speak with him. And he has the President of the European Association with him."

Everyone groaned. The visitors were arch conservatives and, if anything, becoming more conservative when the situation demanded flexibility. The editor campaigned relentlessly against the political reforms. The President of the European Association, a middle level manager in a small rubber company, was among his strongest supporters.

"Why are they here unannounced?" asked Wilson.

"Sir, they say there is a rumour that Lieutenant Walsall's death is connected to that of Miss Carstairs, and that narcotics are involved."

Another groan. Le Fanu knew it was impossible to prevent rumours, Madras was a small community disguised as a big city, and the police force poorly placed to maintain confidentiality.

Habi went off to search Winterton's quarters. Wilson's secretary brought in the unwelcome guests.

Arthur Barrett was the editor: weedy, pinch-faced, bald, top lip with a straggly thin moustache. He wore a crumpled, brown suit patterned more with cigarette burns than checks. Winston Andrews, the President, gruffer and more stolid than his companion, was dressed unimaginatively in dark blue suit, white shirt and plain blue tie. Unlike Barrett, the fingers on Andrews' right hand were not stained yellow.

Perhaps Wilson spotted those yellow fingers because he did not offer to shake hands with the pair, simply indicating them to sit in front of his desk while he remained seated behind. Le Fanu stood to Wilson's right and was not introduced.

"Gentlemen," the I-G began, "your presence is not a pleasure at this moment. We have too much to do, so tell me why you are here."

"Inspector-General," began the editor, pulling a notebook and pencil from an inside jacket pocket, "you have an obligation to…"

"Listen, Barrett. I have no obligation other than to deal with police matters to the best of my ability, and that does not involve tolerating interference or gossip from members of the public who imagine they have a role. Neither you nor the European Association has a role in what we are dealing with, so your visit will be brief."

Barrett leaped to his feet, waving his notebook. Andrews tried to restrain him but Barrett pounded the desk.

"You, sir, are a menace," roared the newspaper man. "You openly support all these dreadful reforms, promote Indians into senior positions, and thumb your nose at the rest of us. Well, we've had enough."

Andrews tried further to calm him but Barrett was still on his feet, shouting. "You have two Europeans dead, one of them a woman. There are rumours of immoral activity and drugs. The mill hands are out of control and European interests threatened. And you dare lecture us."

"Oh shut up, for God's sake" retorted Wilson. "You're a jumped-up little twerp with no idea of what's going on here. You cosy up to your like-minded Club chums, confuse gossip for fact, and print it all in that rag of yours. And you've not even mentioned the dead demonstrators. But then, you don't recognise their right to exist let alone get justice, do you?"

For the second time that day, Le Fanu watched his boss acting aggressively and openly as never before. It was as if these incidents were becoming a test case for how India might develop. Wilson was taking on the conservative forces directly and openly.

"Inspector-General," cut in Andrews, "we know you have a lot on your plate, and we all have different views on the broader range of matters that concern us. But you will understand that many of us are, indeed, worried by the events of the past few days, coming as they do at a time when great changes are upon us."

This man wants to get into the new political assembly, if it eventuates, thought Le Fanu, he speaks like a politician already. He was probably too far down the social and commercial ladder to stand any chance of success, but he was ambitious. Le Fanu wondered if Wilson had picked that up. He had.

"Nice speech, Mr. Andrews," smiled Wilson, "but wasted on me, I'm afraid."

Barrett was still on his feet, trying to interject, but Wilson ignored him and simply spoke louder.

"If at any point," the I-G continued, "there is a need for your Association to know anything particular, then I will ensure that happens. But right now there is nothing you need to know. Superintendent Le Fanu here is in charge of the Miss Carstairs matter, and we will also give him charge of the Walsall matter. If we have to contact either of you, we'll do so. Otherwise our business is done." He stood, and waved his arm in the direction of the door.

Andrews was unhappy, Barrett was incandescent. "You'll regret this, Wilson, I warn you. We'll not be ignored," said the editor.

Wilson shrugged his shoulders, waved again towards the door while shouting for his secretary to show the "guests" out. "See you at the Club?" he asked Le Fanu as the door shut behind the departing civilians.

"Sir, perhaps not. You can handle that without me, and I should spend time this evening working out how all this fits together, or not."

He left the I-G's office, collected papers from his own, and strode towards the stables and a liberating bike ride home.

Twenty-eight

It was just after seven when he rode through the gate, and a few minutes later had showered and "changed for dinner." Elsewhere in Madras that evening, hundreds of other Europeans were doing the same, but wearing full formal dinner dress even if they were eating at home alone. He was once that conventional, especially during his earlier days in India when stuffiness was even more of an art form than back "Home." The war changed that for him, too. After months and years under canvas and on the march, formality became less important, even though it was maintained in the mess. Now, being comfortable with himself was the priority.

So here he was on the verandah, dressed in simple cotton shirt and trousers and wearing light canvas shoes. He thought about some putting practice on the semi-dark green, but opted instead for a whiskey and soda, spreading his papers and thinking more systematically than was possible during day. His first whiskey disappeared, a servant brought another, and Ro asked when dinner should be served. Having settled on eight-thirty, he sat back, listening to the last of the birds before they settled for the night. Thinking about the cases somehow turned to other things.

Watching and listening to Wilson, Barrett and Andrews, Le Fanu wondered what might happen next in India and in Madras, and what his lot might be. He was good at what he did, but had no plans to be a policeman all his life. That thought led to place, because if not a policeman in India where would he go? It was seven years since he was last in England and he had not enjoyed it then. He remembered yet again the latest letter from his wife, which he must do something about. And those thoughts all led to Ro. What did that relationship mean and how could it develop? It had no future in India, so if they stayed together, where would they go?

Constitutional reform and Indianisation were controversial within Madras European circles. A few weeks earlier, at the Club, Le Fanu found himself in a discussion. One senior ICS man, a long time District Collector recently come into the Secretariat, was forthright. This was the end of the line in India. The man had expected to take a senior position, shore up his pension rights, then retire to Bath to write his memoirs and inform the British public about where their political leaders had gone wrong on India. Now he would leave early rather than answer to Indians instead of directing them. His latest scheme was to go off to Australia where, he thought, his funds were sufficient to buy a sheep farm in northern New South Wales, have someone else work the place, profit from the wool clips, play the local squire, and still write the memoirs.

Others still thought returning to England a good idea, though it was much changed after the war. Others again believed posts elsewhere around the Empire were worthwhile, especially in Africa, but sceptics suggested that if change was imminent in India it was not far off elsewhere. Then there were those who thought Canada or New Zealand good alternatives, although climate was an issue with one and distance the other, even if the Land of the Long White Cloud was still renowned as England away from home.

What else could he do, and did he really want to be with Ro? The garden was now in darkness, the night sounds surfacing. The first question was easier than the second. One thing he learned in the army was that he could adapt to all conditions, and that he had analytical skills that could be widely applied. He found leadership easy if onerous, he could read and understand instructions, and balance details with big ideas. He could fit into any business or civil service slot and could contemplate a farm in Australia or New Zealand, but not writing a memoir. He liked physical work, and could apply his analytical skills to the business.

But what about Ro? He had slipped into the relationship haphazardly. His wife had been gone a couple of years, making it clear she would not return. Even if he returned to England, she would not re-join him. He had no idea what she was up to, and no desire to know. The divorce would have to be finalised, he knew, and the letter in his pocket confirmed that. He was celibate after she left, even though he missed the sex, such as it was, and heard all the Club whispers about which city establishments catered best for men in his position.

Madras really was a strange place, he thought, strait-laced on the surface, but underneath… The same chaps who dressed for dinner would later be undressing in any of the houses featuring local or foreign women, and it was all discussed in muted tones, though never condoned publicly. And that applied to this relationship of his as well. It was a private matter, but if it became public he would be disgraced more than some married man found in a local brothel. Like much in British India, this made little sense.

Was he in love with Ro? God, how could he know that? Yes, his analytical skills were good, but that did not include being honest about his feelings. Ro was attractive physically, and he enjoyed her far more than he had enjoyed his wife or the few prostitutes he visited during the war, when life was uncertain. She was well educated and intelligent. He could have a good discussion with her on the few occasions possible. Did that add up to love? And even if it did, how could it become permanent and open? He really did have to deal with that letter, he thought.

He had no idea how Ro thought about this. Did she have ambitions? Was it simply part of her routine to keep the master of the house happy? He did not think so, but wasn't entirely sure.

By now it was dark and the night sounds cacophonous, led by the toads. He got up and turned the light out as a servant returned with his third whiskey. Better stop after this one, he thought, having still to think about the cases amidst the introspection. He enjoyed the challenge of investigating crime in the way that Wilson made it possible. His mentor was about to retire, however, and the IPS had a well-established tradition of incoming I-Gs overturning initiatives introduced by their predecessors, so the Crime unit could be disbanded and Le Fanu sent off to the country as a District Super. He didn't mind that prospect, depending on the district, but he had done all that and the crime work was a daily challenge. Would he be happy without it? Probably not.

That returned him to the current cases. For some reason, he thought they were close to making major advances, but was not sure why he thought so because he had no supporting evidence. He needed to review the papers after dinner.

He did not. All his thinking delayed dinner being served until nine-fifteen so that it finished at ten. By then he had seen enough of that day, so slipped into bed at ten-forty-five, and Ro at eleven-fifteen.

Twenty-nine

Over breakfast, he decided the day's main task would be detailing the precise connections between Winterton, Walsall and the Misses Carstairs and Campbell. He would talk with Winterton and Campbell again, meaning another journey to the city's south. That made a bike ride attractive, but he remembered Habi would search Winterton's rooms during the morning. They could travel out by car, search Winterton's rooms using a big team, then move on to Wark's and speak with Virginia Campbell. The more faces she had to deal with in the room, the more comfortable Le Fanu would feel.

He rode into HQ and met Habi in his office. Wilson had squared the Winterton search with the Governor. Willingdon was unhappy at the prospect of the search, but keen to resolve any doubts about his Private Secretary. Le Fanu and Habi reviewed the previous day's events, updated their boards, and identified further information gaps. They framed their questions for the day.

Le Fanu was summonsed to Wilson's office, where the I-G contemplated the day's Madras Mail edition. The headline was predictably stark:

POLICE INCOMPETENCE LEAVES CITIZENS AT RISK

The citizens, of course, were the Madras Europeans and not the population at large. The gist was that because of Wilson's allegedly weak leadership, the police were making no headway on the Carstairs case. The incompetent handling of the demonstration not only caused more deaths but put the city's entire European population at risk. Sensationalist and inaccurate, the article failed to mention Jepson was in charge at the beach. All responsibility was assigned to Wilson. Arthur Barrett had honoured his threat.

"You knew this would happen, sir," Le Fanu said.

"Of course, but it's another matter seeing it there. You're going well on this Carstairs matter, I know, but any quick advances would be welcome." He smiled at Le Fanu. "I could use some good news."

"We'll do our best, sir. Would you like to come with us to interview Winterton again?"

They both laughed.

"Couldn't think of anything better, LF, but the Chief Secretary has called me and some other worthies in, so I must trot along and be condescended to on how to run a police force."

Recalling his previous night's thoughts, Le Fanu added being I-G to the list of the many things he did not want to become.

He and Habi were back on the now too familiar route to Adyar shortly after, discussing the morning's tactics while the driver negotiated through animals, people and vehicles. Le Fanu was certain that the number of obstacles to be avoided on the road doubled every day. They agreed Winterton should be present at the searching of his rooms. After that, they would re-interview him.

Winterton was waiting, having ensured no servants were present to witness his embarrassment. He led them through the front entrance, along a corridor past the room where they first encountered him, and into the back area of the house where he climbed some stairs onto a landing.

"I'm in here," he said, leading through a door. His rooms

were spacious. Le Fanu realised immediately why the monotonous job of being Private Secretary was pursued so relentlessly by so many. Besides the prestige, the living arrangements were excellent, and free.

They stood in a small reception room from where a door opened to a short corridor that led to Winterton's main quarters: a small library, two large bedrooms with attached bathrooms, a big sitting room with windows opening to verandahs overlooking gardens to the rear of the house, and another bathroom. A large book collection, mostly on India, and innumerable artefacts gathered from major southern archaeological sites like Hampi and Warangal and elsewhere in India, clogged shelves in all the rooms. Paintings and ornaments crowded the other spaces. He must be privately well off or he has an income additional to his ICS salary, thought Le Fanu, reminding himself to check.

"Mr. Winterton," he said, "we'll search first, so perhaps you and I can go out on the balcony and wait there."

Winterton was flustered. "But I should watch the search – that would be right."

"No, you and I will wait outside."

Reluctantly, Winterton stepped out onto the verandah, indicating a couple of cane chairs. Soon they heard cupboard doors opening and closing, drawers being searched, books and objects moved, items placed on tables.

"Don't worry Mr. Winterton, my men will place everything back where it belongs."

"They should not even be doing this."

The PS was distressed, sweating and increasingly anxious. Winterton took a handkerchief from the breast pocket of his tan linen suit and wiped his face. Then he rose from his chair, paced along the balcony, found and lit a cigarette. He didn't look like a regular smoker. Winterton was more worried than he should be if he had nothing to hide, thought Le Fanu. Perhaps this search might be more productive than they had imagined.

Winterton fretted and Le Fanu watched him do so for several minutes, before Habi emerged and asked them inside. Several small packets were lined up on a low table, an open one revealing a powder.

"However clever your choice of hiding place, Mr. Winterton, it would never be clever enough to fool Sergeant Habibullah, I'm afraid." Habi beamed.

"Where did you find this, Habi?" asked Le Fanu.

"Sir, in the library there are bookshelves at the top and cupboards underneath, then between the cupboards and the floor what looked like an ordinary piece of board. But it was not a board. It was a front for some small spaces under all the cupboards. There is just one release point, a small piece of wood under the second cupboard that has to be shifted. Then all those boards swing out."

"So we have these packets, and what else?"

"These are the first things we found, so we will keep searching."

"So, Winterton," said Le Fanu, "what do these packets contain?"

Winterton admitted reluctantly that the packets contained morphine by-products. He had discovered the concealed spaces soon after occupying the rooms. Finding an 1892 letter in there, he knew the spaces were unknown to anybody else in the house so used them to store the packets.

"There is a lot here. Have you been selling morphine?"

"Yes."

"And you also use it yourself?"

"Yes."

"Why did you keep it here when you knew we were coming to search? Seems you underestimated our abilities – Sergeant Habibullah's in particular."

Habi beamed again, eager to resume the search.

Winterton was defeated. "I couldn't think of anywhere

else to put the stuff, and I was under orders not to destroy it, so I trusted to luck."

Habi broke the short silence as Le Fanu silently signalled him to take over.

"You say you were ordered not to destroy the morphine," said Habi. "Who gave you that order?"

Winterton realised his slip. "Oh, I simply was trying to say that I could not bring myself to destroy the opium and…"

Habi cut him off.

"Please don't waste our time, sir. We have more searching to do but we can already charge you with possession of drugs. That will wreck your career. You are finished, but at least finish with some style."

"I can't tell you." The Private Secretary quivered.

"Mr. Winterton," said Le Fanu, "we will finish the search now. That will take ten minutes. You have that time to think. If you don't then answer the question, I'll arrest you and put you in a cell down at HQ. You have ten minutes to decide."

Ten minutes later, when they had found nothing else, Winterton still refused to answer. Le Fanu arrested him, and had a vehicle from HQ transport him to the cells. Whoever it was gave the order about the drugs, he or she had terrorised the Private Secretary.

Thirty

Deliberately, Le Fanu had not warned Virginia Campbell of their arrival, so he was intrigued to find her dressed more elegantly and provocatively than any other woman seen in Madras for years. She was in the same room as before when found by the servant, and apparently reading, because a book sat on the small side table along with a glass of white wine. When she stood, the full line and length of the red silk sheath dress became apparent, as did the mid-thigh slit on each side. Virginia Campbell knew the effect. She turned side on as if looking out over the lawns, emphasising the silhouette of her breasts and, effortlessly, posing in a way that had the dress falling away to display a splendid leg bearing no stocking. The black high-heeled shoes reinforced the impact, as did the long cigarette holder.

Had she anticipated their arrival, Le Fanu wondered. Habi did not know where to look.

"Miss Campbell," Le Fanu began.

"Oh really, Superintendent, how many times do I have to say it? Virginia, please."

"Miss Campbell, protocol requires that we address you formally during official questioning. This is official questioning, about two murders and morphine trading."

Did her eyes narrow at the mention of morphine? He wasn't sure.

"Two murders, Superintendent?"

"Miss Campbell," said Habi, having regained the power of speech, "we believe Lieutenant Walsall was also murdered, probably in connection with both the morphine trading and the death of Miss Carstairs. We think the three matters are connected."

She sat slowly, theatrically, ensuring that legs and breasts were still on show to full effect. To his alarm and annoyance, Le Fanu felt the beginnings of an erection. No woman had affected him that way in public for a very long time.

"Perhaps we might all sit," he managed, sliding into the nearest chair to hide the predicament he was sure she had spotted. She was smiling. Habi looked at him oddly but followed suit, finding a chair. She made herself the controlling focus because the men were in a semi-circle around her, fixed.

"Gentlemen." The smile was even wider. "There are so many of you, I feel so important."

Le Fanu felt this slipping away.

"Miss Campbell," he began, in what he hoped was a firm tone, "there are several important matters you didn't mention to us previously. We want to know why, and we want you now to tell us absolutely everything you do know."

He knew he sounded desperate, and the erection was lingering.

"Superintendent, I do apologise if I neglected to tell you anything. It must have been the stress of my friend being murdered. I'm in a strange place and confused by what has happened. Of course I will tell you everything I know."

She lowered her eyes, towards his crotch.

Habi broke in. "Miss Campbell, what exactly do you know about the morphine use?"

She turned her gaze from Le Fanu. "Sergeant Habibullah." The voice was quiet, low, compelling. "The only thing I know is that James, Mr. Winterton, asked me if I would like to take some at Jamieson's party, because he had it in his pocket."

"And you didn't think to tell us this?" queried Le Fanu.

"Well, I didn't know if the morphine matter had emerged when Superintendent Le Fanu spoke with me last, so I didn't want to give away anything that might cause trouble for my friends."

"Enough!" Habi rose from his chair. "You," he said, "had better start talking. Enough of this stage drama. Your dress will be unsuitable at Police HQ, but if we take you straight from here that is what you will be wearing. Now stop wasting our time. What do you know?"

Le Fanu's erection subsided rapidly. He had not seen Habi this agitated – she clearly had a very different impact on him.

Over the next ten minutes, Virginia Campbell was more forthcoming. Soon after she arrived in Madras, she met Walsall at a house party. They got chatting, had a few drinks, went for a walk in the garden, he kissed her and asked if she would go home with him. She refused. He then asked if she liked things other than alcohol, and turned the subject to morphine. It would help her relax, he said.

"I knew why he wanted me to relax, of course." Smiling, she looked directly at the pair of them, especially Habi who was churning in his chair. Le Fanu felt the erection returning.

She had, in fact, taken morphine before, once, at a party back in England but had not become a regular like some of her friends. When Walsall raised the subject, she was not shocked. A few minutes later, however, Jane Carstairs came to her, distressed, because having failed with one, Walsall had approached the other. Jane Carstairs had led a sheltered life, said Virginia Campbell, so something like drugs was well beyond her comprehension. When Virginia Campbell suggested that Walsall had a sexual intent in offering the morphine, Jane Carstairs became even more distressed, and angry.

Habi broke in. "If she was so upset, why was morphine found in her bloodstream after her death?"

"I have no idea, Sergeant." She spoke dismissively.

"Do you really expect us to believe that? Habi responded. "We know you saw her later. She was living under the same roof. She turns up in a filthy canal with her neck broken, her veins full of morphine, and you think we'll believe you know nothing?"

"I can see how that must look, but that's the truth. Jane was shocked and embarrassed by Walsall's suggestion she take the drug. She was even more shocked by the idea he wanted her to take it so he could fuck her."

With her modulated tones, the word slipped effortlessly, almost elegantly into the conversation that stopped immediately. Habi's eyes were shut and he was rocking his chair violently. Le Fanu was fully erect.

More awkward now than in any situation he could remember, Le Fanu somehow rearranged himself enough to stand, but he knew she knew. He gestured the others to stand. Habi was visibly angry.

"Miss Campbell," Le Fanu said, "we'll return later to resume this conversation. That will be your last opportunity to talk freely with us. If you don't, we'll arrest you, here in Sir Roland Wark's house, and take you to HQ and a cell until you're ready to tell us what you know. Please think hard about what you do next. Good day."

He started for the door, hoping Habi would not notice his awkward walk.

She stood, the dress still following her contours, which she emphasised by smoothing the silk with her hands. "Thank you Superintendent, I will think hard about that." She knew, definitely. "You are welcome any time. In fact, may I have a word with you alone?"

Habi took the hint and walked to the car. Le Fanu, standing uncomfortably, watched as she approached him. The snake image returned.

"Are you quite alright, Superintendent? You look uncomfortable." The voice was playful.

"Quite alright, thank you. How can I help, apart from saying you really must tell us everything you know, because right now I don't believe you."

"I'm sure all this will be resolved, which is why I want to speak with you. I've another six weeks in Madras so, once you clear all this up, perhaps you might ask me to dinner one evening?"

She posed again, smoking through the cigarette holder, the other hand smoothing silk between hip and buttock, the slit again revealing bare leg well up the thigh, the smoothing ensuring that fabric was tight over the bust. She was good at this, he thought, full erection back and on which she was gazing.

"Miss Campbell, I can't even begin to consider that until these developments have been determined." His real answer was, "Yes, and bugger dinner", but he knew that was impossible given the cases, not to mention Ro. Why was this woman affecting him this way? She was hypnotic. He escaped to find a room where he could rearrange his trousers before going out to the car. They set off for HQ.

"What did she want, sir? Habi asked.

"She wanted to arrange a dinner appointment, which I refused."

"That must have been difficult to do."

Le Fanu looked up, surprised. Habi was looking right at him.

"She's extremely attractive, sir, possibly the best looking one in the city now by a mile. She knows you are on the market. Any man would be tempted. And you know that Gross stresses the need to cherchez la femme."

Le Fanu was speechless as Habi continued. "What is happening with your wife anyway? Not coming back?"

How did Habi know about that, Le Fanu wondered.

"Sorry sir," Habi continued, "I know this embarrasses you and that you don't want to talk about this sort of thing, but the whole force knows the story. Miss Campbell has made her intentions clear enough now. You might even find out something useful being with her in a social situation."

"I don't know Habi, but I doubt I will take up Miss Campbell's offer. My wife has asked for a divorce and I'm trying to decide what to do, so I don't need any more complications at present."

"Perhaps just give her the divorce, and get on with your life. I am a Muslim so divorce is not for me, even though it is allowed for in the Koran. Your housekeeper isn't the answer, either."

Le Fanu was stunned. "How did you..."

"I didn't, really, but you've just told me. One of my servants is friendly with one of yours. Apparently there's been some discussion in the house lately, Miss Roisin being alone with you there, creeping about at night sometimes. You know what servants are like."

"Habi, I..."

"Sir, there's no need to explain to me. You've been on your own for a couple of years, Miss Roisin is attractive. But it's not the answer, not here anyway. If you stay in India, you'll need to deal with all that. But get rid of your wife first, that would be sensible. This Campbell woman isn't the whole answer either. She looks a handful, in more ways than one. But she might serve some short-term purpose."

Le Fanu could not believe he was having this conversation with a subordinate, let alone Habi, in a car travelling from Adyar to the beach, dodging carts, cows and pedestrians, being told to divorce his wife, get rid of his housekeeper, and sleep with a woman currently a suspect. He would wake from the dream soon, he thought.

He did. A message awaited at HQ. He was to go directly to the Commissioner's office in Egmore. Whatever was left of the erection disappeared immediately.

Thirty-one

As the car carried him towards Police Commissioner's Road, stopping occasionally in traffic jams caused by animals that were either wandering alone or pulling laden wagons, Le Fanu pondered Habi's advice.

He had to finalise the divorce, obviously, so he would reply to that letter tonight. It was sensible. He did not want to return to England, and the marriage was finished anyway. But Ro was a different matter entirely, because he was beginning to think he cared about her. He knew it would be a difficult relationship when he began sleeping with her. She was smart, funny and attractive, and Anglo-Indian. The more he came to know her, the more impressed he was by the depth of her knowledge and the sharpness of her mind. She was better educated than most of pukka memsahibs who thought they ruled the roost in Madras. When he first arrived before the war, many of those biddies kept him waiting in the hot sun, dressed in full morning suit and top hat, before they would deign to call him in so he could present his card. If he got the divorce, married Ro and stayed in Madras, then his now restricted social life would become monastic – the biddies would see to that. No European would speak to them, making his police work even more difficult, because he would lose respect, even trust, among his own community. Most considered him too pro-Indian now. If he married Ro they would think he had gone "native".

As they turned into the Commissioner's compound, he realised he had not thought once during the journey about the imminent meeting or the case. He was derelict in not keeping Jepson informed, and it was tactically dumb. He could scarcely remember what he had told Jepson or even when last he had seen the Commissioner. Surely it was just a couple of days ago? So much had happened, though, and as scene of offence commanding officer, he should have informed the Commissioner. What was about to come could not be good, and Le Fanu knew his predicament had as much to do with his personal as his professional life.

Hans Gross wrote nothing about the need for good communication up the chain of command, concentrating instead on the search for a superhumanly skilled Investigating Officer. Even so, Le Fanu had been around long enough to know that in British India, keeping one's superior informed was not only sensible, but mandatory. He knew that from his military days, so he deserved whatever bombs Jepson was about to throw his way.

Smartly turned out constables saluted him into the building, and he climbed the stairs deliberately, reluctantly if he was honest, reviewing his thoughts and the evidence. He was shown straight in. Jepson and three Assistant Commissioners were waiting.

"Good morning sir, I hope you haven't been waiting too long. We were out at Wark's and I wasn't aware you wanted to see me."

Jepson glowered. "Le Fanu, I've been waiting to hear from you for two days. Meanwhile, the press is going mad, and you are tearing about all over Madras making no headway whatsoever."

"Sir, I apologise…"

"I'm talking, Le Fanu. Sit down, shut your fucking mouth, and wait until I finish."

Le Fanu subsided into a chair. The Assistant Commissioners squirmed. Unconnected with the case, they were there simply to form an audience. Jepson had learned something from Wilson, at least. The ACs knew their role, so did Le Fanu, but that mutual knowledge did not ease the tension.

Jepson stood up. He was dressed in dark jodhpurs and polished black boots, his khaki dress tunic complete with ribbons. The riding crop smashed the boots incessantly. The verandah doors were open, traffic sounds and bird cries filtering in to accompany the persistent lash of leather on leather as the Commissioner began his tirade.

"Le Fanu, I made it abundantly clear that you might be the I-G's favourite, but you would report to me daily because this is my city."

None of Le Fanu's previous four Commissioners had owned the city like this. Jepson's ego was a considerable work in progress.

"I'm this close to sacking you from the case and sending you off to the back of Broken Stick Bellary where you can rot for the rest of your pitiful career."

Bellary was a notorious "punishment" station for police and ICS officers fallen foul of superiors, so whenever they sensed they were in strife, comic relief came from preparing to "bugger off to Bellary." That was funny most of the time, but Jepson was serious, and Le Fanu prayed for the chance of a reprieve. Having the I-G's ear was his only trump card, even though Jepson saw it as a threat. Jepson would not want to cross him, really, for fear of upsetting Wilson so soon after the beach shooting. Le Fanu breathed deeply, awaiting the rest of the speech.

Over the next ten minutes Jepson's face turned increasingly purple, waves of invective streaming from his mouth. If he did not have a health problem now he soon would, thought Le Fanu. Did Jepson have life insurance, he wondered idly, trying to distract himself from the barrage. The

Assistant Commissioners were wriggling furiously, no doubt sensing a preview of the ticking off they would inevitably receive at some point. Jepson commanded by bombast and fear, not constructive leadership and inspiration. He and Wilson could never work well together, which made Jepson's appointment all the more inexplicable. And the man delivered this spray with no embarrassment, oblivious to the carnage he had caused at the demonstration. The man had no conscience, it seemed. As Habi had warned, the Commissioner made an especially bad enemy.

"So, Le Fanu, I'm ordering you now to tell me and my Assistant Commissioners everything you know, immediately. And if you're to have any possible future, you'll advise me daily on developments."

Le Fanu rehearsed the latest details on the two deaths, and the barest outline of the morphine angle, suggesting that as a new line of inquiry, it had little substantial evidence as yet. He would say more as the information improved later. Le Fanu knew it was just the angle Jepson would use to initiate his own clumsy searches, further complicating the investigation. For the same reason, he provided a sketchy account of Virginia Campbell's involvement, depicting her as someone simply caught up in events. She was far more than that, of course. As he brushed her aside to Jepson, in his mind he shifted her closer to the centre of events.

"For the amount of bloody time you've been on this, Le Fanu, you have fuck all to show for it." Jepson warmed to his theme again.

In relaying so little detail, Le Fanu risked looking inactive, but that was better than revealing his full hand to Jepson. whose ability to grasp complexity was diminishing by the day.

"I'll keep you right up to date, sir, and I apologise again for not having done that so far."

Jepson waved him away as if swatting a mosquito, and as he left Le Fanu heard the thwack of crop on boot resume, as the Commissioner practised some other dressing down. As he descended the stairs, one of the Assistant Commissioners caught up with him. Le Fanu knew him, though not well, because their careers took them to different places, but the man was honest and straightforward.

"Sorry about us being there, Le Fanu. We didn't want to be in the room, but had no choice, as I'm sure you realise. To be honest, these days we spend far too much time witnessing these charades and not enough at our desks reducing the case load."

"Thanks for that," Le Fanu replied, "and I'm sorry you had to witness it all."

The Assistant Commissioner nodded, then continued. "That wasn't the only reason to catch you. Just keep walking, so we look as if we are naturally on our way out together. This place is becoming very conspiratorial. I just want to suggest strongly that you watch your back, literally. Something Jepson said before you came in suggested he might have someone looking into your personal affairs and past cases. Can't be sure, but be careful. The man has no principles, and he is increasingly dangerous."

They shook hands on the step as Le Fanu's car arrived.

He asked the driver to return to HQ through Georgetown rather than across Mount Road and along the Cooum out to the Marina. It was a longer route and slower because of the traffic, and gave him more time to think. His mind scrambled to accommodate all the competing thoughts, oblivious to the beggars appearing at the windows asking for money at every opportunity. Similarly, he was unaware of the enterprising kids emerging at intersections to clean car windows for a fee, or the new and alarming-looking buses thrown up on Ford truck chassis and to which men and boys were hanging one-handed on the back step. He did not see the cows lying in the middle of the road, the roadside food stalls, or the smoking piles of rubbish lining the high walls of public buildings.

Jepson had threatened him, and the AC suggested he was being watched. By taking him on, was Jepson also preparing to take on the I-G? Solving the case was no longer Le Fanu's only problem.

Thirty-two

Habi was waiting, having spent two hours revising notes and updating the progress boards. He also had news for Le Fanu.

"Sir, that American, I think we have found him. Some constables took that basic list and visited a few of the more obvious hotels, and one of them found a likely suspect at D'Angelis'."

"That's great news, Habi, I was beginning to worry about that one. Who is he?"

"One Chester Watson, sir. One of the constables tells me he has been there for a few weeks, seems to have been moving in the film circles, and splashing some money about. A large gentleman apparently – even larger than some of our locals."

Le Fanu thought that an odd comment, given Habi's own bulk, but he got the reference to size – the south Indian diet was saturated in oil and fats even if it was predominantly vegetarian, so many locals did gain weight fast.

"We'll go and see this Watson sometime tomorrow then Habi, thank those constables for me. Great work."

Winterton was in a cell downstairs, but he could wait until morning. If nothing else, he might be more forthcoming after a night in the company of the drunks and vagrants he would meet, a far cry from his normal companions. News of

Winterton's incarceration would be all over the Presidency by now and that might also persuade him to talk.

They would interview Winterton first thing in the morning, then try Virginia Campbell again, and hopefully between the two of them determine the shape, extent and makeup of the morphine ring. The ring had to be central to the killings, and Le Fanu suspected Virginia Campbell knew more than she was admitting. So did Winterton. Increasing the pressure on him might provide results. If both of them held out, then the investigation was in trouble.

What a long, troubling day, he thought, wheeling the bike out of the stables, but there was still more to come. Needing to think, he rode out onto Elliot's Road, turned right, then immediately right again onto the beach road. A little way towards San Thome church, he turned left, riding slowly along the largely unmade road towards the fish market. Most of the sellers had left but their open boats sat up on the sand, awnings strung between them, providing shelter to the fishermen and their families. Small kids peered out at him, surprised by the rare sighting of a European in their vicinity. A few of the adults called out and he answered or waved back. They had a hard life. A few years earlier, more than a hundred boats got caught at sea in a huge storm, and over two hundred men died. Yet these families carried on. The calamity was just another of the many expected hurdles in their life path.

They were fatalist, he thought, believing their lives to be inevitably foretold and unaffected by any amount of effort or thinking. That bothered Europeans, he reflected, because Western thinking argued that the individual could determine a life course through thought and deed. Much of the Western belief was illusory of course, but individuals still tried to control their circumstances.

Like now. He must go home and change the course of his life, or one of its parts, at least. He realised that as he turned into Luz Church Road, taking an even more circuitous route home than normal. Habi's comments about Ro had shocked but not surprised him. He had been waiting for this moment to arrive, he realised. The relationship would become public knowledge sooner rather than later, doing neither of them any good. Arguing that what he was about to do was in Ro's best interests was rationalisation, he knew. His real concern was that his career was at risk and he was not yet ready to leave the police, or Madras, or India. He was not sure there was a future, but he was ready still to be convinced, and if this relationship went public, then his prospects would diminish even further. It was unfair on her in the extreme, he acknowledged. She deserved much better.

That thought raised the other complication, his physical response to Virginia Campbell. She mesmerised him, even though his sex life with Ro was excellent. What did that say about his commitment, or his state of mind? He never betrayed his wife despite the several opportunities to do so, temptation sharpened by his frustration with their arid relationship. Yet he could have easily bedded Virginia Campbell that day, even though Ro would come to him that night.

As he reached the narrow lanes of Mylapore, the street lights disappeared and the silence grew, emphasising the bike's growl. This was the only time he regretted having it. In these localities at night, the engine became the modern version of the medieval flags marking the approach of strangers or notables. He preferred to be incognito away from the office, but the bike made that impossible.

He reached the driveway. Even knowing what he had now to do could not supress the pleasure of seeing subdued verandah light spilling onto the lawn. It was home, something he had never enjoyed in his earlier days. The terrible living conditions of wartime were dreadful, yes, but even before that, the house shared with his wife was atmospherically cold, his days at boarding school restricted, and the his earlier family house mean-spirited. This was the only place he had ever enjoyed coming back to.

A servant wheeled the bike away, and he went upstairs to shower, draining two neat single malts while standing under the water, and feeling the day's dust and anxieties recede. His clothes were laid out on the bed. He changed, went back downstairs. It was eight, dinner was ready. He took it on the verandah, dismissed the servants who went off gossiping, and asked Ro to join him.

She had changed from her working clothes, too. Her hair was oiled, hanging loose rather than pinned as normal. A white shirt spilled over the dark blue skirt that fell to her ankles, barely covering the matching flat shoes. She had never looked so attractive. He felt worse. Sitting down, she accepted a glass of wine, a rarity. He took a few mouthfuls of the food but pushed the plate aside. It would be a difficult enough conversation without trying to eat between comments.

"Aren't you hungry?" she asked.

"Ro, we need to talk. Well, I need to talk to you. It's all my fault. I'm not good at talking about these things, so it's difficult."

"Let me say something first," she said.

Le Fanu stared into the garden, trying to find a soft opening.

"Chris," she said, "I'm leaving your house."

He was stunned. "Leaving?" he said. "Why?"

"Oh Chris, you know why. That's why you've sent the servants away and asked me to sit with you. You want to say something but have no idea how to do so. Your conversational and personal skills are much less developed than your professional ones, darling." She laughed. "This has been coming for a while, but you haven't realised I've been thinking about it, too."

Thinking of nothing to say, Le Fanu poured another glass from the wine bottle stuck in an ice bucket.

"These last few weeks," she said, "have been the best ever

for me. It's not just about the sex, though I've really enjoyed that. You have a terrific body. It's more about having been needed, feeling helpful, being important to you. That's been missing from my life. Also, you're a genuinely nice man, which is astonishing, given that you're a policeman."

"But," Le Fanu cut in, "what's changed?"

"You have, of course. You have to decide on the divorce, you're under pressure at work, I'm a social liability and if we continue, we'll be Madras gossip item number one. You don't yet know whether to stay in India or leave, so you don't need a scandal. Add all that up and I'm a problem."

Am I that transparent, he wondered.

"I want to stay in India, I have to," she continued, "because there's nowhere else for me to go. I've no future with you, as much as I like you. So I must leave, and if you agree that will be tomorrow."

He was dazed. This was not the conversation he had imagined. The result was as intended, but a part of him did not want the relationship to end.

"But where?" he stammered.

"A friend has recommended me a general's wife up in Secunderabad. They need someone there quickly to get the household back in order, and my friend sent me a telegram yesterday saying they would take me as soon as I could start. I said I would travel up by train tomorrow night and be there the next day."

He sipped the wine, glancing between her and the garden. Ro was smiling, her wine untouched. She was in control, not him.

"Chris, don't say anything because you know it's right. You needed to tell me it was over but had no idea how to do that. I knew it was over, and I'm happy with the new opportunity. I need a wonderful reference from you, of course, but you would have given me that anyway. I have no regrets, and hope you feel the same. I will miss you very much."

He could only nod, in tears for the first time since Shaiba.

"I have one other request," she said. "I want to stay with you all night, but there won't be much sleep. It's right that I go, but I will miss you, a lot, and I want as much of you as I can before I leave."

He stood, went over to her, helped her to her feet, and kissed her. They went inside, arms linked.

Thirty-three

At seven the next morning, a sleep-deprived Le Fanu sat in an HQ interview room across a table from Charles Winterton. He had promised Ro he would be back at six that evening to see her off to the railway station. She was more on his mind than the interviewee.

The ICS star now back at earthly level, had not enjoyed his jail stay. Eyes bloodshot from lack of sleep, hair unkempt, and body seemingly as crumpled as his clothes, he slumped in the chair.

"Mr. Winterton," began Le Fanu, Habi seated beside him, "perhaps this night in the cell has persuaded you to talk more freely. In particular, will you tell us who gave the order on the morphine?"

"No, I cannot, I'm afraid, sorry."

Habi wiggled his chair. Le Fanu kept gaze on Winterton.

"Alright," continued Le Fanu, "we'll get there eventually, but I hope it doesn't take all day."

Uncomfortable, Winterton's eyes flitted between his interrogators and around the small room's walls that closed in by the minute. He was hyperventilating.

"Mr. Winterton, drink some water and take a few deep breaths. You'll be here a while if you can't or won't answer that question." Le Fanu looked to Habi, who responded quickly. Winterton would hate taking questions from an

Indian, Le Fanu knew.

"Sir," rasped Habi, "we know you stored morphine in your rooms. Where did you get it from?"

"Superintendent, I should not have to answer questions from this man, it is bad enough being asked by you." Wild-eyed, Winterton was breathing shallowly again.

"You'll answer questions put to you by anyone here now, and anyone whom I might ask in later. You're under arrest, with no right to decide who will or will not ask you questions. I will decide that. Now answer the question, or we'll throw you back in the cell for a couple of days and forget about you. Carry on Habi."

Winterton wilted. "I discovered morphine here in Madras about two years ago, just after the war ended. Two soldiers en route to England brought some across from Burma, and shared it with me. That was when I first started using it. I hated my work, and it gave me an escape."

He looked exhausted and older. Over the next few minutes, Habi drew the story from a now-deflated Private Secretary, who had become dependent on the drug soon after that first experience. He found his way into city social circles with access to supplies. They were mainly military figures connected to the medical supply chain. But one was Billy Walsall, who quickly became Winterton's main supplier. Walsall accessed large quantities of morphine. That meant, Le Fanu thought, Walsall must have had supply lines other than the medical one, where quantities were small and well-guarded.

"So there were other sources of supply?"

"Yes," Winterton slurred, "the medical chaps couldn't keep up the quantities because more and more people were coming into the group."

"We'll need names," Habi noted.

"I can't give you any."

"You don't have a choice," said Le Fanu," but we'll pursue that later. Where else did the stuff come from?"

"It took us a while to find more, but we chanced on some local Indian users."

Leaving aside the identity of the "we", also be detailed later, Le Fanu realised that Winterton and friends must have been desperate because they would not normally have mixed with Indians.

"How did you come across them, exactly?" continued Habi, taking notes, Le Fanu watching Winterton intently.

"Strangely enough, that came through Misses Campbell and Carstairs."

"How so?"

"Somewhere on their travels around Madras, they met an Indian man who is by way of a filmmaker."

"You mean the movies?" interjected Habi, eyes lifting interestedly from his notebook.

"Yes. They met him at the Connemara. He was seated next to them at dinner one night and introduced himself."

"And," said Le Fanu, "can you name him?"

Winterton nodded reluctantly. The Indian was evidently less of a threat than the so-far unnamed person. "His name is Rajan Mudaliar. He went to school in England then on to Cambridge. He arrived back in Madras just after the war ended. You may know his father, Venkat Rama Mudaliar."

All policemen knew him. V.R. Mudaliar was a successful criminal lawyer who came in from Madura to practice in Madras, where he upset several prominent prosecution cases. He was now defending several leading political agitators, had a large house in Nungambakkam and drove about the city in a huge Ford. Le Fanu thought Wilson would take this news badly.

"So the women talked to Rajan Mudaliar, but how did that lead to the morphine?" asked Habi.

"Mudaliar was making a film and he asked the women if they would like to appear as actors," Winterton replied, hesitantly. "He had written in two roles to be filled by English women. The pair agreed, and went to his house in Kilpauk."

"Get to the point, sir," said Habi.

"I am. While they were there, he asked if they would like morphine to help them relax into the roles. Virginia told me later that she did, but Jane refused. They did the filming, went home, and I met them at a party later where they told me what had happened. At that point they didn't know I took the stuff."

"And what did you do then, sir?" asked Habi.

"The next day I slipped around to Kilpauk while on the way into the Secretariat to get some papers for His Excellency. Mudaliar was there, we talked, and he agreed to get me some supplies at an agreed sum. I returned next day with the money and he produced the goods. That was about three weeks ago. He's been supplying me a couple of times a week since then, allowing me to augment the medical supply source."

If this became public knowledge the Governor, his senior officers, and the medical establishment would all be seriously embarrassed. Le Fanu had to deal carefully with this information and connect it to the deaths quickly. At least, he thought, the deaths are now linked directly to the morphine, but revealing that might produce more problems than solutions.

"You'll need to give us Mudaliar's address," said Le Fanu, "and the names of anyone else you met there."

"The only other people there were either working on the film, or house servants. I saw no one else."

Le Fanu let that slide but doubted it was the truth.

"How much did you pay?"

"Over a thousand rupees."

The policemen looked at each other.

"That's a lot of money, Mr. Winterton, well above your pay scale."

"I have private means, and have been dipping into them heavily to support the addiction."

This life was ruined in more ways than one, Le Fanu reflected.

"We'll leave it there for the moment, Mr. Winterton" he said, "but you'll remain here until we clear this up. Buying and consuming morphine is a serious offence, so at the very least we'll be charging you with that."

Winterton nodded, having aged even more during the past few minutes.

"I don't suppose," Le Fanu said softly, "that you're now prepared to name the person who gave you the orders about the morphine?"

"If you charge me with the drug offences, will I be let out of here?"

The question seemed straightforward but Le Fanu sensed a deeper purpose.

"We'll keep you here if you're charged, because there'll be no bail. Given what you've said so far, we'll charge you so there is little chance of you getting out before trial and even less after. You'll be in jail for a very long time. The only question is whether it will be here in Madras, or back in England, if some judge looks on you kindly."

"So I'll be in a cell from now on?"

"Here at HQ for the present, then in the city gaol."

"So no one could harm me?"

"We could have you guarded to be sure."

"If you guarantee that, I'll give you the name."

"I'll have to confirm with the Inspector-General but I'm sure he'll agree."

"In that case, I'll trust you." Winterton paused for what seemed like several minutes.

Le Fanu and Habi sat rock still. It must surely be a dramatic name given Winterton's anxiety.

"It was Sir Gordon Wark."

Thirty-four

"That can't be right LF, surely?"

It was still pre-lunch, but Wilson had reached for the malt stache again, and they sat contemplating their glasses.

"It's hard to disbelieve Winterton, sir. He's genuinely frightened and wouldn't give us Wark's name before getting assurance he would be permanently behind locked doors."

"Even so, LF. Wark? He's the paragon of virtue here. How can we touch him?"

"Same as we always do, sir, and as you always told me. Evidence."

Wilson grinned at the rebuke, but still aghast at the thought of pursuing the city's leading businessman.

"You'd better be very certain before you do anything, LF. I'm already unpopular but you're even more so."

"What do you mean, sir?" asked Le Fanu.

"A couple of things. For one, Jepson's spreading tales about your alleged incompetence. All nonsense, but he's stalking you and some of this stuff always sticks. Then, somehow, he got wind of your housekeeper. God knows how, but he's spreading that, too."

Le Fanu took a long sip at the malt, wondering how long Wilson himself had known. "That's ironic. She's leaving tonight for Secunderabad, permanently."

"In many ways, LF, I'm sorry to hear that, because you

deserve some peace and contentment. But in your very best interests, it's a good thing. I'll get that around, if you don't mind, it'll help counter Jepson's campaign."

For a moment, Le Fanu resented the idea of Ro being used as a political trading card, but deep down, knew it was inevitable. At least she would be away from the rats' nest, as he wished he might be at this moment.

"Thank you, sir, I appreciate that, though I'd hoped her name might be kept out of all this."

"Wishful thinking in this town, old man, as you well know. Come on, finish that and we'll decide what happens next."

That turned out to be Le Fanu and Habi visiting Chester Watson then Rajan Mudaliar in Kilpauk. Wilson would re-interview Winterton to learn more if possible, but mainly to demonstrate that priority was being given to the case.

Habi had telephoned D'Angelis' and learned that Watson was still there. The place had a history and in the old days a lot of ICS and other officers had stayed there, some even with families, because it was a lot cheaper than renting a house and servants. These days, though, it was more of a travelling businessmen's hotel. Inside it was a little shabby, but the food was still good. They met Watson in a small meeting room.

He towered over them, his bulk dwarfing everything in the room. His mustard coloured linen suit had matching shoes, and a panama hat sat on the table in front of him. A mustard coloured handkerchief was at hand, frequently applied to the sweating brow atop the florid, puffy face. The hair was fair, shaved close to the skull.

"Mr. Watson, thank you for seeing us, I am Superintendent Le Fanu and this is Sergeant Habibullah. We believe you know a Mr. Rajan Mudaliar and perhaps some other people in whom we have an interest currently. Would you be so kind as to answer some questions?"

"Surely," came the loud reply that echoed off the walls. "Only too pleased to help though I'm not clear how I can.

I'm just a sales guy."

"But you do know Mudaliar?"

"I sure do. Mainly I sell cars, and I arranged one for him, but he wondered if I might be interested in investing in the movie business and I am. If I can get a start here, I might get in more easily back home in Los Angeles, California."

Le Fanu wondered why it was that Americans always did that, attach the state name to that of the town.

"And what did Mr. Mudaliar offer you?"

"He wants me to become a partner in his film production business, a fifty/fifty investment with a fifty/fifty return. I've put that money in and that helped him get the equipment. The first films are now in production."

"Did you meet anyone else through him? A couple of English women, for example?"

"I've only been to his house a couple of times. I think those women were there the first time but I didn't meet them."

"What about a Mr. Winterton or a military officer called Walsall?"

"Nah, never heard of them, Lieutenant."

Not great listening skills, then.

"How long have you been in Madras, Mr. Watson?"

"About six months, and that is six months too long. The sooner I am back Stateside the better, in the good old US of A."

They left soon after, neither thinking Watson would likely be much further help. Hopefully, Rajan Mudaliar would be.

A premier European residential area Kilpauk also hosted a few very rich Indians, so the houses were enormous, set in large grounds. The driver took them through Georgetown , over Elephant Gate Bridge into Egmore, past the Museum and Library before turning towards this haven for the well-off. The surroundings softened as the big garden houses loomed up, tall and shady trees filtering light down onto the wide, well maintained streets. There were no beggars or street dwellers here. Most of the mansions had nine or ten bedrooms, large lounge and dining areas, billiard rooms and other entertainment areas, wide verandahs upstairs and down, with expansive lawns and tennis courts. All these were maintained by armies of servants in distinctive household uniforms.

Habi had scouted Mudaliar's address for the driver, so they soon entered what seemed to be an even bigger property than the others. The house sat well back, fronted by manicured lawns lined with banks of shrubs and flowers behind the high hedge that ran along the street front. Several cars were outside the entrance to the house, with three more lined up neatly in an open garage off to the side. People came and went, several in costumes. It seemed there was a film being made now, or at least Le Fanu assumed so. If not, then this was a section of Madras society he had not yet encountered.

Habi looked puzzled. "Sir, I wonder what is happening here?"

Le Fanu laughed. "Habi, I think we have entered filmmaking country."

A liveried servant met them at the door, asked their business, and showed them into a drawing room with walls plastered in movie posters, along with photographs of a man Le Fanu took to be Rajan Mudaliar. He kept good company, because Le Fanu recognised some leading London society figures and some senior Madras ones.

The man himself entered. Of average height, he was slim, fashionably dressed in white linen suit and white shirt set off by brown and white two-tone brogues. The face was light-coloured, rounded and fleshy, the eyes dark and the hair thick and black, swept back from the front and brilliantined into place. He was the match for the average London fop, thought Le Fanu.

"Gentlemen, I am Rajan Mudaliar. I understand you wish to see me? Let me say I'm a little busy as I have a shooting schedule to complete today, but I am happy to assist. I just hope that we can get this over with quickly." The voice was cultured and condescending, the mark of the self-appointed VIP.

"Shooting?" Habi asked.

"A film term, Habi," Le Fanu responded, while Mudaliar smirked.

"I see your sergeant is not up with modern times, Superintendent," he said.

"Sergeant Habibullah is much too busy solving crimes to be bothered with these modernities to which you refer, sir. And it is a crime, or rather two crimes, murders in fact, we wish to speak to you about."

Mudaliar was jolted.

"Superintendent, I'm sorry, I did not mean to…"

"No matter, sir, perhaps we can go somewhere and discuss things privately? I'm sure you would prefer that." For some reason, Le Fanu suspected this man immediately.

Rajan Mudaliar led them down the corridor. In the rooms either side, people rushed about carrying costumes, pieces of equipment, what looked like stage settings, and sheafs of paper. Mudaliar entered a small, well-furnished sitting room and directed them towards chairs. He himself sat in the only high backed chair, picked a cigar from a silver box, lit up, and sat back breathing out richly scented smoke. He did not invite his guests to join him. Unbidden, a servant arrived with a tray carrying water, tea, coffee and snacks. Things were done on a grand scale here.

"How may I help you?"

The superiority complex had returned quickly.

"Easily, sir" replied Le Fanu. "You can tell us what you know about the murders of Miss Jane Carstairs and Lieutenant Billy Walsall."

Mudaliar straightened in his chair, the hand holding the cigar fell away to the side, ash dropping on the floor.

"I know nothing of those murders, and must protest at

your tone."

"Protest away, sir. Habibullah will note that and we'll report it to the Inspector-General. But I should warn you he's as anxious as I am to discover what you know."

"I repeat, I know nothing." The self assuredness was slipping.

"Well, that's untrue for a start, sir. You knew the two people, I believe?"

Mudaliar considered the question, staring at Le Fanu. The smoking stopped, the cigar threatening to peter out. The face seemed impassive, but Le Fanu detected anxiety.

"Not a difficult question, sir. Perhaps you might answer?"

"I did know the two, as it happens, Miss Carstairs a little more than Lieutenant Walsall. They both came to a couple of parties of mine over the past few weeks."

"That would be during the past three weeks, sir?" Habi commented.

"Yes, it would." Rajan Mudaliar did not enjoy being questioned by a Muslim sergeant. The answer was calm enough but Mudaliar was hesitant, Le Fanu thought. Why?

"Perhaps you might explain to us, then," Le Fanu asked, "why you didn't come forward and give us this information voluntarily, instead of letting us find out about the connection and having to come to you days later. To me, that looks suspicious."

Le Fanu was pressuring the man and, he admitted to himself, not only because there was a question to be answered. He did not like Mudaliar. Looking closely, he saw Mudaliar beginning to sweat.

"Come now, sir, it's another easy question," Le Fanu bore on.

"I did not want to compromise myself."

"Again, that appears suspicious."

"Superintendent. My father disapproves strongly of me being involved in the movies. He thinks it is something a gentleman should avoid, and he would be happier if I followed him into law where he has given your people hard times, I believe. He already thinks I'm wasting my money, and his, and if he thought there was even the vaguest connection with these murders he would shut me down immediately."

Le Fanu understood the problem. Out of curiosity, a few weeks earlier, he visited one of the new tents appearing around the city to show these new films, and immediately understood how they could captivate people. He also knew, however, that several prominent Europeans, including the Chief Secretary, thought no well-bred European should grace such populist venues.

"But the two people who are now dead were here, sir?" Habi queried.

"Yes."

"And Miss Carstairs even appeared in one of your films?" Le Fanu continued.

Mudaliar looked surprised that Le Fanu knew, but nodded.

"Yes," he said, "she and Miss Virginia Campbell, Miss Carstair's friend, agreed to appear briefly in a couple of roles for English women I wrote into the script."

"Why did you do that?"

"Actually, they asked me. They saw us filming and wanted to be involved. I can show you the film if you like, it came back from processing in Bangalore this morning."

"Answer me something else first. What do you know about the circulation of morphine in Madras?"

Now Mudaliar was definitely worried, searching for an answer.

"Perhaps we can go and see that film while you think about it," Le Fanu suggested, thinking Mudaliar would be off balance out of the comfort of the room.

The movie man led them into a small darkened room with a projector on a table, a screen, and a few chairs. An attendant started the projector and in a second or so, flickering images of both women appeared. Oddly, to Le Fanu, Virginia Campbell was attractive but Jane Carstairs dominated the screen. She was attractive, too, but with a personality that sprang out. She stared down the camera, oblivious to its presence. Naturally graceful, she flowed rather than walked across the set. She had charisma, an allure. Le Fanu realised why she had attracted so much attention, but felt odd watching the vivacity of a woman now dead, murdered and shoved in a canal. The images faded.

"Where was that taken?" he asked.

Silently, Mudaliar led them to another room dominated by three enormous cameras. After his tent visit, Le Fanu read up about this new phenomenon, so recognised the cameras as Williamson Tropicals, made to operate in hot and humid climates. They were large, oblong wooden boxes with a lens at the front and a crank handle to the side. They each stood on a tripod to which they were fixed by a solid iron connecting ring.

Each camera was aimed at a set featuring furniture unnaturally placed against a backdrop depicting windows overlooking a garden. That was odd, thought Le Fanu, there was a perfectly good natural setting a few steps away, but he guessed they could control light better here.

"How often did the two women come here?" Habi asked Mudaliar, who by now was sweating profusely.

"Several times over a couple of weeks."

"So you knew them better than vaguely?" Le Fanu followed.

"Well, yes."

"And Walsall?" asked Habi.

Mudaliar looked surrounded, having to switch focus and concentration as the alternating questioning swept over him.

"He came a few times as well."

There was obviously something here, Le Fanu decided, but as yet no direct suggestion Mudaliar was involved with the morphine.

"Sir, your answers really are unsatisfactory. So my suggestion is that we give you more time alone to think further, and we'll talk again soon."

Mudaliar looked relieved, Habi puzzled.

As they drove away through the pleasant streets, Habi asked why they had left so abruptly.

"Because, Habi, let's have someone watch where he goes and, more importantly, whom he sees. As soon as we get back to HQ, I want you to detail one of your most reliable men and get him here quickly, in plain clothes. I have a feeling Mr. Mudaliar will show us more than he tells."

Thirty-five

It was not yet five when he swung into the driveway, the earliest he had been home from work ever, but still leaving minimal time before Ro left for the railway station and Secunderabad.

He was sad, guilty, regretful, relieved, even remorseful. Because Ro had made the decision for him, he was also embarrassed. After all, he wanted to end it, but she anticipated that. Had she sensed his thinking? He did not know and, really, that did not matter. The breakup he wanted had occurred, and he was glad. But part of him wondered whether he might have simply defied anything Madras society threw at him and them, because Ro was special.

She sat at the verandah table overlooking the lawn, bags piled by the front door. A long, dark grey skirt to the ankles, flat black shoes, a loose dark grey jacket buttoned to the throat where a white shirt collar showed through, matched by frilled cuffs showing through the jacket sleeves. Her hair was pinned, a small gold brooch at her left collarbone the only evident jewellery. She was beautiful, he thought, and smart – why on earth was he letting her leave? He remembered Wilson's blunt warning about the consequences of continuing the relationship. Madras was a hard enough place to navigate friendships let alone a love life, he thought. It was such a hypocritical place.

"Chris," she said, "I do so appreciate you coming back early. It means a lot."

He felt even more guilty.

"Ro, of course I'm back to see you off, I still can't believe you're going. I will, well, you know, miss you very much."

She smiled at his awkwardness, and touched his hand lightly.

"You poor thing. Like most men here, you are just hopeless at all this, aren't you? Mind you, it seems men in general are hopeless at it, not just those of you lurking in Madras."

They laughed, and sat at the table where a teapot, cups, spoons, sugar, milk and baked biscuits were set. She poured the tea.

"Ro, I'm so sorry this has happened and that you are leaving. The house will be empty without you."

"So will your bed, at least for a while," she replied mischievously, her eyes glinting.

He blushed deeply, but laughed all the same. "You are right on the first comment. But on the second, it will be empty for quite a while, I can assure you. There was more to it than that. You're a smart woman as well as a beautiful one."

"Ah, Chris, here I am about to leave and you suddenly find the power of speech. How wonderfully ironic."

They sipped tea, a comfortable silence setting in for a couple of minutes.

"I'll miss this place, a lot, and you", she said. "It's the happiest I've been for a long time. But I don't regret leaving, you've given me the confidence I need to take this next step. You'll always have been an important part of my life, and I won't forget you or what you have done for me. You gave me a chance when no one else in this city would. What came later was a wonderful bonus."

He was embarrassed, again.

"Ro, you were and are an easy person to help because you're a terrific one. Good things will happen in Secunderabad,

I know that. And anyway, I got the better end of the bargain – you stopped me feeling sorry for myself, and now you are leaving I worry some of that might come back. Can we write from time to time?"

"I would love to hear from you."

The car Le Fanu had ordered turned into the drive and stopped outside the main door. The other servants, to this point discreetly scarce, reappeared to help load the bags.

They stood together, smiled, hugged, and walked towards the car, where he opened the door while she got in. Their hands touched briefly, he shut the door, and they waved to each other. The driver set off, she waved through the back window as the car disappeared into the street, and then she was gone.

He stood there, looking at the empty driveway, waiting a minute or two for the tears to pass before he turned to deal with the other servants. The house already seemed empty.

He ate the light meal she had left and there was still light, so he had a servant bring the Robert Forgan putter, a mashie niblick and a few golf balls. As he chipped balls across the lawn he remembered again how much he enjoyed and now missed golf. One of his Cambridge friends reckoned Le Fanu and golf were made for each other, a mutual loner's society. Back then there was a truth in that. The times he enjoyed most were when out alone on a course, in this sort of light, shadows lengthening across the undulations found on a course like the wonderful Boat of Garten he had played on the Speyside in Scotland one autumn before the war. He could think, walk, play and savour the atmosphere.

His back lawn was a long way from the Boat, but he still enjoyed the pleasure of feeling golf balls fly from a club's sweet spot - though that was not happening as frequently tonight as in the past. He really should play more. If nothing else, it would put him back in the social web, as he always thought of it here in Madras, though he was never entirely sure who was the spider at the centre. Of ten putts from ten feet he made just two. He had to play more. And of ten chips from thirty feet, just three finished within three feet of the hole. That did it. He would have to practice much more before braving any course. Dreadful game, never mastered.

A servant interrupted.

"Sir, there is someone being on the telephone for you."

It was Virginia Campbell, when he had expected perhaps Wilson or Habi.

"Miss Campbell, is there some way I can help you?" he asked, warily.

"You really will not call me Virginia, will you?"

"As I explained, you're part of an official inquiry so protocol demands I treat you formally."

"I understand, but could we reach a compromise?"

"Doubtful, but I'll hear what you have to say. I should warn you though, I will still be the policeman leading this investigation in which you are a key principal."

"And suspect?"

"Until proven otherwise, yes."

He wanted this conversation ended quickly, not liking its direction.

"I understand perfectly," she replied, the voice as warm as ever. "I was wondering if we might have dinner together? I could explain further some of the matters we have discussed."

"Miss Campbell, I really can't agree to that. If you have anything further to say, the best thing would be for me to come out there. That would at least avoid you having to visit the police station."

Why did he make that concession, he wondered. His groin was reacting again.

"I would appreciate that very much," came the instant reply, and he wondered if he had just been stymied. "Sometime tomorrow, perhaps?"

"That might be possible. I'll have someone from the office

ring you in the morning to confirm once I check my timetable."

"Thank you Chris." The touch was light, but insistent, treating herself as his close friend. Ro was the only person who called him Chris, he remembered, and wondered if her train had left. He checked his watch. Fifteen minutes ago.

"Miss Campbell, you must address me formally too, please. That will make things easier for both of us."

"Of course. Until tomorrow, then. I do hope you have a pleasant evening. Good night."

Replacing the receiver he wondered how he could have a pleasant evening. A woman he cared deeply about had just left his life, a more calculating one was trying to enter it, his cases were becoming more rather than less complex, and his golf game was a shambles. Could all that combined be pleasant? No.

The whisky tasted bland, the food more so, and his bed felt cold. It was a long rather than pleasant night, and a sleepless one, because he kept waiting for the door to open.

Thirty-six

The next morning, unusually, when Le Fanu entered his office, he found Wilson there already waiting. "Sir, I am sorry. Had I known…"

"Good morning, LF, and no apology needed," Wilson replied, rising. Le Fanu noted the full dress uniform. "I had a call from the Chief Secretary last evening, just as we were about to have dinner. We, and I mean you and me, are bidden to his presence this morning, as in now."

Le Fanu gathered papers from his desk, shoved them in a briefcase and fell in step with Wilson who was already near the door.

"Do I need ask the subject, sir?"

"No. These damn cases, naturally, though I have no idea what tack he's on. He's certainly not interested in the police work, so there'll be some other angle I don't know about."

As they went along the corridor and down the stairs, Le Fanu noticed how much busier people were when Gorilla Wilson was about. They walked faster, looked more serious, more purposeful. The man still had an effect, then. Would that remain when he retired? And who would replace him? No date was yet announced and Wilson himself did not discuss it with anyone, because he clearly did not want to retire. His replacement, however, could have a big impact on Le Fanu's position and work.

Those thoughts were still in his head as they motored along the still-quiet Marina. A few fishing boats were pulled up on the sand in the distance, back from their overnight adventures. On a clear night, the horizon seemed filled with the lights boatmen carried to mark their presence. They would appear and disappear on the swell, and on heavy nights could disappear for seconds at a time as they fell into then rose from the troughs, a reminder of their daily dangers.

Wilson was quiet until they drove into the narrow gateway at Fort St. George and were checked through by the armed soldiers.

"LF, I've no idea what this is about, but rest assured I'll back everything you say about these cases. You've done an excellent job. If there is any witch hunt about, it's not being run by me."

Le Fanu wondered if the I-G had heard some Club gossip, because this was a rare

statement. They entered the Secretariat and were escorted up to the Chief Secretary's expansive office by a senior clerk.

Sir Charles Witney was waiting for them and had them in immediately, so this must be important, thought Le Fanu.

"Good morning Wilson, Le Fanu, thank you for coming."

Witney must have come in very early because even though a fresh sea breeze was coming through an open French door, the warm fug of a cigar or two was evident, and another was already in hand, glowing.

"Thought I'd better get you in to see where things stand."

It was an offhanded comment but Le Fanu knew better than that, so let Wilson begin.

"Of course, Sir Charles. Perhaps you might give us a lead as to the things you want most clarified?"

"Oh please, Maurice, forget the titles in here, we're away from prying eyes and open ears. Don't mind if I call you LF, do you Le Fanu? Seems all the important people do."

"Of course, sir, I'd be honoured."

There really was a purpose here, then, given this bonhomie.

"Good man. Now, tell me exactly where we are with these cases, and where things might lead?"

Wilson signalled to Le Fanu, who for the next fifteen minutes gave the Chief Secretary a full account, with one omission – Winterton's accusation against Sir Roland Wark. He and Wilson had discussed it on the way but were still developing a strategy for dealing with it, knowing any mistake would bring heavy career punishment. So they agreed to keep silent on this point for the moment.

"That all seems clear enough," said Witney, fanning away a plume of rich, scented smoke. Morning coffee arrived, along with some vadas, which startled Le Fanu, who imagined the Chief Secretary as a tea, toast and marmalade man.

"I've surprised you, eh, LF?" Witney was smiling.

Irritated that his surprise had shown, Le Fanu vowed to work on concealing his thoughts. "Not really, sir. Well, perhaps a little."

"You're not the only one who likes things south Indian, you know, though I doubt these vadas match those at your house where you have a splendid cook, I gather."

Le Fanu now was bothered. If Witney knew about his cook, then surely he knew about Ro. If so, what message was being passed here?

"I'm sure these are excellent, sir," he said, and reached for one. It was nowhere near as good as his, but he was not about to say so. Something strange was happening here.

Witney read his mind.

"I do apologise if I'm being mysterious and elliptical. There's a lot of pressure about concerning these two cases, LF, and, of course, Maurice, your name gets into dispatches for all the obvious reasons."

"I imagine so, Charles, so perhaps you'd better tell us what's going on here."

Witney led them to the balcony, closing the door behind him. This was planned, too, because a small table with a white cloth bore another coffee pot, and three cups. He indicated them to the chairs. In the distance Le Fanu could hear the waves, and closer in the sounds of traffic along the Marina road.

"I am sorry about all this," Witney said, "but the further we're away from anyone else, the easier it is to talk."

He had brought the vadas with him, offered the plate around, and Le Fanu took another out of politeness. Witney smiled, then poured more coffee.

"In fact," he said, "I will share a little information with you, but you'll need first to be more expansive on one matter than you have been so far. What do you make of Wark's position in all this?"

The question was nonchalant, but Witney's eyes did not leave Le Fanu's face.

Wilson answered immediately.

"Charles, one witness suggested to LF the day before yesterday that Wark might somehow be involved. LF discussed it with me, and we're working out how best to determine a strategy and test the assertion against what else we know."

"Fair enough," the Chief Secretary commented, "so, LF, can you give me the detail?"

Le Fanu recounted the Winterton statement, finishing with the claim that Wark had warned the PS against mentioning the morphine.

"Well, I can tell you," said Witney, "that the statement confirms some suggestions we've been hearing."

The two policemen looked at him, astonished.

"Sorry, Maurice, but we heard a whisper about Wark a couple of months ago. By "we" I mean the Governor got a rare telephone call from his counterpart in Bombay, suggesting Wark was up to something. Because of Wark's position, His Excellency thought the utmost discretion was required. It was not that he doubted your chaps, Maurice. It was just that with the potential embarrassment being so great if this got out unproven, he wanted it as secret as possible. I got one of the military intelligence chaps in New Delhi to do some work. He came back with strong suggestions that Wark is up to no good. That information came in two days ago, the same time as Winterton spilled his guts to you."

Le Fanu suspected the Chief Secretary was now under as much pressure as he and Wilson.

"Charles," said the I-G, "I appreciate you letting us in on this so quickly because, as you say, it means we should look at Wark very closely. Did your Delhi chap produce anything concrete?"

Witney reached for his inside jacket pocket and pulled out an envelope. "This is his full report."

"Sir, " said Le Fanu, "Winterton was frightened to the point of terror about mentioning Wark, and it was only after we assured him he could stay in a cell for the foreseeable future that he agreed to give up Wark's name. Do you know why he might be so scared?"

"Excellent question, LF, and the answer is, yes. It's all in there, but Wark has been in this business for some time and there have been casualties along the way. Nothing connected directly to him, but he probably ordered those casualties. Winterton has good reason to be afraid."

Wilson took over. "The question now, then, is how do we approach this? The morphine is a root cause of the two deaths, so is a legitimate line of inquiry for those deaths and as a crime in its own right. For Wark, however, we only have Winterton's allegation and no concrete evidence, is that right LF?"

"It is, sir. The only other angle we have is that Wark tried to have me dismissed from the case, and on reflection, that might have been more a ruse than an apparently drunken stumble."

"I was thinking the same thing, LF" said the Chief Secretary. "Wark might be a lot smarter than I've been giving him credit for."

"Do we interview him? Is that the question you want us to consider, Charles?" asked Wilson.

"It is, indeed, and my feeling is to not do that yet. Let's stalk him for a while. My suggestion is the two of you read this report fully, then work out how to keep an eye on Wark. Might be difficult, but I have another little surprise for you that might help."

Wilson and Le Fanu looked up at Witney who had risen from his chair and was looking out across the ramparts of the fort.

"You talked to Mr. Jackson Caldicott, I believe, LF?"

Le Fanu nodded.

"Well, there's more to him than being a pretty cricketer and ambitious businessman. During the war he didn't go to the front because he was too busy being an intelligence agent, and he's still on the books, an old friend in London tells me. He might be just the chap we need to keep that eye on Wark."

Le Fanu wondered, yet again, how it was this case became more rather than less complex. By the time he and Wilson left the Chief Secretary, Le Fanu had agreed to approach Caldicott about conducting covert surveillance on Wark.

Thirty-seven

Caldicott, tipped off clearly, awaited Le Fanu who ascended the stairs in the merchants' commercial block. The cricketer was pensive as he showed Le Fanu into the office, closing the door. The tea was there already. At this rate, Le Fanu would be awash by lunch time.

"I thought I was leaving all that when I came to India." Caldicott was rueful.

"Were you surprised to find your past known here?"

"Not really. As a matter of courtesy, the Governor was advised when I came, but I was not to be called into service on intelligence matters. However, this is different, I see that."

Le Fanu wondered whether or not Winterton knew about Caldicott, given the Governor was advised. If he did, had it altered his plans and activities?

"It is different, Caldicott," continued Le Fanu, "and I'm grateful you've agreed to help."

Caldicott explained that he saw Wark regularly through cricket at the Club, talked to him a lot, so this new task was simple enough. By chatting with Wark, Caldicott could refer any helpful information on either the deaths or the opium ring. Le Fanu doubted much would emerge, because if all the information so far was right, Wark was unlikely to say much. Winterton's fear suggested Wark was serious. If he threatened others, he would not be rash himself. That might depend on whether or not he did drink too much. Has that been an act? It seemed genuine enough, but this case had produced so many surprises already, Le Fanu would not be surprised if someone confirmed Wark as a teetotaller.

"Given your background," Le Fanu said, "I don't have to tell you what to watch out for. But one key witness is petrified of Wark. The man could be dangerous, so take care of yourself."

"Thank you, Superintendent"

"Call me LF."

"Thank you again. It's a while since I was in the field, so I'll keep your advice in mind. Not really sure I want to re-awaken all that, but as it's necessary…" His voice faded.

"What did you do, because you were obviously at senior level?"

"I'm under a code of silence on detail, but I spent most of the war chasing German spies in England, and some of them were dangerous enough. Towards the end, though, I was under cover doing the same thing in France, and that was more dangerous. The bosses kept telling me it was important and I suppose it was, but I'd have preferred to be in combat."

"You feel the same way now?"

"Yes, in some ways. I'd be happier joining you in the direct work."

"Not thinking of joining the police, are you? It would wreak havoc on your cricket, I can tell you."

The tension broken, the two men spent the next half hour swapping war histories, and discussing exactly what Caldicott was looking for. The pair would meet daily late in the afternoon to debrief at the Madras Cricket Club pavilion, not far from where Jane Carstairs was found. That moment seemed a long time ago now. If anything urgent arose, Caldicott would phone Le Fanu and they would meet.

Back in the car, the driver picked a way through the narrow alleys and lanes of Georgetown, where enterprise never stopped. Goods were loaded on and off lorries and bullock-drawn drays whose respective drivers were swathed in turbans and invariably wore long shirts over grubby lunghis. It was a hard life for many, Le Fanu remembered. This was fertile ground for politicians trying to mobilise mass support for independence that would push the British out of India. Many thought that day far off, but Le Fanu was not so sure. It also occurred to him that people like Wark had a ready stream of volunteers to do their dirty work, at low cost.

They straggled onto the Esplanade and drove back along the beach towards HQ. The information boards were updated with the latest findings, and Habi reported verbally on the developments.

Mudaliar left his house soon after their visit, and Habi trailed the film maker for the rest of the day – he reckoned their reconnaissance activities would remain confidential if he did the trailing himself. Le Fanu agreed. Much of the journey was uneventful as Mudaliar went to a restaurant near Egmore Station for lunch, then visited Higginbotham's on Mount Road to buy books and writing materials. His driver then took him to a Triplicane house where he stayed for a couple of hours. Habi's inquiries revealed the place to be a high class brothel. Before returning home, however, Mudaliar made one more interesting call, to Sir Roland Wark's where he spent time with Virginia Campbell. Habi knew that, because a friend of his was a friend of a servant at Wark's, and information flowed freely because the Wark employee did not like her treatment in the house.

"So", said Habi, "this Mudaliar fellow definitely knows Wark's house, and Miss Campbell. We know two of those three are in direct contact with the morphine. It seems likely, then, that Sir Roland Wark knows about the stuff as well."

"That, Habi, is a fair conclusion," noted Le Fanu. "Wark is getting closer to the centre of this, but we still have no direct evidence of his involvement. Even so, very good work.

Nothing so far this morning?"

"A constable is keeping a quiet watch on Mudaliar's house, and Mudaliar has not left there today yet."

"Fine, get over there ready to follow him when he does, and let me know later what happens."

Wilson had left a report on his Winterton interview, and the man had produced extra details about Wark.

"According to Winterton," Habi reported "Wark is right in the middle of this morphine trade, and has been for some time. While he takes a good salary from the company, it seems he doesn't have shares in the business. His father-in-law, all those years ago, did not want Wark marrying the daughter, and tried to stop it by refusing the prospective son-in-law a share. The daughter married Wark anyway, but the share arrangement stood. The salary is Wark's only income."

"But," said Le Fanu, "he must make a princely salary, thousands of rupees, surely?"

"Yes, indeed," Habi, "but he has expensive tastes Lady Wark doesn't know about, including a house out at Mahabilipuram with an Indian mistress and a young child."

"Did Winterton reveal all this to the I-G?" asked Le Fanu, astonished. He had not expected that of Wark.

"Well, Winterton knew about the house somehow, and it was mentioned in the report, so I followed up from there. A police friend of mine is posted at Chingleput and knows all the comings and goings at Mahabilipuram. Apparently all the Europeans out there know about Wark."

"Yet no one here in Madras does?"

"Surprising, isn't it?" Habi shook his head. "Princely fellows making such big money should know better than to have an extra family. It is very expensive. And it is also a very complicated thing to have in your life. It leads to bad decisions."

Le Fanu nodded. At the very least, Wark would get a hard time at home because this would become public knowledge. Madras European society tolerated most things, but not if they became public. The vultures then swooped in quickly.

"So just how much financial stress does he have?" he asked.

"I can help there, sir," Habi responded. "His bank manager is another friend who owes me some favours – I helped him avoid a bad investment a couple of years ago. He was not keen to talk, it being Wark, but he gave me the general outline. Wark has an overdraft of twenty thousand pounds, big money even with his salary. Over the past year or so, however, he has made heavy and regular repayments, up to two thousand pounds at a time. It would be interesting to know where that money comes from."

"Well you have been busy, Habi," said Le Fanu, "great work, my friend."

"Sir," the sergeant said, "it does look like Sir Roland is a very naughty fellow. But we are no nearer to connecting him directly to all these events. Perhaps we should spend some more time on the morphine supply channels to see if we can connect him."

Le Fanu informed Habi of the new Caldicott involvement, telling him to keep it confidential.

"So now," said Habi," we have this cricketer keeping an eye on Sir Roland, and we know from Winterton that Wark is a threatening person. Does Caldicott know how dangerous this might be?"

"He does, Habi, and he is well prepared for this work. We may even get him in our team after all this is over, but why he would want to give up a promising and wealthy business career, I don't know."

By now they had covered everything, so Habi set off to follow Mudaliar.

Le Fanu needed to talk to Virginia Campbell again.

Thirty-eight

She was on the verandah at Wark's when the car pulled up at the steps. They greeted each other and she led him in, past the room of his earlier embarrassment and down a corridor towards the rear of the house. Following her, he was mesmerised by the dress, a lime green silk affair that stopped just below the knees and clung to her provocatively. Watching her hips and buttocks sway, he felt like a cobra watching the snake charmer's pipe.

This new room was darkened, curtains drawn and two table lamps in opposite corners casting dim light and shadows. A small library, it had a reading desk and chair backing onto a window, itself opening to a terrace. The shelves lining the walls were packed with books almost to the ceiling. Wark's wife must be the reader, because he did not look the sort. Another small table sat off to one side, two chairs beside it, bearing a tray with two crystal whiskey glasses, a soda siphon and an unopened bottle of Bruichladdich.

She stood, hip tilted, one hand resting on the table and the other closer to the swell of her bottom than the other hip. The dress strained taut because her feet were spaced apart, and it was cut far lower than normal for this time of the day. A generous sight of upper breast was complemented by prominent nipples standing out against the silk. Le Fanu remembered their last encounter and feared a matinee rerun. She knew her effect, and smiled.

"Ah, Miss Campbell, perhaps we could sit and I could ask some questions?" He knew he sounded unsure, and fumed.

"Superintendent, surely there's no rush?"

She opened the bottle, poured two good measures, topped them with soda then undulated towards him, glass trailing in her fingers. Her thighs stood out against the dress which was moulded to her body everywhere, and because he had already sat down his gaze was almost directly at her crotch. She swayed, switching balance to the other hip.

"Ah, I probably should not have a drink," he spluttered.

"No one will know, I won't tell." She handed him the glass and her fingers left it to trail along the back of his hand, cobra replaced by spider.

He took a strong sip, if only to do something, anything to break the pattern. She stayed in front of him, and what he dreaded began to happen – which she noticed immediately, staring straight at his trousers, and smiling.

"Are you sure you're comfortable there, Superintendent?" she asked archly. "Would you prefer the other chair?" She was willing him to move and reveal his predicament.

Le Fanu stuck to his chair, sitting so that his erection was at least not blatantly obvious.

"No, comfortable here, thank you," he croaked, pulling again at the whiskey.

She leaned forward and stroked his shoulder, her hand moving from there down his arm. The cobra was back.

"We could go somewhere else if you preferred."

Her voice dropped a register, the eyes half closed, and she shifted weight from hip to hip, emphasising not only the contours of the dress but also what lay beneath the fabric.

"Quite satisfactory here, Miss Campbell," Le Fanu managed. "Please, tell me what else you have decided to reveal."

The words were out before he thought. She smiled, using both hands to smooth the dress from neck to thigh, barely bothering to avoid touching her breasts. He hardened more, squirming to try and rearrange himself.

"Reveal, Superintendent?"

"That is to say, ah, is there anything else you know about the case I should know about." He knew he was close to inarticulate.

She looked at him, sipped her drink, then slowly moved over to the other chair to sit down, crossing her legs at the knee so that the fabric parted well up her thighs.

"I don't think so" she replied.

"Perhaps start by telling me the truth about how you and Miss Carstairs came to be staying here. And don't bother with the old friend of the family version."

He regained some composure as the tightness in his trousers eased.

She lost some swagger. "What are you suggesting?" she said, brushing hair back from her eyes.

"You know the answer." Le Fanu replied immediately. "We know Wark is involved in this, so it is too much a coincidence you turn up and become involved in the morphine circle."

"Are you sure you wouldn't like to go somewhere more comfortable?" The invitation was blatant, so he knew he had control back.

"No, I need you to provide credible answers."

She looked away, sipped more whiskey, turned back to him.

"Alright, it was no accident. The ring here has been active for some time, and was even shipping supplies back to England using willing couriers who need the money and free passage. I knew about it from the other end."

"So you were already involved before you arrived in Madras?"

"Yes, I began using about three years ago, got involved in trading, and came across the Madras contact in London about a year ago. That was a man Sir Roland met when he first came to Madras but who had returned home before the war."

"You mean Wark was or is supplying from here into London through this man?"

"Yes."

"Why did you have to come here?"

"The men I was dealing with wanted to contact Sir Roland to see if they could become his new agents. They sent me because they thought I might have more effect."

Le Fanu understood that logic, even if the cobra had slithered off temporarily. "Did Miss Carstairs know about this?"

"Not before she arrived here. I had her come along because it was a more convincing story – we were travelling together on a possible last mission to find husbands. I knew her at school and university, but looked her up deliberately in the three or four months before I came over."

"How did she find out what was going on?"

"By complete chance, unfortunately. Winterton was at a party just after we reached Madras, and had taken some morphine to get him through the evening. He spied Jane, propositioned her on the spot, as the drug can make you do, and she was shocked. She came to me and asked why he would do that. I made some lame excuse but she had done some reading and accurately described what she thought was going on. She threatened to go to Sir Roland, so I had to tell her what was happening."

"Which was what?"

"That I was here to persuade Sir Roland to switch trading partners. If he knew one of his local men like James was indiscreet, then he might shut down altogether and all would be lost. Jane didn't care. She was all for going to Sir Roland and/or the police."

Jane Carstairs was tricked into coming to India, then stumbled into something she was not supposed to know about. She was an unlucky young woman.

"What happened after that party?" Le Fanu prompted.

"Those of us involved got worried, because Jane wouldn't let it go. I spoke with Sir Roland and he thought she'd forget about it, but she didn't. If anything, she got more determined to expose the whole thing. After a couple of weeks, Sir Roland was as worried as the rest of us."

She looked drained, temptress replaced by a slumped figure sipping whiskey absent-mindedly. The shadows cast lines over her drawn face, her eyes almost dead. Le Fanu reckoned he was close to learning how Jane Carstairs died.

"What was the plan?" he asked.

"Sir Roland knew Ranjan Mudaliar somehow or other, Ranjan takes morphine, so they must have met through that. I'd already spoken with Sir Roland, who was adamant Jane had to disappear. I didn't want that, but she was a real problem. Ranjan was also worried, Sir Roland asked if he had any ideas, and Ranjan said he knew people in the country who might help."

Le Fanu could imagine what happened next. There were large numbers of people willing to take a life for not much money at the best of times. What with food shortages and lack of work, those numbers were rising and the cost of their labour falling. Many willing hands would have lined up to despatch Jane Carstairs. Le Fanu grew angry.

"She was your friend. Why not just tell her to get on a boat and go home?"

"Because Jane wasn't like that. She was morally outraged by the drug use, and by the involvement of people appearing to be respectable. She talked about going to the police, even to the press. She wouldn't listen."

Le Fanu suspected Virginia had not tried too hard to convince her friend, and became even angrier.

"What happened next?"

"Ranjan went off to a village near Madura, and came back with a man he said would help with the problem. Sir Roland took me to a meeting with them late one night near Elliott's Beach."

Most judges would consider this a conspiracy, Le Fanu thought, so that might toughen the sentences for those not directly involved with the killing.

Virginia Campbell was close to tears, the most vulnerable he had seen her. "The original plan," she said, "had the man raping then killing her, to suggest it was a sex crime that got out of hand. I talked them out of that so she had at least some dignity."

"Whose idea was that original plan?" Le Fanu was now clinical.

"Sir Roland Wark."

"And your alternative?"

"That it be made to look like a random bashing that went too far."

"But she was your friend."

"Not really, though I did rather like her."

Le Fanu had to get out and confront Wark. He knew, though, that he was leaving for fear of what he might do if he heard much more right now. As he left the room she was pouring another drink, and looked broken. He was still unconvinced he had heard the full truth from her, or that the cobra had truly disappeared.

On the way back to town he had the car drop him at the Madras Cricket Club where he was out of place in his civilian clothes among all the players in their whites. The club had a match coming up against Mumbai in a few weeks, competition for places was intense, and practice sessions were serious affairs. He watched Caldicott play for a while, confirming earlier impressions that the man was several levels above all other local cricketers. Caldicott had the easy style of someone to whom it all came naturally, but Le Fanu knew that a lot of coaching and effort had gone into that style.

They met about half an hour later, on the verandah of the clubhouse and off to one side so that the conversation could be private. After some idle chat about the other players, the real discussion came up.

"Le Fanu, I think you can quite confidently say that Wark is implicated in all this. I had a couple of friends in London do some work for me, and Scotland Yard has his name on a list of people doing business with a drug ring."

Le Fanu was astonished, because he could not get that information.

"Don't ask me how I got this, you know my background, but I can assure you the information is sound."

"What about Wark himself? Have you talked with him?"

"Yes, a couple of times, and I think he's guilty as sin. For one thing, he is agitated about something, can't concentrate on a conversation for long. There's something big on his mind."

"Anything else?"

"Yes, he's very evasive, even about business things he should know. A friend of mine who works for Wark says there's some chat around the office that the boss is losing touch, or whatever touch he had before. Wark's wife has been seen in the office a bit, and people are wondering if she's running things behind the scenes."

Le Fanu had wondered that himself earlier.

"The club chatter is rising, too," the cricketer continued. "Wark is a known bully but even by his standards he is now very rude to all and sundry. There is definitely something amiss, and my London information seems to provide the answer."

"Nothing about Jane Carstairs, though, I assume? And what about Virginia Campbell?"

"Nothing on the former but a bit of talk about the latter, naturally – some idle speculation about why she is really at Wark's."

"What about Wark's country family? Anyone know about that?"

"Oh so you do know about that. I had wondered. One or

two are getting to know about it and he is losing face, which will not help his mood."

"Caldicott, thanks for this, very helpful, and sorry to drag you in but it has been worth it."

They parted and Le Fanu walked to the gate and had the driver take him straight home. It now seemed a cold and empty place compared to a few days earlier.

Thirty-nine

Habi was waiting when Le Fanu reached his office.

The sergeant had followed Ranjan Mudaliar again, further afield this time because the film maker travelled to Conjeevaram. Habi had somehow followed in a friend's car, trying to look inconspicuous. Mudaliar's excuse for the travel was to investigate possible film sites, and he took actors along to test them in those sites. Habi soon worked out, however, that the main purpose was to contact men in the depths of the silk making centres for which the town was famous. Amidst the swirling colours of the saris, Mudaliar looked ill at ease according to Habi, perhaps because some of the characters he met would have cast well as villains in one of his films.

"They were definitely goondas, sir," the sergeant said. "They will have records with us or our colleagues in Conjeevaram, or both. I have some of their names and will check them with my friends in records."

"Habi, was there any obvious reason why he was meeting them?" asked Le Fanu.

"Not that I could see, but one fellow there I talked with said that Ranjan Mudaliar had been in the town several times over past weeks. He certainly had business with those goondas. We will find out what that business was when I have some of those names checked."

Wilson had interviewed Winterton yet again, but the ICS

man was silent, realising that his career was ruined, he would spend a long time in jail before being deported, and would have to rebuild his life once all that was finished. He said no more about Wark, and mention of the man's name turned him pale, because he doubted he was safe even in police cells.

Le Fanu wondered about the different attitudes displayed towards Wark by Virginia Campbell and James Winterton. She did not fear the man, he did. What did that mean? An answer would help determine the best way to trap Wark, no easy task given his commercial and social position. There was no choice but to confront him, and that would need very senior officers present.

Wilson was in his office, and agreed promptly to help Le Fanu interview and possibly charge Wark. The I-G had less cheering news, though.

"Bad news for me, LF, and possibly for you, depending how things turn out."

"Sir?"

"The Chief Secretary is under pressure from the European community to find a scapegoat for the demonstration fiasco, and he's settled on me."

"But, sir, it had nothing to do with you. I was there. Jepson lost control, completely. That was why the shootings and the deaths occurred, and it made Billy Walsall's murder possible. How can they blame you for that?"

"LF, you know how it works. I'm a senior public figure. Execute me and it looks like resolute action. It's alright so far as I'm concerned, the reactionaries now have an influence here I don't like and are impossible to work with. They'd get me sooner or later, so taking the pension and going back to England is no bad thing. Different matter for you, though, and I regret that."

"Why?" Le Fanu was puzzled.

"This Crime Unit was my idea and you've led it brilliantly. But a change of command risks a change in attitude. If they select an unsympathetic replacement, the unit might disappear and you could be back in the depths of routine policing."

"That might be no bad thing, either. But is there no chance of you being reprieved?"

"No, the agreement is I will retire, that will be made to look like a forced stand down because of the shootings, and all will be well. That announcement will be three days from now."

Le Fanu's immediate thought was that the cases must be completed by then, no matter who Wilson's replacement was, otherwise complications would abound.

"Sir, all I can say is that this is a serious injustice and I'm extremely sorry you're going. You've made all this possible for me, and I'll always be grateful no matter what happens next. This work you have allowed me to do has been wonderful."

They shook hands, Wilson placed a hand on Le Fanu's arm.

"LF, you'll do well whatever's thrown at you. But watch your back for the next while – be careful. Now let's go and see if we can pinch that sod Wark. Never did like him, especially his behaviour in the Club. If I can get him exposed, I'll happily announce my retirement."

They walked to the entrance and joined Habi. Le Fanu proposed strength in numbers dealing with Wark who, strangely, wanted to be interviewed at the Club. He did not want the police at his office, and being in the club might restrict publicity. Le Fanu, however, thought he could heighten the embarrassment: Habi would never be a member of the Club given he was Indian, and a Muslim to boot. Having him there officially would sharpen the moment, and the attention. He had even arranged for two cars to transport them there, attracting even more attention.

The I-G and Le Fanu were in the first, Habi followed. As they skirted the Cooum heading towards Mount Road, Le Fanu pondered how much the past few days had changed his view of Madras, especially its European community. He had never set great store in the vaunted "reputation" of this European community, but the past few days had exposed just how shallow and vicious it was. Senior ICS officers were involved with drugs, military personnel were trading those drugs, a young woman was killed because she wanted to expose those activities, a senior business figure was the mastermind, and a really good I-G was retiring so it could all be covered up. Away on the right, the Gymkhana grounds now seemed less imposing, and the buildings on the left housing senior officials insignificant.

They reached the broad expanse of Mount Road and turned towards the Club, passing the Madras Mail offices. What would the conservatives there and those in the European Association make of all this when the truth emerged, if it ever did, Le Fanu wondered. Madras had a way of papering over infelicities, and it took a major crisis like the 1906 Arbuthnot banking crash for serious penalties to be handed out to senior civilians. Back then, the Governor lost much of his personal wealth, so justice ensued swiftly and easily. This time, too many senior people had too much to conceal, so it was doubtful that Wark would get to trial. Perhaps he would be asked to "retire," too, thought Le Fanu, bitterly and still regretting Wilson's departure.

As they turned into the club driveway, he readied himself for what was to come. Looking across, he saw Wilson doing the same.

"Don't worry, LF, you don't have to make the running here. I've nothing to lose because I know where I'll be. Let me take on Wark, I'll enjoy it, for one thing, and it gives you leeway for another. We still don't know what will happen with you, so let's not give the diehards more ammunition than necessary. I'll take the lead, you chip in where necessary, and your other chaps can look menacing. I doubt Wark will enjoy this."

As they climbed the entrance steps Le Fanu saw the puzzled

faces of the Indian staff – what were the police doing here, and why was an Indian among them? The club manager appeared and attempted to turn back Habi, but Wilson swept him aside almost physically.

"This is serious police business," he said, "and we're here to see Wark, who's waiting for us."

The manager winced at the harsh use of the surname without title, and Le Fanu knew this news would sweep the city in minutes.

"Where's Wark?" demanded Wilson, ratcheting up the harshness.

"Ah, he is in the Committee room, I thought it best to place you all there."

"Good, now get out of the way."

Wilson strode ahead, turned into a corridor and passed the billiards room where several members halted their games, hearing heavy footsteps and serious voices. Wilson slowed as he passed the door, Le Fanu admiring his ability to create a presence. A little further along, they found a door signed "Committee." Wilson stopped and waited for the others to catch up.

"All set?" he asked. "Good, let's see if we can get this villain."

He opened the door.

Forty

The room was large, dominated by an oak table with matching executive chairs. High windows on the outside wall filtered in early afternoon light. Oak display cabinets showed off trophies, books, documents, photographs and souvenirs. The walls carried large portraits and photographs of Presidents and Committee members dating back to the club's foundation in 1832. Honour boards remembered individual services and achievements, and those Club members who died in the South African and European wars – a surprisingly large number. This was the formal record of Britain's domination of Madras that began three hundred years earlier.

Wark was sat at the head of the table, thinking that gave him an advantage, or perhaps he was just used to being there. He faced a whisky decanter, a half-full glass and a plate of wilting sandwiches. Folklore thought the Club had improved greatly in the later nineteenth century by rearranging the kitchen on English rather than Indian lines, but Le Fanu thought that the biggest marker of ignorance of all time. The Club food was dreadful.

Wilson fixed things by taking a chair and placing it side onto Wark who had either to turn his own chair or twist sideways. Wilson motioned Le Fanu to occupy a similar position on Wark's other side. The tycoon was stuck - now he had to face straight ahead, turning either way to deal with whichever policeman then questioned him. His awkwardness was made complete when Wilson asked Habi to sit angling his chair into Wark's sightline. Wark was surrounded, Le Fanu thought, marvelling at Wilson's tactical speed.

"Now, Wark," began Wilson, "are you sober enough for this or is the apparent drunkenness just another ploy?"

Wark placed his hands on the table and started to rise but the I-G was too fast, leaning over to shove him back by the shoulders.

"Don't bother playing the outraged patrician, Wark, we know too much about you."

Sir Roland looked them over, lip curling noticeably when staring at Habi. The only Indians he dealt with were servants, yet this man was sitting in judgment on him.

"Wilson, this is an outrage, I'll see to it that you…"

"Oh give it up, man. If you were paying attention you'd know I'm finished anyway, so I don't care. Why did you order Jane Carstairs to be raped and killed, and why did you have Billy Walsall killed?"

Le Fanu was surprised by the blunt directness. They had discussed the Carstairs issue and Wark's connection, but not the link to Walsall where they had no real evidence.

"How dare you accuse me? I'm a respected member of this community and…"

Wilson returned fire. "You might be prominent but I can assure you, you're not respected, not by the community, not by your employees and certainly not by me. So, I ask again, why did you order those murders?"

Wark lost confidence visibly. He made another futile attempt to deflect the attack, but knew he was on the wrong end of the discussion.

"Look here, Wilson, I know you have a job to do, and I know what it's like to have to make the big decisions, but let's try to be civilised about things."

"Wark, I'm never civilised with murderers and manipulators

and you're both. Just get on with it. Start with your little morphine trade sideline, because that's in the middle of this mess you've created."

Mention of the drugs removed Wark's resistance. Now he knew they were not bluffing.

"Alright, I can talk about the morphine, but that doesn't mean I'm connected to the murders."

Wark was looking to bargain his way through this, Le Fanu thought.

"Sir Roland," he interjected, "I should let you know that we have you connected to these killings, and we can connect those killings to the drug trade itself."

Wark slumped in his chair. "The morphine thing started by accident," he began, in a voice so quiet the others could scarcely hear him. "About halfway through the war, as you know, we started getting wounded European officers from the Indian brigades arriving in Madras hospitals and nursing homes. It was obvious that many of them were addicted to morphine following treatment in Europe. They had to find supplies."

Wilson was impatient. "We know that, we don't know why it involves you. Explain yourself."

"Simple, really. I hadn't told anyone, not even my wife, but I'd lost a lot of money on a couple of bad investments at the start of the war, and it involved company money as well as my own. The auditor was a friend and covered the trail but I needed money to cover the losses."

"But," said Le Fanu, "how did you of all people find the solution in trading morphine?"

Habi slipped a folder across the table.

"Habi, you can help here?" asked Wilson.

"I think so, sir. It seems Sir Roland has a servant who is a friend of one of the clerks in the medical stores. That clerk wanted to make money, and suggested the servant contact Sir Roland to raise some possibilities."

Wark loathed being exposed by a Muslim, but could only nod. "Yes, that's it. The opportunity was there, and I took it. My servant set up the supply lines, then we got a couple of people as distributors. That fool Winterton was the first. He'd got himself addicted, so was happy to do anything to keep up his own supply."

"Not any more, I am afraid," said Wilson, "we found his hoard, and yours, in his rooms in the Governor's house. It's all locked up back in the medical stores."

Wark looked almost relieved. "Well, at least people who really need it will have access now," he said.

"And where did Virginia Campbell fit into all this?" asked Le Fanu.

"That cold bitch!" The truculent Wark reappeared. "What a conniving cunt." The vituperation stilled the room.

"We thought she was your partner," Le Fanu continued.

"Only because I had no choice. She's connected to some serious London crime gangs. They heard what we were doing here and asked us to supplement their supplies. The arrangement was she would come out to do the liaison. The fishing fleet smokescreen gave her access to all the necessary places and people. I was told she'd stay with me, I'd no choice."

"What about Jane Carstairs?" Wilson queried.

"I liked her, "Wark replied, "she was a really nice person betrayed by Virginia Campbell. That bitch even tried to get Jane to take morphine so she'd end up in bed with one or other of the men hanging about frustrated by Campbell's cock-tease routine."

Wark refilled his glass and talked through an alcoholic haze, but Le Fanu recognised the behaviour he was talking about, remembering his own recent experiences of being alone with Virginia Campbell. Le Fanu flushed too, but not from the drink.

"So," said Wilson, "the London gang sent Campbell out here to firm up the pipeline, she introduced you to new sales and income, and you and your pals like Winterton and Walsall were doing nicely. What went wrong?"

"Virginia Campbell. She had to be in the spotlight. If she'd kept quiet it would've all been fine. But no, she had to get obvious, having people take the stuff at parties and behave oddly. She doped up James Winterton and Billy Walsall whenever she could, and they started propositioning women openly all over town. There were ugly scenes at important parties. Walsall damn near got cashiered, forced a colonel's wife out into the garden with him at one show, and got insistent physically. Got thrown out of the party, and took me a lot of talking for him to avoid a court martial. Cost me a fur coat I had to give the cow to keep her quiet."

Wark was slurring his words, and not enjoying the memories. Le Fanu realised that the past few weeks had undermined the man.

"So what happened to Jane Carstairs?" Wilson was now just steering Wark, who had given up on any defence.

"She was propositioned earlier by both Walsall and Winterton separately, but when they both tried again on the same night at Jamieson's it was too much for her. She told me she was going to the police because it had to stop. I tried to talk her out of it, but she was adamant and started off out of the house."

"And you rang Ranjan Mudaliar?" Le Fanu guessed.

Wark was surprised. "How'd you know that?" he asked.

"We know more than you think," Le Fanu replied, "but arrangements must have been made earlier because Mudaliar already had someone ready to silence Miss Carstairs."

"Yes," said Wark, "but I didn't know that. I just wanted someone to frighten Jane, make her go back to England. I had no idea her murder was already planned."

Wilson was puzzled. "But if you didn't order her killing, who did?"

"Virginia Campbell."

Forty-one

They had now to revisit Ranjan Mudaliar in search of further evidence against Virginia Campbell. Le Fanu was still unsure about whether she or Wark ordered the killing, but leaned towards her. Wilson favoured Wark. Le Fanu realised he and the I-G were both driven more by sentiment than fact, and that made him uncomfortable. He suspected Virginia Campbell simply because she was so close to seducing him. He remembered the green silk dress, and the cobra. There was no telling how this would end.

Wilson returned to his office to prepare for an audience with the Governor and the Chief Secretary, part of the ritual easing him out and salving other consciences over the demonstration deaths. Le Fanu raged at yet another manifestation of the great Madras hypocrisy.

Habi prepared to re-interview Winterton in search of more information on who ordered Jane Carstairs to be killed, but was pessimistic.

"Sir, I don't think he'll tell us anymore, because I'm not sure he has any more to tell. He wants to stay in the cell. I've never seen anyone so keen to do so. He'll hold out on us to avoid being released, even if he does know something else."

"Habi, I'm sure you're right," Le Fanu replied, "but we have to test the possibility, and you know him better than anyone. See what he says about Jane Carstairs, especially, it could be either Wark or Campbell or both. They've both lied to us so who knows?"

"Alright, sir, but only because you're asking. I think we are getting near the finale, and I don't want to miss that."

"If it looks like being finalised I'll have you contacted and a car ready to get you to wherever necessary."

Habi was mollified, but had something else on his mind. "Sir, the I-G skewered Wark, but there's something else on his mind, I think. Do you know what it is?"

"That's why you are a detective. Keep this to yourself. He's taking the blame for the demonstration deaths and his retirement is being engineered."

"Sir, these people are impossible. The Gorilla is the best boss we've had in the force, and these idiots get rid of him. Who replaces him?"

"Well, I don't know," replied Le Fanu, "and I'm pretty sure Gorilla doesn't, either."

"They'll complicate it, we can be sure of that. It should go to you."

"We both know that won't happen."

"My point exactly, the obviously good decision won't be made."

Habi rolled off towards the car.

Le Fanu's driver set course again for Kilpauk, passing over Anderson's Bridge, which Madrasites still believed harboured devils ready to leap out upon careless travellers. Le Fanu considered his present devils enough to be dealing with.

The house/film studio was as frenetic as before, but Ranjan Mudaliar stood out. He was wearing a Harris tweed hunting suit, complete with plus fours, matched with a white shirt and tweed tie. His shoes were tan and highly polished, the hat a slouch cap usually worn by golf caddies. He was shouting orders through a red megaphone, but no one was paying attention so he looked exasperated, lips pursed, nostrils flared, eyes flashing, free hand gesticulating as he shouted orders that were ignored.

Le Fanu tapped him on the shoulder. Mudaliar spun around, ready to shout at the interloper but recognised the policeman just in time.

"Oh, Superintendent, you catch us at a most busy time. We are about to start filming the final scenes on what will be my most magnificent film yet. So it is not convenient for you to be here now. Return tomorrow."

Nice try, thought Le Fanu.

"Sir," he said, "no one is listening to you, so you might as well have a chat with me somewhere quiet. Or perhaps you want me to drag you across to Police HQ?"

Mudaliar nodded, and led off deeper into the house, towards the back, then up stairs to where the film industry appearance disappeared. He entered a small drawing room full of family photographs. In one corner, two Victorian lounge chairs were separated by a small pedestal table. Mudaliar flopped into one without inviting Le Fanu, who wanted to stand anyway, looking down at the pretentious film director.

"You," began Le Fanu, "need to answer quickly and directly, because this is serious. If you don't, the consequences and the publicity will be severe. I don't think you want that."

Mudaliar rang a bell and the door opened, a servant seeking instructions.

"Coffee, and quickly," ordered Mudaliar.

Playing for time, thought Le Fanu and, on cue, Mudaliar began dissembling.

"Superintendent, I've no idea what you're talking about, but I'll do my best to help. We can have some coffee, then you can be on your way."

"I don't have time for this," Le Fanu flashed. "How about I go on my way now, visiting your father's chambers en route to inform him about your involvement in drug trading and murder?"

The servant returned with the coffee as Mudaliar tried to

mask his astonishment.

"Superintendent, these are, well, you know, very, um, serious matters and I would…"

"Don't bother, Mr. Mudaliar, we know all about the morphine, and we've just had a long, helpful chat with your friend Wark."

Like Wark, Mudaliar crumpled. "I wish I'd never met any of these people," he whined, "I'm just a film maker and now I'll be ruined, my father will disown me and I'll be poor."

"You should have considered that when you began dealing in drugs."

"I had no choice." That was a constant refrain, Le Fanu thought. "They gave me no choice." The cap was crushed shapeless.

"And who might 'they' be?" asked Le Fanu.

"Virginia Campbell and Sir Roland Wark."

Mudaliar said he had loaned Wark money four years earlier, which matched Wark's own account of financial stress. They kept in touch. When Wark started dealing he contacted Mudaliar, assuming the film community and its hangers on might be interested. Mudaliar himself became a morphine enthusiast. It was the drugs rather than the film career that upset Mudaliar's lawyer father, so the young man tried to cut ties with the drug ring. Then Virginia Campbell arrived in Madras. She and Wark visited Mudaliar in Kilpauk, making it clear he would stay part of the chain. If he did not, considerable money would be lost and important people upset. That, they said, would mean big trouble for him.

"They threatened you?" asked Le Fanu.

"Yes, especially that dreadful woman," Mudaliar replied.

"Virginia Campbell?" Le Fanu no longer trusted her but could not think of her as a killer. If she was, then his judgment had been swayed by her sexuality and that worried him. Given the problems that would emerge with Wilson's departure, he had to be able to trust his concentration and judgement.

"Yes, her, she is dangerous."

"How do you know?"

"Because she ordered me to find someone to kill her friend, Miss Carstairs. If I refused, she threatened to have me killed."

"Are you prepared to say that in court?"

"Yes, because it's the truth. I found someone for her, because I feared for my life."

"What happened?"

"I gave her the name of some fellows I know from a village near Madura. She and Wark discussed it with me. Wark was to send his servant off with a message for these men to come to Madras and meet Miss Campbell."

"Did that happen?"

"Yes, two fellows arrived two days before Miss Carstairs was found dead. One went back the following day, one stayed. The one who stayed killed Miss Carstairs."

"Do you have a name for this killer?"

"Yes, he is one Kadiravan from Umbattar village near Madura. The police there know him because he's been in trouble before."

Le Fanu was almost there. They knew the organisers and the killer. The final strands would emerge, including how the killing was ordered and completed. But he was uneasy, Wilson's news undermining his confidence in predicting anything that might happen. It was time to go home.

Forty-two

He was not there for long. A call from the I-G led to a call to Habi, telling him plans had changed. Le Fanu, Wilson and Habi would now meet at the central railway station at eleven-thirty pm and catch the midnight service to Madura. The District Superintendent of Police would take them from the railway station to breakfast before they went to interview Kadiravan who was already under arrest. Hopefully, he would reveal who ordered the killing of Jane Carstairs.

Packing a few things for the journey, Le Fanu remembered that Ro packed his bag for the last such excursion while he sat on the verandah with tea and snacks. That seemed long ago, and he missed her. Since her departure, he realised, he'd avoided home, staying late at the office or going to the Club for an hour or two after work, joining all the other soulless souls. He had to do something about that.

The car came at eleven and he was at the railway station by eleven-fifteen, amidst the normal chaos of Madras Central. A police porter met him at the car, commandeered his bag, then found a way through the hordes of passengers and itinerant sellers who seemed never to sleep. Hundreds of other people were sleeping on the floor though, surrounded by their few possessions as they awaited trains to destinations all over the Presidency and elsewhere in India. A million or more people travelled by railway in India on any given day. Tonight it seemed like they were all here. He was badgered to buy tea, coffee, snacks, meals, cakes, magazines, tobacco, combs and or hair cream, medicinal cure-alls, soap, biblical and other texts, newspapers, political pamphlets (some of which berated the police for the deaths of the demonstrators), shirts, sandals and other things he did not need.

When he reached his first class carriage and assigned sleeper, already made up, he took a sip from the hip flask he had brought along. As he did so, Habi arrived in from the next sleeper, tired and unhappy.

"My wife will have a word with you next time you see her," he said.

"Sorry Habi, I-G's orders."

"I know that, sir, but my wife still thinks the job should be ten to five and home for lunch."

"Is that all that is bothering you, Habi? You're not your normal self."

"This business with the I-G is very worrying. I think they'll disband the unit. I'll get posted somewhere back in the wastelands and my wife and family will be unhappy."

"It may not come to that, let's hope so anyway. Any rumours you are hearing about Wilson's replacement? You seem to have very good sources."

"Nothing concrete, sir. The usual wishful thinking, but with no obvious name, apart from yours if they were sensible, it is a real concern. Anything might happen."

Normal rules would have had Habi in second class, but Le Fanu won permission from Wilson earlier to have Habi travel in the same class as his colleagues when on official business. Le Fanu saw no reason why Habi being Indian should make his travel any harder when his contribution was equal. Some of Le Fanu's colleagues had complained officially about it, but Wilson held firm. That arrangement would also come under pressure once Wilson was gone.

They chatted for a while, then Habi left as the train pulled out at midnight. Le Fanu watched out the window for a while, seeing the last of the sleeping figures on the long platforms, then watching the few lights still shining as the train wended through the suburbs southwest towards Madura, three hundred miles away. He settled in, listening to the rhythm of wheels on tracks, and drifted into sleep.

He woke about five-thirty as the sun appeared, and looked out on green swathes of rice fields dotted with small villages and temples. People were already in the fields, many squatting at their early morning ablutions. When he first came to India and was posted up-country, the shitting in public bothered him, as it did most of his contemporaries. After a while he became used to it, and then totally oblivious after living in close proximity to other men during the war when privacy disappeared.

As the train entered the Madura outskirts he glimpsed the first of the giant temple towers that made this city a national Hindu worship centre. No matter how many times he saw them, their age and detail overwhelmed him, as did their difference from any other form of worship he knew. The hundreds of colourful of god figures parading across these towers, and the bewildering numbers of stories told in the panels, conveyed the richness and texture of Hinduism. The last time he was in England, his wife insisted they visit Winchester cathedral. After the lavishness of south Indian temples Anglican cathedrals were boring, even uninspiring. That started him thinking about religions seriously, and becoming less a Christian believer, he thought. However, he could never abandon himself to the fatalism of Hinduism. He preferred to exercise direction over his own fate rather than leave it to some god.

Madura station was even more crowded and chaotic than Madras, but having few bags, they were soon in a car and carried off to a hotel for breakfast. They ate, the local police chief telling them Kadiravan was talkative. The coffee and breakfast were excellent, so by the time they got back in the car, Le Fanu was almost cheerful and Habi beaming.

It was like any other district police headquarters: set in a walled compound, two storied, a rabbit warren of offices and papers, long lines of complainants and accused outside, hundreds of lawyers rushing about brandishing files, while food and drink sellers tried to cater to everyone, and all this amidst a constant din. The District Superintendent led them upstairs into a small meeting room next to his office. The room was lined with shelves overflowing with papers. That was familiar, at least. They took the three chairs behind the desk, and waited.

The door reopened a couple of minutes later as two constables led in a short, tubby, young man with a bottle blue complexion and thick, luxuriant black hair that flopped forward over his face, meeting the flourishing moustache that spread from top lip almost over his entire mouth. He was handcuffed and barefooted. The constables shoved him into the chair on the other side of the table.

"You are Kadiravan?" asked Habi, in Tamil. "Are you able to speak in English?"

"Yes, and no," the man replied in Tamil.

"We should interview him in Tamil," Habi said to Le Fanu.

"Take the lead then, Habi. You found him," said Le Fanu. "We'll come in where necessary."

The smile returned to Habi's face. "Now then, you goonda, you must tell us what you have done and who it was told you to do that. Speak up, now."

Kadiravan's eyes flickered uncertainly from one to the other of them.

"I am just a simple village man," he said, "A very big mistake is made here."

Habi sprang to his feet, leaned over the table and thumped his fist on it in front of Kadiravan. "Now do not give us this nonsense. We know you are a bad fellow, and we know what you have done in Madras these past few days. So start talking."

Le Fanu leaned back, content to let Habi make the running.

The man blinked several times, shuffled his feet and waved his manacled hands as best he could.

"Could I be having one cigarette?"

"No you cannot," barked Habi, "we do not want you making the air in here impossible to breathe. The sooner you talk, the sooner you'll be able to smoke."

"Now tell us," Habi continued, "who paid you to kill Miss Jane Carstairs in Madras?"

"Sir, I am having to say that I did not kill anyone."

"More nonsense," roared Habi and repeating the table thump, "We know you did it."

"I was contacted here by one Mr. Ranjan Mudaliar, who lives in Madras. You are perhaps knowing him? His family comes from my village area and his father is an important man."

"Good, you are talking," said Habi. "Why was this fellow talking to you?"

"He gave me money for a third class fare to Madras, where I met him and another person, at his house in Kilpauk late one night."

"And who was this other person?"

"It was a woman, I did not understand her name. But she talked and gave me a photograph of another woman, and asked me to be killing that other woman."

Le Fanu produced photographs of Virginia Campbell and Jane Carstairs. "Were these the two women?" he asked in Tamil, "and which one was the victim?"

The prisoner could not really understand this version of Tamil, and looked at Habi, who translated. Kadiravan identified Virginia Campbell as the woman he met, and Jane Carstairs as the victim.

So it was not Wark, Le Fanu reflected. That resurrected

the question of why Winterton was so scared of the businessman.

"And what did you do then?" Habi asked.

"They paid me some money, so I stayed in the city that night, in Triplicane, and it was agreed to be killing her the next evening."

"And what happened?"

"The next evening I was being left near a house in Adyar. A European fellow was driving the woman home, but he had agreed to stop in a dark place so I could grab her. As soon as he stopped, though, she was getting out of the door and running off, and I had to follow her."

"Who was this man?" asked Le Fanu.

"I am not knowing his name, but he was a soldier."

Walsall.

Kadiravan continued. "The man was of a panic, and got the car going again. I chased the woman, but had to hide sometimes when other cars came by, but then caught her and put her in the car when it arrived. I was putting her in the back seat and choking her while the man drove."

"Why did you go to the canal behind the Chepauk Palace?" Le Fanu asked.

"I am not knowing that, because the man did not speak. He just stopped there and told me to put her in the canal."

"And who raped her?" asked Le Fanu.

"I am not knowing anything about that," Kadiravan shouted.

"Someone had sex with her," Le Fanu shouted back.

"It was that soldier fellow," Kadiravan spluttered. "Before I could finish choking her, he was stopping the car near the river. She was conscious. He forced some morphine tablets into her mouth. I knew what they were. He'd told me about them. She nearly vomited but he made her swallow them. She was crying. It was cruel. He dragged her out of the car and off into the dark, his hand over her mouth. A few minutes later he was coming back, carrying her. She was dead."

So, according to Kadiravan, at least, Walsall raped and murdered Jane Carstairs.

They now had the killer, they had Virginia Campbell and Billy Walsall, they had Mudaliar, but where did Wark fit?

"Habi," said Le Fanu, "very good work. Charge this man with attempted murder and with being an accessory to the murder of Jane Carstairs, then inform the desk sergeant while I advise the District Superintendent."

Habi summoned the two constables and they all trooped off down the stairs. After a brief discussion with the District Superintendent, Le Fanu and Habi returned to the railway station.

As the train rolled back across the flat, green landscape, Le Fanu wondered how it was that life now was so cheap that a young woman with a sense of what was right had her life stopped by a hired killer from an Indian village on the orders of her best friend. It was a long trip back.

Forty-three

After another night in a barren house, Le Fanu wheeled out the bike and set off for the office. Even the bike gave him little pleasure now, he thought, as he rolled along under the shade trees that blocked much of the early morning light. Churches and temples streamed out bell sounds, street sellers were out already with their flowers, snacks, papers and tea. As he reached the beach and turned towards HQ, the sea air lifted him briefly before the looming shadows of the building took over, as he entered the grounds and surrendered his bike to an attendant.

His mood fell further when summoned once more to Egmore and the Commissioner's office. Walking around to the I-G's office in search of advance intelligence, Le Fanu considered the paradox: the murder case was largely solved, yet he might be about to receive his marching orders to Broken Stick, Bellary or some other such site to serve out his days counting stolen bicycles. As India pushed for more independence in the twentieth century, its British rulers seemed intent on reverting to the nineteenth whenever possible.

Wilson's office was already half packed, sealed boxes stacked along one wall and a few remaining open ones clustered around the desk, behind which the I-G sat sorting through piles of papers.

"Good morning LF, the worst thing about this is ensuring

that any incriminating papers stay with me, when I have no idea what might make them incriminating now or in the future."

They laughed, and Wilson offered tea.

"What are you going to do, sir?" Le Fanu asked.

"Immediately? Take some leave. We're going down to Australia for a month or so, stopping in Singapore on the way. Then I'm coming back."

"To Madras?" Le Fanu was surprised, imagining Wilson would return to England as soon as possible.

"Not Madras, no. News of my resignation spread fast, and I received a visit from an envoy of the Nizam of Hyderabad. Turns out the Nizam needs a new Chief of Police, and I fit the bill. I start a month after we come back from holiday."

"But that's marvellous news, sir, congratulations." The fabulously wealthy Nizam was India's leading prince, and Hyderabad one of the country's most developed cities. It was also next door to Secunderabad, and Ro.

"Thank you, LF, and I need you to keep in touch. There's a job there for you, too, if you ever need or want one. I'll be introducing Hans Gross to proceedings there and you'd be just the man to do it for me."

"I'll definitely keep it in mind, sir, and after this next meeting I might be back here discussing prospects with you faster than either of us imagined. Do you have any idea what he wants?"

"None whatsoever, I'm afraid. Haven't seen him in days, but I hear he's been haunting the Chief Secretary's office, and the European Association as well. There's a bit of chat at the club about what he's up to, but nothing definite. Needless to say, mind how you go."

As the car made for Egmore, Le Fanu imagined the possible scenarios, but could not concentrate because of Wilson's latest news. Hyderabad would be a good option. He liked the city, the work would be good and easy, and Ro was there. It would mean leaving Madras having lost to Jepson, and that would rankle, but he also realised he would miss the city, and he had not anticipated that.

Jepson kept him waiting for an hour with no tea, coffee or lime juice. When he was shown in, he saw Jepson, again flanked by his Assistant Commissioners, but also in the company of the Chief Secretary who raised a hand and a smile. Le Fanu was not asked to sit.

"Le Fanu," said Jepson loftily, not looking up, "be so good as to get us up to date on what you know and, more importantly, what you don't know."

"Sir, on the last point, almost the only thing we don't know is Sir Roland Wark's precise role in the death of Miss Carstairs. Time permitting, we'll determine that today."

Jepson ignored the veiled barb about Le Fanu being kept waiting, and attacked.

"Pretty easy thing to determine, I'd have thought. Wark is not Invisible Man. What on earth have you and your chaps been doing? Went off on a picnic to Madura, I hear."

"It was a productive picnic," Le Fanu retorted, "We arrested Miss Carstairs' assailant and established Walsall's direct involvement in the killing. We also know why – Miss Carstairs wanted to reveal a morphine ring in the city headed by Wark and involving people like Winterton and Walsall, not to mention Ranjan Mudaliar. We have all that documented and proven."

"But what do we know about Wark, LF?" asked the Chief Secretary. He was more welcoming than Jepson, who looked sideways and displeased.

"We know he was short of money, personally and professionally, because of bad investment decisions. He increased his income by trading drugs, largely accessed through contacts at the medical supplies store here. The rest he got from elsewhere in India, the drugs brought in by couriers on trains. Walsall and Winterton were instrumental, then Miss Campbell came out from England to introduce Wark to another market there. Really, she came to force him to supply that market, because she made threats on behalf of her criminal connections in London. Wark stood to make even more money, so signed up, but hadn't reckoned on the complications caused by Miss Carstairs."

"Very good, but was he directly involved in her death? It's an important question. I know you understand, because of his standing and the delicate nature of the current political condition."

"Sir, I do understand that, of course, but it has no bearing on my investigation. At present, we know he knew about the arrangements to kill Miss Carstairs, and that he was unhappy with those arrangements. He claims he tried to have Miss Carstairs paid off, and that he wanted to avoid her death. He blames Miss Campbell entirely for her friend's death. But as they were both staying in his house, there is some doubt to that story. He knew and was involved more than he claims, I think. And he had a lot to gain by Miss Carstairs being killed. That's why we want to talk with him again today."

The Chief Secretary was about to respond when Jepson cut in.

"That's all hearsay, Le Fanu. Sir Roland can't be implicated in this, you have no evidence."

"Actually sir, we do. He admits to his involvement with the drugs, he admits Miss Carstairs was a problem."

"You seem not to understand, Le Fanu – I didn't think you were so thick. There is no question of Wark appearing in court."

Jepson looked at him directly. Le Fanu looked towards the Chief Secretary while the Assistant Commissioners looked down in embarrassment.

"Is this true, sir?" Le Fanu asked the Chief Secretary, himself now looking awkward.

"Actually, LF, I have to say there's no decision to that effect that I know of, but perhaps the Commissioner knows more than I do?" The sardonic tone was unmissable.

Jepson reddened, working up to another display. "It stands to reason," he blustered, "there's no point having a man like Wark paraded in public, certainly not in court. We have to deal with this quietly, have him go off on retirement or something. Anyway, the real issue here is that Le Fanu has no proof to charge him with murder."

"We can charge him right now with being an accessory to murder," replied Le Fanu, "and perhaps with conspiracy to murder. And after this afternoon we'll know whether the charges can include murder itself."

Le Fanu wondered how the Chief Secretary would line up.

"Perhaps, Commissioner," said the Chief Secretary, "we might conclude this meeting and await those further discussions with Wark, and Le Fanu can report back later."

Jepson had no choice, and less grace. "That's as well may be, but I can tell you Le Fanu, big changes are coming to this force, and one of the big questions concerns your place in it. You'd better come up with some evidence on Wark, quickly."

Surely Jepson was not being considered for I-G? How could that be considered a good idea, given this display that came hard on the heels of his incompetence at the beach demonstrations?

Le Fanu stayed silent. If Jepson was in the running, then saying anything more was a bad idea. He left quickly, raced down the stairs and into the car that returned immediately to HQ. He observed nothing during the journey, preoccupied now with his career possibilities.

Wilson was still packing.

"Sir, have you heard any suggestion Jepson might replace you?"

Wilson paused. "I can't believe it's possible, but I hear the European Association is bombarding the Governor and his advisors with the idea that a tough law and order man is needed. They have no idea what that is, of course, apart from it not being someone like me, or you for that matter. But because Jepson does a good line in bluster and crash-through talk, he's being touted by the Association."

"I know I'm biased," said Le Fanu, "but that would be a disaster and many good people in the force would agree."

"You don't have to convince me," Wilson remarked, "but I'm not the one making the decision, unfortunately. That'll be the Governor, ultimately, but it will involve the Chief Secretary and some Members of the Board of Revenue. You don't have a lot of friends at court there, Chief Secretary aside."

Le Fanu was stunned, but knew he should not be surprised. He had always believed that the system ran on merit and that people were appointed on the basis of ability and performance. Sure, things went awry occasionally, but it was a big organisation and things like that happened. But if Jepson was appointed, then that belief and confidence was destroyed. So, too, was his belief in the value of his work at this point in India's history.

"Hyderabad's still an option, LF," Wilson murmured with a half-smile, "So really, you have little to lose – see what you can get out of Wark, go back to the Chief Secretary and if necessary the Chief Justice, then we'll know what to do. I have another couple of days left in this post, so still have some influence. Go off and finish Wark."

Le Fanu left in a daze, knowing this final discussion with Wark had more riding on it than the straightforward question of whether or not the man was guilty of murder. Depending on what he could determine, then convince Jepson and others of this afternoon, this could be his last case in Madras.

Forty-four

Sitting in his office with Habi and looking at the evidence boards now full of information and diagrams, Le Fanu thought about how best to finish this quickly, and give himself more than one career option. At the same time, he thought, any option must also consider what would happen to Habi. The latter was philosophical when told of the possibilities.

"The only certainty is that I will not be going back to Nellore. Apart from that, I will go almost anywhere else if I have a job."

Gloomily, Le Fanu focused on how they might resolve the outstanding case questions.

"What about, "he said, "we interview Wark and Miss Campbell together? Get them here, in a cell, see what happens?"

"Would the Chief Secretary or the Commissioner allow that?" asked Habi.

"The first would and the second not, so the obvious thing is to inform the Chief Secretary. But is it a good idea in the first place?"

"We have incomplete answers from both of them at present," Habi observed. "We would not lose anything by putting them together."

Le Fanu phoned the Chief Secretary.

"LF, I hope you realised during that awful meeting that I

reject any idea that Wark should get a free ticket. The truth is that he happens to be a dreadful person. If he is in any way connected directly with the death of Miss Carstairs, then I want him charged with murder. I'm not sure who Jepson's speaking to, mind you, so I've no idea what other schemes are being dreamed up."

"So you've no objection to us interviewing the pair of them together?"

"None at all, good luck."

Two separate police cars full of senior officers went to collect Wark and Virginia Campbell. During the hour of waiting, Le Fanu and Habi prepared, arranging their boards for what might be the final time ever let alone on this case, reviewing the evidence, and rehearsing questions.

Wark and Campbell arrived at three-thirty, and were installed in a cell where they sat until four, when Le Fanu brought them to a ground floor room at the back of the building. It was bare apart from the table and chairs. The door was solid iron. It was sparse, with solid whitewashed walls and no windows, apart from a row of narrow panes near the top of the roofline that let in some natural light. A single light bulb in the middle of the large ceiling added to the gloom. Le Fanu doubted either interviewee had ever experienced anything so bleak, and hoped it would dispel their remaining confidence.

"Thank you for coming," he said.

"Oh Superintendent," Virginia Campbell said in her warmest voice, "as if we had a choice, or would even have wanted to miss this."

She was in black: shirt and scarf, silk slacks, high heeled leather shoes. No jewellery, hair tied back and tight, which lifted her forehead even higher to accentuate the angles in her face. Wark was far less distinguished, his dark blue pinstriped suit crumpled as was the white shirt. The dark paisley tie was knotted at an odd angle, his hair was dishevelled and he had not used a razor for a couple of days. His eyes were sunken, bags billowing beneath.

"Can we get this over with?" grunted the businessman. Le Fanu was lifted by the thought that even if Wark escaped the murder charge, his professional and personal life in Madras was finished. The establishment would not reintegrate a drug dealer and fraudster.

"Very well," said Le Fanu, "Perhaps you might start Habi?"

The sergeant took his time arranging papers, aggravating Wark in particular. "Sir Roland," he said, "do you still maintain that killing Miss Carstairs was all the idea of your accomplice here?"

"She's not my accomplice and, yes, it was all her idea. I wanted no part in any killing, things were bad enough already." His voice was quiet, his manner resigned.

Virginia Campbell turned her head, considered him disdainfully. "Oh you are not so much the tough man now, are you?" she said. "What happened to the person who threatened to open James Winterton's face with a razor?" she said.

"That was all talk and you know it." Wark returned the contempt.

"When you had the razor in your hand?"

Wark looked uneasily at Le Fanu. "This woman is calculating to the point of being insane," he said.

Habi resumed. "Miss Campbell, it seems you are officially the organiser of a murder."

She turned her contempt on the sergeant. "You may think whatever you want, but you've no evidence that connects me directly to the killing."

Habi consulted the file. "But you do know a goonda fellow called Kadiravan who comes from near Madura. You know him because you had a meeting with him a few days back."

She was shocked, surprising Le Fanu, who assumed she would have worked out they now knew who actually killed her friend.

"You seem surprised, Miss Campbell," he said softly. "The

man identified you in a photograph as the woman who hired him to kill Miss Carstairs, whom he identified in another photograph. So we can link you directly to the killing. At the very least, we can charge you with involvement in planning a murder, and the court will accept the man's testimony as proof that you directly arranged the murder."

Virginia Campbell's mask disappeared.

Le Fanu continued. "I see you realise that. Put us all out of our misery and tell us what you know. And, Sir Roland, you should do the same."

Wark replied quickly. "I've told you all I know and all I did, but can tell you no more about the murder, because I had nothing to do with it. I told this bitch not to do it, to find some other way, but she knew best. I knew you could trace any killer fast enough. She was not even smart enough to use an intermediary, apart from that flamboyant film type who was as discreet as a purple hat."

"The only mistake I made," she hissed, "was to think you were a lot tougher than you turned out to be. Jane was a liability and we had to get rid of her, so I did."

"What about Billy Walsall?" interjected Habi. "Did you have him killed, too?"

"Of course, the fool thought I was in love with him. He had complicated things by his silly behaviour, and by being drugged up and raping Jane. That was never the plan, because it drew too much attention. The man from Madura joined the crowd at the demonstration, and it was easy enough for him to shoot Billy in the middle of all that confusion."

She had shed any sense of defence.

"Tell me," said Le Fanu, "where did Winterton fit into all this, and why is he so scared of you, Sir Roland?"

"That's easy," said Wark. "This cold cunt discovered he was homosexual. She tried to seduce him, found out he was not interested, so blackmailed him into running even more drugs. Then she said I would come for him if he resisted.

Poor sod was more frightened about being outed as a homosexual than as a drug addict. Made no sense to me, but it gave her power over him."

Within half an hour they had all the information they needed. Virginia Campbell was charged with ordering the murder, Wark with running a drug operation.

The I-G was delighted, but cautious.

"Just brilliant, Chris," a rare use of his name. "But watch out for Jepson, he's after you."

Forty-five

He rode home early, taking the longest possible route along the beach road. The weather was still pleasant, the warm sun and cooling breeze easing the headache that had built over the day and the weariness accumulated during the case. By the time he reached home, it was the best he'd felt in weeks.

Two letters awaited, the first from his wife. Their divorce was now complete, the papers for signing would reach him soon. For the first time since she had left, he felt relief rather than regret, and opened a bottle of Riesling to celebrate.

The second was from Secunderabad, Ro telling him that everything was working out well, that she liked her new place and job, and that she missed him. The celebratory drink turned sour because he missed her, too, he realised.

He took the putter out on the green and practiced for an hour, frustrated again at his loss of skill. He would go and play this weekend.

Dinner was set for seven, so he showered, sat on the verandah with some more Riesling and a selection of London papers full of bad news. Perhaps being in Madras was not so bad. He had just finished dinner when the phone rang. It was Wilson.

"LF, sorry to bother you, but thought I'd better let you know."

"No, that's alright. What's happened?"

"Jepson's the new I-G. Sorry to be the bearer of bad news. I tried to get you up, but the powers that be think you're too young. Doesn't matter you are the best person for the job, apparently. I've managed to protect the crime unit for the next six months, but during that time you'll have to shore it up. He'll be looking for any chance to take you out. I'm sorry, Chris, the compromise candidate wins again. But don't forget about Hyderabad."

When the conversation finished, Le Fanu took his glass and walked around the garden, in the dark. He had a management problem, again

Brian Stoddart is a writer, academic, blogger and commentator with forty years experience of Asia. He grew up in New Zealand, completed a PhD in Australia in the history of modern India, became a senior university executive in Australia and has lived and worked in India, Malaysia, Cambodia, Lao PDR, China, Indonesia and elsewhere. Brian Stoddart is also an acknowledged international authority on sport and culture, being a frequent keynote speaker at international conferences on issues like the governance and politics of Asian and other sport. In addition to working on aid and development projects dealing with higher education reform, he also lectures on passenger cruise ships. He has written or co-authored sixteen non-fiction works. His A House in Damascus: Before the Fall won gold and silver recognition at the 2012 eBook Lit Awards. A Madras Miasma is his first fiction work. Dividing his time between Australia, New Zealand and elsewhere he reads crime fiction avidly, watches international affairs and sport, and collects Asian antiques.

>Word-of-mouth is essential for any author to succeed.
>If you enjoyed A Madras Miasma, please consider
>leaving a review on Amazon.
>Even a couple of lines would make a difference
>and would be extremely appreciated.

If you enjoyed reading **A Madras Miasma** why not check out **The Pallampur Predicament**, the second Superintendent Le Fanu Mystery, also published by Crime Wave Press.

The Pallampur Predicament– Brian Stoddart

The second Superindentent Le Fanu Mystery sees our intrepid British policeman on the trail of the murderers of an Indian Rajah. Under pressure from his superiors, pining for his lost love and allergic to the sight of blood, Le Fanu must navigate through a political mine-field of colonial intrigue in 1920s Madras.

As the British tighten their grip on the sub-continent, Gandhi's peace movement, British secret agents and armed pro-independence rebels complicate Le Fanu's investigations further and he soon finds himself in a quagmire of violent opposing forces that are unwilling to compromise.

If you enjoyed **A Madras Miasma** you may want to
check out other exciting books on our website:
http://www.crimewavepress.com
Subscribe to our newsletter and you will be amongst the first
to learn about new **Crime Wave Press** titles and
free advance readers copies.

Crime Wave Press is a Hong Kong based fiction imprint
that endeavors to publish some of the best new
crime novels from around the world.

Founded in 2012 by acclaimed publisher Hans Kemp of
Visionary World and seasoned writer Tom Vater,
Crime Wave Press publishes a range of crime fiction –
from whodunits to Noir and Hardboiled,
from historical mysteries to espionage thrillers,
from literary crime to pulp fiction,
from highly commercial page turners to
marginal texts exploring life's dark underbelly.

Follow us on Facebook:
http://www.facebook.com/CrimeWavePress